NOETIC GRAVITY

Written by R. P. Gage

Published by Gage Force Publishing

AFTERDEATH™ – What Are You Doing After Death?

You mastered college, retirement, and life's little surprises. But what about after? At Afterdeath Inc., we engineer a seamless transition beyond biology—because life is the demo. What comes next is the full, uncut experience.

READER ADVISORY

This novel explores death, grief, and the unresolved boundaries of digital consciousness. It includes emotionally intense content and an early depiction of violence and loss that may be distressing for some readers.

Please read at your own pace. If you need to pause or speak with someone, you're encouraged to reach out to someone you trust—or contact a mental health support line in your region. You are not alone.

Your safety and wellbeing matter more than any story.

ABOUT THIS WORK

This story was built from the ground up—every word chosen with care. The same goes for the art on the cover: created in collaboration with Engin Akyurt, whose vision helped shape the mood and invitation to step inside. No part of this publication may be reproduced, stored, or transmitted in any form without prior written permission from the author, except in brief quotations for reviews or critical commentary.

For Helene, the first one who saw the shape of this.
And for the ones still learning to stand in their own
ruins.

We go on.

PROLOGUE

A mind is a terrible thing to waste, she thought—so
most mornings were already a tragedy. Adrift between
bells, a student walked on, her mind already
elsewhere—not on this step, or the next step, but on
the ones that would never come.

Cold air snaked down the corridor, collecting
at her ankles. In the alcove's polished glass, her
reflection watched her pass—same face, same eyes.
Someone she should recognize.

Remy Moreau.

She was a few minutes behind, like most
mornings. It was quiet, which made sense. That didn't
stop it from feeling wrong.

Mr. Haskins' English class hadn't changed
since her mother's time—back in the 20s. The desks
were askew—enough to irritate anyone who needed
rows and order. A dozen students filled the room,
heads down, tablets propped beside matching copies of
The Odyssey. The whiteboard had been wiped recently
but never fully cleaned—faint outlines of old lessons
clung to the corners.

Remy slid into her usual seat at the back.

"Thank you for joining us, Ms. Moreau," said Mr. Haskins, his tone flat but patient. He turned the page without further comment.

"As I was saying," he resumed, flipping open his worn copy. "When we left off, Odysseus had survived the sea—only to suffer again the moment he reached land."

Something outside the window caught his attention. He paused, gaze drifting with the light sliding across the glass. His voice trailed as he turned the page.

"Much have I suffered." He delivered it with the rehearsed weight of someone who knew drama was part of the point.

"Laboured long and hard by now in the waves and wars." He sighed—the kind teachers do when they want the line to linger.

She didn't hear the hero in it—only the tired part, the part that kept going without knowing why. That part she knew all too well. At sixteen, when everyone else moved as if the future had already been mapped, she stood at the intersection, unwilling to fake it.

From the next row over, a hand reached—bracelets gently clinking as it passed a folded note into Remy's hand.

MALL AFTER?

As much as she'd love to spend a few hours at the mall with Jess and Darby after school, her brother came first today.

Mathieu, her little brother, was her anchor in a world that never stopped changing—loud, goofy, and loyal to a fault. Once a week, usually on Sundays, she read to him—long stories about spells and monsters and worlds larger than either of them. It had become their small ritual, a thread she feared might fray with time, though Mathieu seemed to savour it. They'd only recently reached one of the last books, where the story darkened, and the heroes began losing things they couldn't get back.

Jess waited, expectant, her class notes aligned like coordinates, already well on her way somewhere. Since sophomore biology, she had worn med school like a second skin, diagnosing injuries both seen and unseen with an ease that left Remy feeling unmoored by comparison.

Darby's chair balanced on its back legs, boots up, arms crossed—perfectly at ease, as though gravity worked for him, not against him.

The career fair last year had been a joke—a parade of brochures and fake smiles—until he glimpsed a High-Risk Skilled Trades flyer that promised hazard pay and was always in demand. That, at least, sounded real.

"Underwater welding," he'd told them afterward, confident it had been obvious all along. Plain as day, as his voice rose: "Dangerous, insane, and pays stupid money? Sign me up." Somehow, even Darby had found his way—without flinching, without doubt.

She shook her head at Jess and pocketed the note before she could second-guess it.

Jess didn't press. She gave Remy a look—one that saw straight through to the reason—and returned to her book.

Darby rocked his chair once and shrugged—he'd seen it coming from the start.

That's when something tugged at her attention. A crumpled letter-sized sheet pinned to the wall. Marker on paper, block letters shaded to stand out.

OFFLINE IS TRUTH

Remy had seen those words before—on a subway sticker, scrawled on a washroom stall, half-erased on a library desk. People had opinions about the phrase, even if they couldn't agree on what it meant. Some called it rebellion. Some called it obvious. Some merely rolled their eyes.

This one was signed—Jacob.

Strange. He wasn't someone who put his name on things. He barely spoke.

She searched for him in his usual place. Tension braided up behind her sternum as he crossed the room, each step steady, like the path had been traced days ago. The guitar case sat behind her, but the way he moved, it could've been her he was approaching. Maybe he had something to deliver, and she was in the way.

With his back to the class, Mr. Haskins continued: "It's not the dying he fears—it's the drowning."

Jacob passed close, and her body locked. Fear. Paranoia. To hell with drowning—death too. She wasn't ready for either.

He reached the back wall, where an old guitar case leaned against the cabinets, and set it down. A tremor sparked through her arm the moment the latch snapped open—a click that struck, clear and final, bypassing thought.

Her brain reached for reassurance: it was just another Monday. That's what she told herself—before she looked.

What he lifted wasn't a guitar—too sleek, too black, undeniably real. He faced the front of the class, moving with deliberation. Light caught the barrel. Then came the commitment: a step into his own darkness to light up the room.

The first shot cracked through the morning like drywall snapping. The second came before the first could even unravel. By the third shot, her mind had barely grasped what was unfolding.

The first bullet struck Mr. Haskins. He jerked back, arms lifting halfway—reflex, not realization. A torn gasp escaped him. He crumpled in place.

The second shot hit Darby. He went down hard, chair buckling, boots skidding out.

Remy saw the gun clearly now, the kind of object that felt printed rather than forged. A shape dredged from the depths of her nightmares.

Then the third shot hit her. The force punched through her gut, folding her in half. She dropped hard—her head slammed against the tile, and the world cut out.

Sensation flooded in. It came raw and fragmented. Her vision stuttered—edges first, then centre, fragments coalescing reluctantly. She gasped—hard. Pressure mounted in her gut, her body desperately sealing itself shut.

The room pitched. Chairs scraped the floor. Jess's wail sliced through the static—raw, unravelling. Remy tried to answer. Her lips parted, her jaw tensed, but no sound came. Every neural signal felt scrambled.

Shots followed—tight bursts, spaced too close to separate.

Jess's voice stopped mid-syllable, swallowed by the noise.

Figures flashed past her vision—bodies staggering, falling, fleeing—blurred and wrong, as if the room itself had torn loose from meaning.

Overhead, the lights hummed without pause—bright, sterile, unaware.

A shadow loomed over her, backlit and unmoving—somehow larger than the space around him.

She said it before thinking. "Jacob."

He drew back at the sound of his own name—and raised the gun.

The room receded, sounds retreating, until all she could hear was her own pulse, marking out seconds already lost.

The hammer dropped, the sound of metal striking metal like a death knell. The firing pin clicked. A suspended breath. Then the flash—blinding.

Her chest jerked. The world fractured—then stopped making sense.

She felt nothing after that, like she'd been taken somewhere else, not drifting, not dreaming—gone.

ACT ONE

CHAPTER ONE
THE INDUCTION

A chill prickled Remy's skin—sharp, sudden, and waking. Panic faded out, but an iron taste clung to her tongue. Every detail landed with strange clarity, as if her body was trying to convince her she was here. What met her shoulders wasn't fabric, but packed earth—almost like her backyard.

Where the hell am I? How did I get here?

She blinked up into white light, sky bleeding into sight. A tilt of her head brought tall grass into view—and a treeline she didn't recognize. Warmth rose from the earth, light poured across her vision, and something deep inside her eased—like her body had been waiting, unknowingly, for this.

She traced both hands over stomach, back, the curve of her thigh, searching for the heat or sting of injury. Nothing hurt. Not even her wrist—the bicycle crash last summer used to send pain shooting up her wrist. Now—nothing.

A figure appeared near the treeline—humanoid, translucent blue, hovering, its shape cut off where legs should be.

"Welcome, Remy Moreau. I am Alma. You have successfully been Inducted into Afterdeath."

Inducted—their word for it. Sworn into a club she'd never wanted. Sanitized, repackaged, painless. Afterdeath. That one landed differently. The name didn't have to explain itself; it sat there, already loaded. It wasn't a promise. It was a brand.

She'd grown up hearing it—in the background noise of the decade. Smooth jazz behind the slogan: What Are You Doing After Death? She used to think you had to live first. But here she was—proof you didn't.

She could picture celebrities hyping their private realm setups on late-night talk shows, hosts nodding like it was normal. Tech moguls with shaved jaws and squeaky shoes embraced it as the final pivot. It was branded as disruptive, like flying cars—demoed for decades, delivered to no one.

That's late stage capitalism for you: surfing Moore's law, sinking into Murphy's. And here she was, at the bottom, dead as a rock. Or as they insist on calling it: Inducted.

"When you are ready, please step into the light" Alma prompted.

Remy rose slowly, every motion intentional, unfolding herself from the earth like someone surfacing from deep water. The meadow opened in every direction. Wildflowers broke the field in no particular order. Trees leaned off-centre, their branches angled toward a soft, sourceless light. Across the clearing, a doorway of light awaited.

The light would not come any closer. If she wanted an answer, she'd have to cross the distance herself. She advanced, drawn through the divide as the world behind her faded.

When her sight finally cleared, she was standing on short-cut turf—the kind you'd find on a school field or museum lawn. Ahead, tall stone structures rose into view. Their surfaces were dark and smooth, with thin lines of circuitry running through the black stone like veins. A clear path divided the field, guiding a slow, orderly queue toward two massive monoliths that stood like sentries.

"Welcome to the Pearly Gates," Alma said.

This was the Pearly Gates? How?

There was no hinge. Nothing to open. Nothing to close. Framed by pillars—but empty. The metaphor had been honoured in form, gutted in meaning. Like someone had followed the blueprint but omitted the point.

Around her, the line shuffled onward with resigned inevitability, the other Inductees' steps syncing to invisible markers, marching toward a final sorting. Near the middle, an older woman laughed hard at something and coughed—a jagged sound that cut the air. Most of the faces were older, dressed like they'd come from retirement parties or rehearsal dinners. A scattering of younger souls threaded among them, but few looked under forty.

Remy stepped into line, scanning the crowd ahead. She spotted one strange pocket of life: a middle-aged man facing the wrong direction, holding court with two older women. His story kept derailing into laughter—half from him, half from them—like none of them cared where the punchline landed.

Alma spoke again, breaking the silence. "While we wait, we can review some options for your personal realm."

A panel flared into view—neat rows of categories and promises. It was staged, like everything else—colour palettes for a life she didn't ask to decorate.

She muttered sarcastically, "Thanks, Alma. What would I do without you?"

Alma, of course, took the query seriously. Remy tuned her out, focusing instead on the settings panel. She flipped through option after option, letting them pile up—non-choices, really. Maybe that was control. Forced through a door of light and into a lineup, now handed a tutorial, she felt the pattern repeating itself. Restless, she scrolled through tabs and labels—until one stopped her.

ALMA SETTINGS.

Her thumb hovered. She tapped it open.

A list unfolded: permissions, language packs, compliance settings. Near the bottom, a word stood out.

DISABLE.

She didn't need a guide to navigate the afterlife. She swiped.

ARE YOU SURE?—flashed on her display. "It is not recommended to disable me before—"

She was. The insult was in the asking.

She re-confirmed, and Alma dematerialized.

Suddenly, the act of lining up, waiting her turn, felt as alien to her as Alma did. What was this? Respawn. Line-up. Get processed. As if grief came with instructions.

"Frack this," she muttered, breaking formation.

No one looked up. Resistance coiled in her gut—whether doubt or instinct, she couldn't say. She didn't look back. Didn't need to. The habit of refusal had survived her. The path remained exposed—no hinge, no gate, nothing left in her way. Each step chipped away at the hesitance—motion overtaking thought. Emotion overtaking motion. The few Inductees ahead of her had stopped in their tracks. Voices rose behind her, blurring into the noise of her sprint. One of them reached, but Remy spun and weaved her way through.

A red band spanned the floor, pulsing low. Not a wall—a line. Meant to make her stop.

She didn't.

Her foot crossed it, and nothing happened—yet. She kept running. Every step struck back. The barrier flared and she braced for impact.

LOADING.

Static.

ERROR.

The simulation withdrew, taking the air, ground, and sky with it.

A form remained behind.

An awareness slipped free.

A body hanging in space while a mind unspooled through a thousand shards of itself, moving without gravity, without time.

She didn't fall. She didn't float. She dispersed. A buried recursion, cycling through everything she'd carried, as if something essential had been dropped in the transition and her mind had been set loose to find it. Her sense of self bled outward, like static peeling from signal.

Jacob lifting a gun.

She couldn't hear, only watch. Again.

There was time—barely, but it was there.

She could have called out.

Could have intercepted.

Could have mattered.

She didn't. Again.

She floated beyond the range of notice—until the water came back.

A lake.

She'd been young, floating in a borrowed life jacket that scratched behind her neck. She couldn't swim yet, but she couldn't see her limits either.

A rope marked the end of the shallow water. She passed it, the sandy bottom floating away from her. She didn't flail or call—she only panicked, flat on her back, eyes to the sky. Trying desperately to look composed while her breath shortened and the cold crept into her limbs.

She was unseen in their periphery.
Drifting, waiting to be saved.
The world didn't fight her—or for her.
She didn't need answers.
She needed something to press against.
Something to prove she had shape.

A dim Christmas tree with two dead strands. The light never reached the corners, but it didn't need to.

She was curled under a blanket too big for the couch, cocoa cooling against her wrist, marshmallows slumping into the heat—softening, breaking down, losing their shape.

The hospital ambiance cut through the warmth.

Sterile, metronomic beeps carved the silence. Hope flared—bright, unsustainable—and sank into the same fluorescent wash.

She could hear voices—urgent, overlapping.

Then her father broke through the static, his voice strained in a way he never let her hear.

"If Max says it's viable, we should listen."

Her mother's hands rested on hers, guiding a pie crust she was too impatient to roll. Flour dusted her elbows.

A song played low on the radio, something older than both of them, and they sang badly on purpose.

She didn't care if it burned.

That was the win—being allowed to try.

Each piece threaded through the next, slower than thought, deeper than recognition. A convergence of Moreau, Remy, and all the fears that weigh her down.

Her awareness began to rethread itself—not fully formed, but gathering.

The numbness of her limbs called to her first. Suddenly, her orientation reasserted—felt as depth and direction.

Time narrowed into a single fixed point.

She was. Here.

A panel opened in the darkness. Glyphs aligned along the left side—symbols, tools, labels she half-recognized. Nested frames formed at the centre—summaries, previews, hints of what was hers. It wasn't something she summoned. It had simply arrived—sent by a guardian, an admin, or both. To save her. Or finish the job. Either way, there was no escaping it. It was time to choose her home away from home. There was no going back.

The heading: PERSONAL REALMS. Afterdeath had been running for years—she could tell at a glance. The options went on for hundreds of pages. The landing page offered mostly manors—sprawling estates with long driveways and high gates, trees flanking the roads like they'd never known a season. Everything looked beautiful, curated, sleeping. She could see why someone might want that. Maybe even live there. But it didn't pull at her. Not yet.

A few pages deeper, she noticed polished replicas of places she barely knew—Santorini rooftops, the Shibuya Crossing, the cliffs of Big Sur. Each one gleamed, preserved, untouchable. She stopped on a preview: sunlit stone, flags mid-snap, undisturbed. Beautiful, probably. Important, definitely. Though, this clearly wasn't for her. She hadn't seen these places while alive; therefore she hadn't earned the right to miss them now.

Her hand kept moving—past private islands with soft shorelines, treehouses strung with lanterns, rustic farms where the seasons changed like clockwork and nothing was ever truly lost. Stardew Valley tugged at her briefly: late nights spent rearranging pixel furniture, modest triumphs stacked like jars of duck mayonnaise. But even that world was a loop, and she wasn't ready to vanish into someone else's version of peace.

Previews blurred past: arcades, neon cities, endless weddings—until a glimpse caught her. Quick, almost subliminal.

Custom.

Simple, unadorned, the only one that didn't demand she settle into someone else's headspace.

A short series of choices appeared—pond, trees, temperate, campsite. It all clicked into place.

She was ready.

Her world crystallized around her, as she slowly descended to the earth. Trees arced upward, their trunks rising out of moss-softened soil. The air slipped through the clearing, light and damp, carrying the scent of rain-soaked bark and crushed leaves.

Along the banks of the pond, a ripple crossed the surface. It travelled clean through the water, reached the far side, and moved on.

Remy exhaled slowly. Whatever this place was—hers or not—it was holding. The world had stopped collapsing, at least for now.

It felt like the end of the longest day of her life. And yet, somehow, she was staring at morning.

She opened her console and scanned the new options. Her gaze landed on a slider labeled Day/Night. She dragged it sideways.

Her custom forest realm transformed in an instant, the world flipping like a storybook page. The air picked up the heft of late sun. Lines of shadow crept farther from their source, claiming more of the clearing. The leaves took on a denser tone, the green receding under a gold tint that signaled the end of a long afternoon.

She dragged the slider farther.

The sky shifted—first to muted peach, then into darker ember, before settling into a dense violet that marked the edge of night. Light receded from the treetops, leaving only a faint glow along the lower branches and the ground beneath.

Time responded like it was hers to shape.

Curious, she tested reverse.

Colour mellowed into morning after cresting at noon. The sky took on a cooler cast. Shadows retracted to their sources. The clearing assumed the clean geometry of a day starting over.

Time had always happened to her. Not here. Here, she slid light across the sky—watched the world bend to her hand.

Before letting go, she drew the world into a dark night—ever watchful. The sky deepened, stars punched through the dark, and the quarter-moon settled into its curve beneath them.

Remy smiled, the kind of smile that arrived before her thoughts could. Grief stayed close. She let it, taking it all in—the dark pond, the gold-tipped trees, the stars easing into place overhead.

Her campsite was modest: a canvas tent, a firepit hollowed into the soil, and an orderly spread of rations—hot-dog pack, buns, a can of beans, and a sack of marshmallows. She nudged a log closer until the flames took it.

A faint display nested in the corner of her view—Health, Rest, Hunger rendered in sterile glyphs. Hunger read ninety eight percent. Rest matched it. She scowled. The fatigue pressing at her wasn't a metric the meters could register. She eyed the bag of marshmallows; she figured an evening snack couldn't hurt. Assuming the simulation even trusted her with real fire.

She held her palm above the flame, feeling the heat gather fast. It rose in waves, curling around her fingers. A sudden bite made her jerk back before she understood why. She stared—at her hand, at the fire—the instinct had arrived before the thought, some deep-wired memory lighting up beneath language.

She lowered a marshmallow toward the flame, letting the outer layer deepen from amber to black. She resisted the urge to blow too soon, then let the flame dim under the slow curl of air from her lips. She peeled the charred layer away, the brittle shell breaking to ash between her fingers. Beneath it, the core held—sticky, molten, stubborn against the cooling air. The heat hit her lips first—too hot to miss. Sugar bloomed in its wake.

The fire, the clearing, the slow turn of the marshmallow—each obeyed her now. She threaded another marshmallow onto the skewer and extended it into the glow. The marshmallow rotated slowly on the stick, but her thoughts refused to burn out with it.

She'd been dead for what—an hour? A day? She wondered if they were planning her funeral. Do they need to say goodbye, or was it her? And if they did—would they say it to the version of her that mattered?

Either way, she wasn't supposed to be here. To be this—Frankenstein in a slip drive. But if the world had stolen her future, she'd make something of the pieces.

The flame curled against the marshmallow. She let it burn—offering one small thing to be ruined on her terms.

CHAPTER TWO
OBSOLESCENCE

Max hunched over his desk, high above the city's outer rim, where towers thinned into parks and the lake's open reach. Toronto shifted in barely perceptible increments, as if oblivious to what had eroded beneath it. Through the panoramic glass, the skyline offered no surprises. Inside, the climate was unwavering; every surface was immaculate except the battered desk under his palm, worn smooth by years of use. Nothing about today felt different—except the part of him that had stopped pretending otherwise.

On the noetic pane, Remy Moreau crouched by a campfire, tending a marshmallow with the calm precision of someone born to flame. She'd chosen the path less travelled—grounding herself in spite of the system, not because of it.

Max exhaled, not from fatigue but from the shame of watching a world that no longer required him. His only act of interference had been a silent backend override—no fingerprints. After that, she was on her own.

He snapped the pane shut.

He'd told himself this was the moment he'd built Afterdeath for. But part of him knew the truth—he hadn't built it for her. He'd built it for someone he couldn't save.

In the corner, a battered magazine framed against the wall. Its headline—The Man Who Conquered Death—felt like a cruel joke now. He gave a dry laugh, the kind that comes when you realize your own myth has worn thin. Beside it, well-thumbed comics leaned against a thick dossier, spines cracked, covers faded. One showed a red-suited hero mid-flight; once, Max had styled himself an Iron Man. These days, even the mask felt ambitious.

Eleven years had passed since the inaugural transfer. A million users now lived beyond Afterdeath's gates; on paper, the numbers screamed triumph. But at the top of a corporate ladder, every season demanded fresh victories—or your enemies would eat you whole. And with the Lazarus Project delayed—the very same system he used to save Remy—the last quarter had been more than painful. His unauthorized, experimental transfer of Remy had only made him more vulnerable. She had already been drawn into the new media spin cycle—less a person, less a girl. More story. More symbol. One feed called her a miracle. Another labeled her a protocol breach. It would be over soon. Once she stopped fitting into any story they knew how to tell.

The living had a knack for rationalizing the dead—easier to file her away as a controversy than sit with the discomfort of what she really was. He wondered how they'd file him. Max had carried the truth long before the doctors framed it; the slow retreat of his bloodwork had already written the verdict in lines too plain to ignore.

When the words finally came, they confirmed what he'd already known: "Bile duct cancer. Stage Four. Months, maybe a year."

For most of his life, he believed science was inevitable. Now, facing his own appointment with the executioner, he saw the inversion he had spent decades denying: Death is inevitable, and science—science never had a chance.

The pain returned in sequence, tracing its worn path with dull persistence. His hand reached the origin point by reflex, confirming its persistence as expected. The taste of the medication remained on his tongue, offering no illusion of comfort.

A knock sounded—firm, cutting through whatever thought he'd meant to finish—Max braced a hand against the desk, half-rising from his chair.

"Mr. Roy," his assistant said in a low, careful cadence—as he added, "Mr. Reeves is here to see you."

His torso felt hollow, like the meds had eaten through something structural.

"Send him in," he said, before the next wave could reach him.

Harland Reeves' entrance was surgical—each step measured. His cologne cut through the sterile air. The suit was immaculate; his posture so rigid it might as well have been ironclad. He moved with the precision of a board-approved automaton, every gesture calibrated to deliver bad news without hesitation.

"You told the press I went rogue," Max said.

"I conveyed exactly the mandated message—no edits, no exceptions." The words landed one by one—clean, exact, stripped of apology.

"Deviation equates to exposure, not innovation. Compliance secures continuity. I upheld every guideline—you did not."

"I was already at the hospital when it happened." He stiffened against the desk. "There was no time to call a meeting."

Reeves' voice dropped. "Strange how we found time to hold one regardless." His gaze fixed on Max.

"Listen, Max. Your legacy will continue to endure outside the headlines. And now, with the board's vote, a burden is being lifted off your shoulders. Your role as our humble leader has concluded."

"This was never about the Moreau girl, was it Reeves?"

Reeves slid his sleeve back with measured composure and replied, "You know how it works—every mistake becomes a weakness, every weakness a liability. The world doesn't wait for decline."

His hands trembled as he added, "You could've given me a choice."

His delivery arrived ice-carved and metronomic. "There are always choices Max. Decide now. Step back—or alternative measures will be enacted." Each syllable was emotionless, but it pierced the gnawing ache at Max's core.

"That's no choice."

"The world sees a brilliant man unravelling. Let them mourn a hero, Max. The alternative is watching them dismantle you when you're gone, not me." Harland's expression didn't crease. "Keep an office if you like. But this one's off-limits. Optics matter."

Savouring the spectacle, he continued: "The record will note you as architect and founder. Your legacy is in good hands."

The words sank inside him—cold, immovable, final. As Harland took his leave, his duty complete, his grin optimised, Max's hand hovered over his desktop display, above a specific command. The override existed for the automatic door—theoretically. It switched the system to manual if anything ever broke. It had never been needed until now.

Reeves strode to the far side of the room with the unshakable confidence of a man who had never needed to look back—until his face struck the sealed glass. A dull impact echoed; a hairline crack spidered across the pane, and with it, the illusion of control fractured. The scent of cologne and metal clung to the atmosphere.

Harland's expression darkened—confusion flashing, irritation following, before his mask reassembled.

"Oh. Darn," Max remarked, a wry chuckle breaking through his resignation. "I've been trying to get someone to fix that bug for weeks. Maybe you'll have better luck now."

Harland didn't give in to a response. He set a hand against the door and pushed. It gave easily, it was only a door now, automatic switched off. Simple, yet effective. Max watched him slip through. Then pressed the button. The door slid shut with a satisfying snap.

He didn't dislike people, but the more he got to know Harland, the more he understood that label didn't fit him. Humanity wasn't a guiding principle for everyone. He knew that. But Reeves counted the living on a spreadsheet and valued the dead on a balance sheet.

Max let the tension drain out of him. He gathered the last of his things, trying to move on muscle memory alone. He touched each object like it belonged to someone else.

His console chimed—a new email: Alan Prescott. Induction scheduled for 10:15 PM. The name landed differently than he'd anticipated. Afterdeath had inducted ambitious scientists before. But there was a familiarity to him—a kind of reckless vision that felt all too close to home. His reputation balanced breakthroughs with backlash, the kind of friction Max once knew firsthand.

He weighed Prescott's scheduled entry against Remy Moreau's sudden arrival. He'd built the pipeline to be self-contained—contacts lined up, documents signed, timelines clear. Remy didn't fit that. She hadn't registered, hadn't consented. She dropped into the grid like a breach, not a client. Alan came with steps to follow. Remy showed up as noise—raw data, a scan, a countdown already in motion. He had argued it was protocol. Beneath that—always—was the need for control.

He hadn't planned it. He opened the file and read on. She reminded him of someone—though that resemblance wasn't supposed to surface. He saved her. No one had stepped in for his mother, and he wouldn't stand by again. The link took time to surface. But once he acted, he didn't stop.

If he couldn't account for others anymore, perhaps his own diminishing future deserved some attention. His condo at Harbourfront was usually home. Bare—and empty. The family home was harder: too many memories, too much left unfinished. His father was as good a reason as any to return to the farmstead. But it was his mother's grave that truly called him back. His brother, well, that was another confrontation for another day.

He took his jacket and keys and headed for the door. The old magazine drew his eye again—The Man Who Conquered Death. A lie built for comfort, he thought. He'd only ever offered payment plans. Death, in the end, always collected.

CHAPTER THREE
QUANTUM LEAP

The monitors hummed, each beep marking the planned descent. Alan Prescott lay motionless, hands folded over the sheet. It was late—well past time for anyone to arrive. Life support had already shifted to its lowest setting, conserving energy for a body nearing its limit.

Outside, the city pressed on. Midtown's endless bustle persisted—automated taxis slipped through barely-there gaps while red lights flared atop unfinished towers. New York's machine never truly stopped, yet lately, it rarely reached his senses.

It wasn't extinction—it was surrender. A trade between muscle and memory. Afterdeath had earned its place—comforting the grieving, placating the cautious. But now, facing the edge, Prescott understood: the test was never simply technical. It was personal.

His worldly affairs were in order. He'd even refined a second will after the pre-humous divorce. His Afterdeath personal realm had been chosen months ago. He was one of the few who'd submitted a complete call list for their newest feature: Legacy Link.

It wasn't the pain that wore him down. It was the erosion. The slow subtraction of abilities once so automatic they'd never seemed worth naming. Holding a spoon. Buttoning a shirt. Breathing without supervision. Trusting a cough or a hiccup not to become something else. His limbs betrayed him—muscles stalled, then quit. His voice thinned out, words slurring and sticking, until speaking required more effort than it yielded.

Some days, the mind inside felt whole—undimmed, alert. But it could only watch as the machinery failed, like a signal with no receiver.

He didn't fear death. Not anymore. What haunted him was the long interval—this drawn-out erosion where the body obeyed its cruel schedule while the self remained, intact but powerless. Not extinguished. Withheld. The ache of being present long after you've gone. He knew what the commercials promised instead: clean exits, perfect uploads, peace. But he couldn't fathom a future without the doom and gloom of extinction looming somewhere. That, at least, had felt honest. His worries gathered force: Could the next version of him preserve what mattered? Would his thoughts, memories, and sense of self—each strand that made him Alan—survive the conversion intact? He couldn't tell if he was truly crossing over—or if a better-behaved version of him would get to live inside Afterdeath's digital snow globe.

The doubt was snowballing. He had no answers. What rose inside him was weariness shaped into direction by the ticking of the clock. Two minutes left. At the foot of the bed the nurse checked the monitors, let the numbers level out, and glanced his way with calm assurance before speaking.

"Values look good—whenever you feel ready, we can begin," she said, more bedside reassurance than procedure.

He eased back against the bed, letting the last of the tension slip loose. "I suppose this is the cue for last words?" he ventured with dry humour.

The nurse looked up briefly, her face remaining impassive yet kind. "Most people have something to say."

A faint pull at his mouth, reflex more than amusement, as his eyes wandered the flawless surface of the wall—smooth, pale, and so carefully anonymous it almost dared him to find meaning in it.

"If I die surrounded by this wallpaper, I want it listed as an accomplice," he muttered.

The laugh that followed surprised them both. Brief, but real. She met his eyes with something lighter.

"You're the dodo guy, right?"

He exhaled a dry laugh. "Unfortunately, yes. Marketing really ran with that one."

Raising an intrigued eyebrow, she continued, "So you resurrected a species humans wiped out—and now you worry about a nickname?"

He recentred himself on the mattress. "I'd prefer a name with a bit more dignity," he said.

She glanced around uncomfortably. "Will anyone be here for your induction?"

He met her eyes. "The stockholders maybe," he said, dry and flat, letting the words speak for themselves.

She didn't get it. Or at least, she didn't correct him.

"No one's coming," he admitted.

Her stance eased, though she hadn't fully relaxed. "I could stay," she offered. "If you want someone around."

A faint change touched her features—genuine, if brief.

"That won't be necessary," he replied, restrained, clinging to some small measure of control.

She didn't look away, but headed for the door—agreement passing between them.

The latch clicked shut behind her, leaving him alone to his fate.

For a while, he stayed exactly as he was. The tension in his hands ebbed away. He closed his eyes and listened—regular beats tracing out time around him. It sounded like breathing. It felt like his.

As the last threads of awareness frayed, the machines took over. Beneath the soft click of monitors, a deeper choreography unfolded. Tiny machines flowed through his blood toward the brain, recording the state of each cell before decay set in. They didn't battle death; they simply mapped his entire neural pattern, logging every cell and signal in his brain. His consciousness, already loosening from its biological moorings, barely registered the migration. The fixative compounds cooled his tissue even as the swarm worked, preserving the intricate lattice of thought before entropy could blur the lines.

Somewhere beyond the haze, quantum relays were primed to receive the full map of him, the stored pattern, waiting for the conversion. Only the sensation of being lifted in transit—weightless, drawn by forces he could neither see nor resist.

The first thing he noticed was his skin—a liminal contour, faintly cooled. It was sunlight, falling in a way that made the sensation cohere and wake him.

Air flowed freely through his lungs—painless, unforced.

He felt the sensations gather: the brush of air across his face, the faint give of earth beneath his hands. Immediate. Tangible. He opened his eyes slowly. A wide, green meadow stretched before him. Realigning himself subtly, feeling the familiar allegiance of muscles responding freely. He let the moment linger, trusting the ground beneath him.

He recalled a line from the early white papers—a concept that had seemed theoretical once: noetic gravity. Consciousness, once patterned and sustained, would keep reaching for coherence, for centre, even after the body let go. Meaning didn't remain in place—it was drawn inward, pulled together by something deeper than consciousness: a noetic force.

He felt that pull now—not as revelation, but as something simpler. Direction maybe. An announcement rose through the low electronic murmur—even, polished, unmistakably artificial.

"Alan Prescott, welcome to your Induction. I am Alma." As it spoke, a figure resolved nearby: the silhouette of a woman, bathed in pale blue, a light-traced humanoid outline.

He lifted an eyebrow but didn't react—he'd seen the proposal decks. He expected Alma, at least in concept.

"Not Kansas."

"Feedback acknowledged." Alma responded reflexively, untouched by the humour, or the irony.

He figured if there was a human at the other end of that feedback chain, they would get it.

He kept his eyes on the horizon, anticipating the engineered veneer to fracture and expose the construct's scaffolding—or a layer deeper he hadn't accounted for. Instead, he watched as a door of light formed.

As if summoned by buried anxieties, a clear panel swung into view at the rim of his vision. His brow furrowed; a chill crept through him.

LEGACY LINK – WIFE.

A countdown began—ten, nine, eight—dragging on with the sting of debts unpaid. His mouth tightened. Of course she was calling. He'd meant to update the details, meant to close that door properly. Instead, he'd left it hanging open. He had no one but himself to blame. Five, Four—Letting it ring would stretch the awkwardness even tighter. Better to take the hit, weather it, and move on. With the kind of breath reserved for root canals and tax season, he accepted the call.

And there she was. Alive. Framed by the lived-in mess of a new house that wasn't his. No reunion, no catharsis—only the strain of distance hung between them. She wasn't doing well. He could see it in the way she sat: braced, weary, half-turned from the camera, as if even now she was holding the world at arm's length. Grief, he thought, didn't always look like wailing. Sometimes it looked like this.

"Alan, we have an issue with the estate." Her voice sounded tired, worn thin by days like this. "The lawyers are debating both your wills."

He rubbed at his forehead. "Figures. Even in the afterlife, the paperwork finds me." The words came out flatter than he intended, another box to check in a life that wouldn't quite let go.

He glanced toward the empty horizon, the pale stretch of promise he hadn't even reached yet. "Can I at least walk into the light first, Priscila?" he added, his patience about as thin as his humour.

She didn't laugh. But she didn't scold either. "Alan—"

His attention slipped to the digital horizon—a pale sky hanging over a pastoral stretch they used to dream about retiring to. "I should've taken care of it," he murmured.

She refused to rush, allowing a fragile honesty to take shape between them.

"You look better than I would have expected." She gave a faint smile. The old kind.

"I suppose it's easier to talk to the man standing than the one fading." As soon as the words left him, he knew they landed drier than he intended. Pain flashed behind her eyes.

"Please, Alan." There was nothing left to fight over.

The connection cut. The final words hung between them. He wasn't surprised—quick exits and incomplete farewells were nothing new. He pressed his palm briefly against his forehead and let the light take him.

Seconds later, the Pearly Gates came into view. He slowed, taking in the layout with a familiar, measured eye. The grass stretched out in immaculate bands, too flawless to feel accidental, leading toward a pair of monument-like pillars that framed the path ahead. It was beautiful. The single winding path offered little doubt about where he was expected to go. Prescott found himself wondering how many focus groups it had taken to get it right—how many committees had reviewed the curve of the path, the height of the grass, the hue of the light, until the place told you, without ever speaking, exactly what you were supposed to do.

He noticed the queue—less a line than a slow gathering, a drift of people finding their way forward. Each stood with an Alma assistant nearby, but there was no order to the movement. Some falling over their previews, fiddling with details or lingering on a choice they hadn't quite finished. Others barely glanced, their paths already long decided. A few exchanged words, small pieces of life spilling into the open, free of pretense.

He tipped his head back and saw the sleek, hovering Afterdeath sign. Its polished surface spelled out a message with brutal efficiency:

YOU NO LONGER MATTER.

He squinted, half-expecting it to vanish—and it did. A new directive slid into place:

PLEASE STAY CALM AND QUEUE.

He stayed frozen—briefly. Was it a logic breach? A delayed fragment of some deeper honesty? He scanned the people around him. No one else seemed to react; their attention stayed pinned to their previews, undisturbed. He let the question hover, unanswered. Whatever it had been—a test, a slip, a break in the mask—it didn't change what he had to do next.

Moments like this, he fell back on basic math. Predictable systems made the unknowable feel structured. The line nudged ahead—one slow shuffle every ten seconds, by his rough guess. That meant roughly six people per minute, assuming no failures in the handoff. Twelve per two minutes. Thirty in five. That would do. He noted the tells—those brief lapses, recalculations, fragments of doubt—and calculated he'd cut their time in half. His decisions were already made. No dithering, no rewrites. When his turn came, he'd cross in four seconds flat.

He slid his hands into his pockets and stepped with it, falling into the rhythm without thinking. Nobody barked orders. Nobody needed to. The path advanced at timed intervals, calibrated to the crowd.

As he waited, he found himself studying the previews blossoming to life ahead of each person—unfolding images of cities, mountains, oceans, grand designs stitched together by longing and unfinished plans. He felt no judgement in it. If anything, he admired it—the impulse to dream in dimensions.

His own preview filled a nearby window, a modest cottage tucked inside a place that looked like a living oil painting. Alan chose Loch Awe because he needed a place that neither required him to matter, nor demanded that he forget who he was.

In front of him, a broad-shouldered man with a square jaw and an almost cartoonish perfection in his hair activated a preview with unyielding confidence, summoning an expansive cavern rendered in crisp three dimensions. The walls were meticulously detailed, carefully lit, and decorated with relics for maximum effect—a giant penny propped against a stalagmite, an oversized playing card near the entrance, and, in the shadows, a skeletal dinosaur poised mid-roar. His lips twitched as he recognized the Batcave immediately—a Silver Age vision where everything was larger than life and logic was optional. There was no ambiguity, no half-measures; whoever had requested it had made up their mind, and the engine had delivered. He respected that determination and even envied it a little.

The man's expression changed as doubt crept in. "Wait," he said, eyes flicking between the giant penny and the skeletal dinosaur. "This—this isn't the Classic Batcave." He frowned. "I asked for the Classic Batcave."

He arched an eyebrow. It looked perfect to him. Now, the word classic carried too much baggage—like asking a room of Star Wars fans to pick a favourite trilogy and watching chaos erupt. He knew exactly what he had prepared for himself.

Before he could take another step, a greeting came from behind him. "Well, I'll be damned—Prescott?"

The name landed like a cue rehearsed. He looked over and saw Barry Linwood stepping out from the queue—standing with the calm purpose of someone who knew where he belonged, tie neatly in place. He looked exactly as Alan had always known him—friendly, tie straight, with a practised ease that almost hid the worry lingering behind his eyes.

"Didn't think I'd run into you here," Barry said almost teasing. "Then again, you always did prefer to arrive unnoticed."

He hesitated, thrown by the sudden familiarity. "Barry? How the hell are you even here? You've been gone for years."

Barry gave a small shrug, hands loose at his sides. "I check in sometimes. Help people find their feet."

Alan gave a short huff. "Help people—or scout all the promising women before they realize they have better options?"

Barry didn't take the bait.

"Maybe both," he said lightly. "Good work either way."

Barry didn't look away yet. "And you?" he asked, not as a joke this time. "How are you finding it so far?"

He shrugged, half defensive. "I asked for a little peace, and quiet."

"Sometimes that's harder to live with than noise," Barry said, slow and measured, letting the words land on their own.

Alan's mind drifted back to the call from his ex-wife. "Depends on the signal, I guess."

They stood with it—Barry refusing to read into the comment the conversation hanging half-formed between them. Barry, with the ease of long practice, let it pass like so many other things unsaid.

"Well. I'll let you get back to it."

He raised an eyebrow. "Back to what, exactly?"

"You'll tell me," Barry said. "Eventually." With that, he walked away—unhurried, confident, as if Alan's tight-lipped response hadn't touched him. He blended back into the queue without looking back.

He watched him leave. The distance felt permanent.

His slot arrived next. He lifted his eyes to the doorway, feeling its invitation rather than any command. The others ahead of him had all passed with green; he found himself wondering if anyone ever saw anything else.

Above him, the signal sequenced in order. A small sign, but a real one: he had been seen, counted, allowed to continue on his own terms. He accepted it, and entered his personal realm for the first time.

In a smooth, unceremonious realm jump, the Gates gave way, and Alan entered his personal realm. Loch Awe unfolded before him—its surface stirred with faint ripples, casting morning light over the mirrorlike water.

The path unfolded before him in broad curves. He walked at his own pace, absorbing the land as it rose and fell around him—hills brushed in muted green, the slopes broken by mossy outcrops and long seams of exposed rock. Farther off, the higher ridges dissolved into morning mist, blurring the boundary between earth and sky. A lone bird cut a wide arc overhead, its call cutting across the open air.

The shore gave way in slow, worn curves, stitched with reeds and patches of wild grass that leaned into the water's pull. The loch spread outward, its surface gleaming, reflection revealing the shapes below. Alan traced its outlines with his attention as he walked. He noticed the water stir—a faint ripple where light followed the current.

Every detail felt lived-in, not imagined—a world built with the kind of care that left no imprint of its own hand. Near the bend, the cottage came into view. Rough-hewn stone, a slate roof darkened by moss, a narrow chimney releasing a thin line of smoke into the pale sky. It stood exactly as he had visualized it, and yet finer, more complete than even memory could claim.

He moved inside, each step deliberate, rehearsing the act of belonging. The air inside carried a steady heat from the fire, neither overpowering nor thin. He closed the door. Nothing moved but the fire.

When the sun dropped behind the hills, he pulled back the blanket on the narrow bed and lay down, the day drawing to a close with the ease of something finished.

He woke at the same hour each morning. It didn't matter, but changing it felt wrong. Waking with the light was stitched into him, too deep to unpick now. Even here, stripped of deadlines and demands, his body followed the old rhythm. Habit had outlived the reasons.

The tea was an act of patience, not comfort. He spent damp mornings wandering the meadow edges, picking meadowsweet blossoms where the stems ran red and the loch mist clung to the banks. He rinsed the flowers clean, boiled the loch water over birch twigs and driftwood, and let the petals steep until the steam carried their faint, honey-almond scent. Sometimes he'd blend in gorse petals or a pinch of mint, the cup blooming from pale gold to green, the flavours hinting at wild hills and sun-warmed bracken. Each sip was more tonic than treat—earthy, sometimes sharp, a taste as much about endurance as pleasure. He conjured old stories of the plants—Cú Chulainn's meadowsweet, the lore about nettles "putting iron in your blood"—and found himself, for once, wanting to believe them.

Fishing was no less a lesson in humility. The rocks along Loch Awe's shore wore slippery coats of moss; the wind cut sudden and cold over the water, rippling the surface and carrying the calls of distant gulls. He started with a fly rod, threading local patterns—Greenwell's Glory, anything to mimic the frantic dance of insects in morning light. When that failed, he tried spinning spoons near the drop-offs, feeling every vibration as he reeled in, hopeful for the thump of a brown trout or the jagged strike of a perch. Most casts returned empty, or with a lure lost to weed beds or submerged alder roots. He watched the water for the rings left by rising fish, learned to spot the perch that schooled in the shallows near the reeds, and listened for the stories of monstrous pike—water-wolves—shared by locals at the pub. On rare afternoons, when he landed a modest trout, he traced its pink, cold skin with reverence, knowing he'd earned little more than an hour's peace.

The driftwood he found was no blank canvas—it had a will, shaped by years tumbling in the loch's current, grain bleached and twisted, knots hiding under the silvery bark. He learned to dry the wood by the fire, feeling the weight ease as water bled out. Some pieces, birch or rowan, split along old scars if he carved too soon; others, especially oak blackened by the peat, resisted the blade and left his hands sore. He used a crook knife for bowls and a gouge for deeper cuts, sometimes rubbing a thumb along the new grain to test for splinters. On evenings when the need to fix something faded, he traced old patterns—a thistle, a five-pointed rowan star, the curl of a salmon's tail—into the wood, finishing each piece with oil and a small hope that it would outlast the season. When the fire was low, he kept a carved spoon or charm close at hand, the touch of real work grounding him in ways nothing else did.

One evening, he sat by the fire with an old Darwin biography—its spine grooved from years of handling, the pages thinned to near transparency in places. The story surfaced easily: Darwin's son asked a neighbour plainly, Where does your father keep his barnacles? As if the presence of such work, such obsession, was natural. Expected. His mouth twitched. He closed the book halfway over his hand and let the fire's slow light illuminate the room.

The kettle began its whistling. He filled the cup and sat down. He drank, the heat tracing a familiar path down his throat. His mind kept moving. He nudged the book higher on his thigh, steadied the cup—futile distractions against a thought that kept circling. The world remained intact around him—the whistle gone, the fire dimmed—but the question kept pacing the outer rim of his mind.

Darwin had spent eight years cataloguing barnacles, a stretch longer than any war, longer than some marriages. Barnacles weren't grand or noble or even beautiful. They were endless—and endlessly unfinished. Each answer bred more questions. The willingness to pour time and care into something that didn't promise applause, only understanding. That was the difference between work that filled time and work that filled a life. He rested the book on his knee, the fire holding the room in place. Where were his barnacles?

He glanced at Alma's avatar—glossy, serene, engineered to reassure without ever saying so. It was purposeless companionship. That presence was the last thing he needed.

"Alma," he said, "that will be all."

She had done nothing wrong. That's what bothered him. She was built to please everyone—and he didn't want everyone's answer. He rubbed at his temple. What he needed wasn't comfort—it was friction. A presence that could check him when he went off course. He rebuilt the settings to match his plan, working through the familiar protocols until only one choice remained.

The name.

His fingers hovered over the entry field. Names had always tripped him—genus, species, subspecies. Ninety-nine percent of the time, they were inherited, not chosen. And when there was room for invention, the naming never belonged to him. A de-extinction expert wasn't meant to create the new—only bring back the old, again. On the rare occasions he did have to name something—a pet, a rare find, a character in a game—he dried up like the time he spent three hours naming a save file "Save1_Final_2." But this one surfaced on its own.

He remembered his old comics—where impossible questions met unstoppable minds. One name rose to the top. He typed it: R—E—E—D. The console accepted the entry.

The image resolved—a tall, slightly rumpled man in a tailored jacket. He looked like someone who'd slept in his clothes, then fixed his collar before walking into a meeting. Casual, almost forgettable—until you saw the eyes. Keen, alert, already scanning the space ahead of him. Not waiting to be told—waiting for the data to start.

"Right. Let's get to it, sir," said Reed.

"First things first. Drop the sir, we work together, not for each other."

"Understood."

"Right then. Workshop, nuclear microscopes, and somewhere to hide from metaphysics."

They drank tea as they planned—supply chains, tool access, and the bitter precision of gunpowder green.

After a vacation in relevance, Alan was a work in progress again.

CHAPTER FOUR
GRAILSPOTTING

Near the fire pit, Remy crouched and brushed aside a trail of ash from the logs. Her fingers hit the rim of a can—shallow in the dirt, swollen from heat. She pulled it free, soot streaking her knuckles.

The can still held warmth; its sides dulled by long exposure to coals. She cleared off the residue with her hand. The lid hissed as it opened, releasing a scent she recognized: molasses, pork fat, tin. Old family recipe—really, just fire, earth, and patience. Another test for the world she built. By smell alone, it passed.

She sat back on her heels and ate straight from the can, the warmth settling into her palms. The beans stayed intact but gave way easily, suspended in syrup darkened and thickened by time. Smoke had crept in through the metal. The pork fat had pooled near the bottom, rich and absorbed by the beans. Nothing had burned. The trick was distance. You buried the can when the fire had worked itself down, not before. She finished the last bite, scraping the bottom, and set the can aside.

Remy scanned her forest clearing. It was untouched, though strangely, that had taken some work. It felt like the beginning of something, not the thing itself. She would need to venture further if she wanted to finish what she'd started.

The default settings and tools could only do so much. She didn't want to replace what she'd made—only take a peek at what's out there to get a better sense of what belongs in here. There were things she simply needed: tools, animals to keep the trees and pond company—things she wouldn't know she needed until she found them.

It was time to go looking. She summoned a panel and brought up public realms. After reminding herself not to get lost in wonderland, she aimed to pick a destination that could help her get what she was looking for.

The first listing shimmered into view: Luvoir Campus—an orbital learning hub suspended above a simulated moon. Classrooms spun at soft rotational gravity, solar sails unfurled like banners, and every subject from particle physics to poetry had a dedicated wing. Inductees could even host lectures, give their own talks, or audit any topic from zero to forever. Remy nearly smiled, then swiped it away. Too soon for school. That one felt like revisiting the scene of the crime. Was an eternal garage sale out of the question? Remy kept looking. The next one snagged her attention, briefly—Pacific City. The preview shimmered, casting up neon strips stitched between glass towers, a city built for visitors and forgotten by the people who worked there. It looked like a paradise—a place that welcomed guests but never offered a way back. Remy flicked it away without thinking. Landscapes spun past her fingertips, most curated to impress but not to stay. A few snagged the mind, marking where her attention slowed.

The next one called her name right as the description unfolded. Everstacks. The largest department store on the network. If you have a demand, they have the supply. Endless options. No checkout. It looked absurd. Exhausting. Perfect. The kind of store where no one could find what they came for—but everyone left with something. This looked like the right kind of mess.

She tapped the icon.

The ground kicked sideways, snapped level. The scent of pine, the rough pull of earth—gone. Replaced by a vast parking lot, the surface broad and faded, paint peeling away in places.

Everstacks dominated the horizon—an ocean of concrete and glass, built to serve anyone, belonging to no one. It felt like any superstore she'd ever visited—endless and neutral, engineered to erase the shopper as thoroughly as the shelves. Remy remembered childhood weekends beneath fluorescent lights, how sound disappeared the deeper you got. Here, there was no echo, no noise at all—only the slow buzz overhead and the shine of polished floors. The windows mirrored the sky back at her: blank, pastel, refusing to sell even the weather.

She looked up at the sign. Not bold, not boastful—there. This wasn't a casino, or a theme park, or even a Walmart with its veneer of welcome and threat. The name tried to pretend it wasn't selling anything. In a way, it almost worked. She thought back to her last memories with Jess and Darby. Mall after. She'd made it, technically. But it felt like there was always another aisle left to cross. The aisles stretched on, promising closure, but offering only more aisles. Remy almost laughed. For all the infinite choices, every line and shelf felt designed to keep her moving, to keep her from arriving. There were no carts, no checkout lanes, no crowds pressing for the last of anything. In this afterlife, the Black Friday clock never started. Everything was stocked, always free, never urgent. Even her economics teacher would've given up trying to explain why.

This was the big box dream, finally untethered from money, from time, from anything human enough to want. The only thing missing was need.

The entrance was open; she went inside. The air carried a faint scent of plastic wrap, and cardboard ink. Shelves stretched outward in all directions—stacked with food, clothes, toys, and tools. Every row stood pristine, and the displays were arranged with a reverent exactness. She wandered aimlessly, her boots making the kind of sound you only noticed when you were alone.

The signs had been hung with intention once—practical, human, a little off-kilter in the way real hands leave things.

She stopped near the entrance and glanced back, searching for the familiar anchor of a checkout counter. The space offered none. Registers had vanished. Conveyor belts, employees, even the hum of scanned barcodes—erased. Aisles stretched farther, each one unbroken, each path without closure.

The carts near the entrance stood in neat alignment, waiting to be used by people who never paused or doubted. She spared them no glance.

She wasn't here to follow the old routine.

Yesterday, she stumbled on a feature called realm storage. It was so simple, she had questioned it at first with a few tests. Anything she tucked inside became hers, silently and without resistance. She could stroll out with a tree—or an entire building—and the world nodded along.

Afterdeath, she realized, prized convenience over conversation.

She entered the maze of Everstacks, somewhere in between PETS and SEASONAL. The next bend led into dimmer light.

A long tank stretched along the side wall. Koi Habitat, Model No. 47C. Behind the glass, three koi swam through the water. One, pitch black, cut a slow arc through the current. Another flashed orange, darting ahead in restless bursts. A third shimmered between hues, never resolving into one colour.

This seemed like as good a spot as any to try out the storage trick. She glanced around, found nothing that looked like a net or scoop. Honestly, she had no clue how you'd even get these in the cart. Did the goldfish in a water bag method apply here? Even in the waking world, this would be a dubious task.

The console shortcut made it easy. The water rippled once, and the koi swam into her realm storage. Her non-existent bank account remained intact. It worked. She'd found something alive—something to live beside her. What else would she encounter?

She passed towers of unopened cookware, rows of bundled winter coats, bins of boxed board games—all neat, all waiting. The maze of Everstacks opened around her, wide but familiar, as if parts of it had already been claimed in her mind.

Overhead, a placard read: PERSONAL CARE.

The hallway ahead dimmed. Mirrors lined both walls, each one reflecting her image down the line. Each mirror angled with retail logic. The mirrors reflected her as she was, but hinted at the versions she might have tried on if she had a moment.

Her reflection didn't blink—same eyes, same slouch, carrying what she hadn't figured out how to leave behind. Her hand hovered near the glass, testing whether it might respond.

Icons bloomed outward, translating stray thoughts into rendered shapes.

She tapped one. Bell-bottoms took form—vivid, dated, wrong. She gave a quick, surprised laugh. The look didn't fit. It felt adopted—somebody else's nostalgia, briefly worn.

She swiped at the pants and a vintage dress appeared—wistful in its folds. A pressed uniform followed—rigid, declarative. A flick upward produced a wide-brimmed hat.

She kept swiping. A few made her grin. Others missed entirely. But beneath the novelty, something surfaced. These weren't disguises. They were pitches—drafts of lives that once might have belonged to her.

Then something clicked: a cloak, thick, worn through in places, built for use more than display. It didn't highlight her features or pose her like a mannequin. It simply fit, as if it had always known her shape. The kind of thing you reached for without thinking. She traced the seam. The fabric resisted—coarse, lined, meant for weather and work. The rest was stagewear. This she would wear into the world.

As the outfit carousel faded, the mirror's edges dimmed—icons receding, others surfacing on their own. First came a discreet bar labeled Hair Colour. Remy slid it once, watching her familiar chestnut fade to silver. The change felt light, playful.

Next appeared Height, and beside it, another labeled: Breast. She winced at the word and paused; her fingers hovered over the control before moving to the bridge of her nose.

She scanned through the icons in a slow orbit, testing some, skipping others. Now and then, a change surfaced that felt true in ways she couldn't explain. She was nearly finished.

Then the Age slider appeared.

Remy's mind nearly stalled. Though her right hand broke through the numbness, easing it backward until Fifteen slid into place.

Her reflection changed: limbs narrowing, posture melting, the guarded precision of her expression softening into a face she hadn't seen in a lifetime.

Okay, maybe she'd earned that joke. It disarmed her, in a way she hadn't prepared for. Freckles dotted her cheeks. Her eyes looked wider—not from innocence, exactly, but from a lack of rehearsal. That version of herself hadn't learned how to brace. She expected things to keep unfolding.

Spoiler alert. They didn't.

She slid past her younger self and became Seventeen. An age beyond aftermath. Her mouth had a slant like she knew what not to say. Carrying knowledge, a balance learned the hard way. Though it wasn't earned, it was painted on.

She stared at that draft longer than she meant to. She looked like someone getting ready to leave home. Or give a speech. Or say yes. Maybe all three.

She couldn't help but catch a glimpse of her Eighteen. She carried herself like she belonged—not here, but wherever she chose to stand. Remy could picture her filling out college forms, staying late for something important, planning a weekend without needing permission. A woman no one would've overlooked.

It all looked complete—but unfamiliar. Finished in a way that felt rehearsed. An image built for interviews, engagement photos, seating charts—everything that required certainty. She looked cast, not chosen.

Remy didn't see herself in that face. A tidy arc of cause and effect, as if this was the version that would have surfaced if nothing had broken the line. But someone had.

She stepped back.

Each face was a drafted future, plausible but unlived. The slider showed progress—but she saw absence. Not the wonder of becoming, but the quiet subtraction of years she never got to fumble through.

What she needed wasn't a resolution. She wasn't working toward a fixed image; she was creating room to stay in motion, to misstep and change her mind. To live long enough to be wrong, to regret something, to repair it.

She looked again at the final image—polished and poised. Maybe she'd grow into her. Maybe not. If that future ever arrived, it would belong to her alone—built day by day, not handed down by any script.

She wouldn't accept some preset.

Keeping only the cloak, she reset every change until she was simply Remy Moreau. Sixteen. Pushing six feet.

Behind her, the mirrored corridor dissolved into recursion. Ahead, the ambient churn of Everstacks took over—insistent, impersonal, and nearly endless. She'd found a few things already. Fish for the pond. A cloak shaped for her. The pieces were starting to fit together.

Her old tent had come with a regulation bag—serviceable, but never hers. She hadn't found real rest since she got here. Maybe what she needed next was a sleeping bag of her own.

Her eyes drifted upward, scanning for signs that might point to bedding—maybe near the blankets, or wherever this place thought pillows belonged.

ELECTRONICS →

HOME & GARDEN ↑

RECREATION ←

None of it aligned. She stood beneath the signs a while, trying to parse their logic—if there was any. Sleeping bags weren't decor, exactly. But they weren't quite tools either. After a long beat, she angled toward HOME & GARDEN, hoping it leaned more domestic than decorative.

The aisles opened around her—bright, endless, reset-perfect. Bedding. Lighting. Planters. She passed each by. Bath linens followed. She scanned the signs again, trying to orient herself. A structure beyond the shelves pulled her eye. Somewhere between drawer pulls and curtain rods, she lost track of time. Several minutes later, another cluster of signs came into view, glowing above a junction.

FURNITURE →

SEATING & ACCENTS ↑

BEDROOM SETS →

The space carried ambient authority—the kind of muzak built to dissolve thought, lighting meant to keep you browsing, digital price tags flickering through numbers like they were guessing what you'd pay.

She had arrived somewhere. Around her, the aisles no longer restocked on demand. Foot traffic was almost nonexistent. It felt like she'd wandered into a dead zone—one of those places in the waking world where no one could get signal. But that wasn't the issue here.

She had yet to figure out how to refer to that other world. The one where her family lived. It wasn't hers anymore. And yet, she referenced it more often than she wanted to admit.

She scanned the signs again, trying to orient herself, when a structure beyond the shelves caught her eye. The displays ended abruptly. The racks gave way. In the open space beyond, structure took form—built, not guessed, each element placed with intention.

A fortress had claimed the bedding section. Not thrown together. Built. Certa and Sealy boxes made the base, lined and stacked with purpose. Mattresses stood as walls, bound with bungee cords and ratchet straps. Full-body pillows curved into archways, each one placed with care. Sheets stretched smooth over surfaces in repeating patterns. Quilts hung over the middle tiers—thick, functional, and balanced. Throw blankets hung as banners. Heavier toppers pressed into the highest points, retaining their shape with enduring compression.

It wasn't chaos. The fortress before her was equal parts childhood blanket fort, apocalypse bunker, and tribute to every mythic sanctuary she'd ever read about or half-built as a kid. Pillows rose like ramparts, boxes stacked with a defender's logic, each gap closed off as if it might face a siege at dawn. Every corner felt mapped, corridors angled not for efficiency but for narrative effect—borrowed straight from Hyrule's labyrinths and reworked through the lens of Minecraft's trial-by-error genius. Quilts draped over archways, weighted blankets anchoring parapets, every layer bearing the visible marks of past failure and revision. Nothing here was accidental; it was a structure tested and rebuilt for a campaign only its architect could fully recollect. It bore the scent of detergent, old ambitions, and a defiance that ran deeper than play. This was not some forgotten aisle claimed by chaos. It was structure—every angle chosen, every fold proof that the builder believed in comfort as defence. Here, the logic of childhood had survived, layered over with the grit of someone who needed to make sanctuary real.

The signs pointed clearly—sleeping bags were inside. She advanced, cloak whispering past endcaps stocked with vacuum-sealed pillows.

At the threshold, Remy absorbed the layout and entered.

The response came swiftly. A gate swung inward with exacting force, two wedge pillows snapping into position with the choreography of ritual.

From the narrowing slit between stacked ottomans, a figure emerged in a fluid, practised motion. He landed in a low crouch, one knee pressed to the floor, one arm raised in greeting or command.

His tunic—two fleece throws artfully secured—draped with the aura of self-made royalty. A weathered name tag sagged near his collarbone, its adhesive failing but its message intact: BOB, KING. He sustained the pose—unshaken, fully committed—as he met her stare. He wasn't measuring proximity. He was reading her intent.

Seconds later, the faint but unmistakable sound of a trumpet fanfare came—from Bob himself, hands cupped, landing somewhere between conviction and comic failure. The proclamation followed, free of volume but full of performance—delivered with the theatrical cadence of a man who'd long since crowned himself and never asked permission.

"You dare approach the Kingdom of the Pillow Aisle?"

She blinked. She understood him. That was the strange part—it actually tracked. EverStacks had already broken her sense of what counted as normal.

But this—this was something else. A man in a folded crown—what looked like a towel and a bathrobe belt—stood in front of a fortress built from bedding. He wasn't joking.

"Um. I'm looking for a sleeping bag."

Bob studied her with the gravity of a dungeon master might appraise a party member who asked to bypass the story. He gave a solemn nod, as though she'd passed some invisible checkpoint.

"You seek the Inner Sanctum. It is not open to visitors or spies."

"So—the sleeping bag section is inside your fort."

Bob's posture contracted, shoulders drawing in the way someone does when they've had to defend the same point too many times.

"Tell me," he said, already certain of her answer. "Are you sent by him?"

"What?" Remy asked. "Who?"

His voice dropped, heavy with caution. "Don't pretend. You know who I mean."

She didn't. Only her shoulders moved.

"Jeff."

She still didn't.

The way Bob said the name, it wasn't fear. It was something larger—a force that warped the room by existing. Jeff wasn't a rival. He was something else.

"Leader of the Bean Baggers," he said, as if that explained anything.

Remy didn't respond right away. Something about the way he said Jeff—like invoking a broken prophecy—made her stomach tilt. This wasn't roleplay. He'd gone past it. Past parody, past logic, past whatever thread had once tied him to the real layout of the store.

He'd been here too long. The way some perishables forget they're perishable. The way a mind can spoil when the expiration date stops meaning anything. He wasn't armed, but that didn't make him safe.

Tread carefully, Remy thought. He's all out of Cocoa Puffs.

"I'm sent by no one," she said.

Bob weighed her response, the calculation obvious in his expression. He inclined his head—less guarded now, more formal.

"Very well. We parlay."

He receded and straightened his back, balancing the invisible grandeur of a crown that may or may not have once been a neck pillow.

"I am King Bob," he announced, tone deepening. "Ruler of the Pillow Aisle. Defender of Proper Sleep. Sovereign architect of this fortress."

She glanced past him. Extravagant, absurd—but beneath it, a reserved brilliance lent the structure its force.

"Okay," she said. "Impressive."

A tension in Bob's posture released—a low, settling relief of being understood. His expression changed—anger absent, but a darker layer surfaced. Intent, fully formed. "Not everyone values peace and rest," he said, finding firmer ground. "Some people would tear comfort to shreds if you let them."

She squared her stance and folded her arms. She picked up the pattern. "Let me guess," she said. "The Bean Baggers."

Bob straightened, as if summoned into conviction by the name itself. The glint returned to his eyes—righteous, weary, a little bit wounded.

"Exactly. They can't offer anyone true support. Only a slow descent into chaos."

He looked away, like he was recalling a moment he wished he hadn't.

For a second, Remy couldn't tell if he was being dramatic or if someone had actually been swallowed by a bean bag chair. She didn't ask.

"I have lost good men to their abyssal grasp," he said.

The smirk never came. The wink stayed absent. He believed it—or needed to. Without warning, he pivoted back to her. His posture stiff, his focus laser-cut.

"You have entered my domain seeking aid," Bob said, voice projected with the formality of a commander too often ignored. "But tell me—would you instead seek glory?"

He approached like a knight announcing his claim, posture formal. Pride sat where threat might have. Maybe even belief. A forgotten desire to fight for someone else's cause stirred in her—but she pushed it down. Her cause was elsewhere.

"Well actually, I'm sort of too busy right now for questing," she said, trying not to mock him.

The shift came small, practised—like a sovereign absorbing loss without yielding the crown. "And what, pray tell, do you offer in exchange for safe passage through my realm?"

She turned, eyes moving from the fortress back to him. He wasn't posturing. He stood with conviction, as though this exchange bore real consequence.

"Right," she said. "For the sleeping bag."

Bob gave no reply.

She could walk away. Say she didn't care. But that felt incomplete. Maybe she cared—though the Holy Quests thing was a step too far. The time for that hadn't come. Maybe he only wanted to know if he could trust her.

Remy straightened her cloak, squared her shoulders, and fixed Bob with a measured look.

"I claim no allegiance to Jeff or his unruly forces," she said, her voice catching the echo of his seriousness. "I've come in search of shelter—a worthy sleeping bag—knowing full well that the path to comfort is never freely given. If you need another to defend the borders of Rest, or to hold the line against the Bean Baggers and their schemes, then name my enemy, King Bob, and I'll serve with honour. Grant me safe passage, and your fortress will have my respect."

Her goal was to avoid overselling it—her tone walked the knife-edge between parody and earnest. A girl between a floor display and a throne made of bedding, offering a vow to a king who might fold if she didn't get the tone right.

He inclined his head—less guarded now, more formal.

Bob closed his eyes, letting the name sink into him like a rite fulfilled. With the deliberation of a man stepping into a role that mattered to him, he reached for the impractical sword mounted like a relic on his back. Its blade was faintly polished, its surface gleaming with the echoes of past battles.

He lifted it with both hands, his grip trained on belief. Whether he'd done this before or only imagined it didn't change the intent. "Kneel," he said, as if bestowing an honour.

She gave him a long, skeptical look, one brow raised, then bent her knees slightly—acknowledging the formality without slipping into full parody.

Bob paused with the timing of an invoked ritual, then lowered the flat of the blade against her left side—near the collar, above the line of the cloak. The contact was light, exact. A breath passed between gestures—silent, intentional—before he raised the blade and mirrored the motion on her right. The act felt studied in the way memory sometimes is: repeated until it meant something, whether born of history or hope.

"By sovereign right of the Pillow Aisle, and the binding laws of Restfulness and Structural Balance," his tone held no irony. "I dub thee—Dame Remy Moreau."

She kept her stance—measured to pass inspection, but not invitation. "An honour."

Bob nodded once and sheathed the sword. "You may rise."

She straightened, brushing her palms over her knees. She felt the same—mostly. She started to step away, but his words followed her. "Stand tall, Dame Moreau. The fight for rest is endless. Day, night, holidays. We defend until the shelves fall."

She lifted a hand in a half-wave, already walking. "Sure. I'll keep an eye out."

The fortress unfolded ahead of her—not as a barrier, but as an interior passage. What had first appeared as a wall now reconfigured itself into a walkway, shaped from the inside. What once served as defence now pointed forward, structured to receive rather than repel.

Inside, the world narrowed again into options. Tidy shelves of rolled sleeping bags lined the walls, sorted by thickness, season, and comfort metrics that didn't mean much here. Remy ran her fingers along a few, tugged one free, and unrolled it partway across a foam ottoman. The fabric was solid, reliable—nothing fancy. She folded it once, tucked it under her arm, and swiped it into storage.

She continued, letting Everstacks fade behind her. The shelves grew taller, stripped of arrangement. Labels dropped their sales pitches and switched to single-word function: THERMAL STRESS, FASTENERS, most of them blending into the background. A ceiling speaker looped twelve seconds of muzak, repetition cycling whether anyone listened or not. The main path had fractured into side corridors. Overhead signs thinned out—plain, painted metal with no branding.

A junction opened ahead. Two signs hung overhead: CONSOLES to the left. FIELD CALIBRATION to the right. Neither one stood out. Neither asked anything of her. The left-hand path looked hazier—like a seasonal display kept beyond relevance. Probably sentimental. The right looked unremarkable. Straightforward.

She veered right. Because it was there. Because it was the right-hand side. Because something in her legs made the choice before her mind did.

Around the corner, a man stood beside a heavily loaded cart, arms folded loosely as he surveyed his haul. It looked like prep for some deep-space assignment: oversized scopes, bridging tools pulsing in trained succession, rugged cases of data gear, and one device tagged Quantum Calibrator. Everything was stacked with the offhand confidence of a person used to moving fast and trusting the load to keep up—for now.

One of the kits near the top slipped free, tumbling toward the floor. Remy snatched the kit without thinking.

The man swiveled toward the sound, lifted one brow, and gave a small shrug. "You can keep it. I packed too much."

She glanced at the cart. His evaluation held—it overflowed with gear no one intended to haul solo. The kit felt different in her hands. Her fingers followed the sides, tilting the angle to catch the label: Manual Coding Kit – For When You'd Rather Build It Yourself.

It was plain. Practical. The kind of tool you picked when you cared more about control than comfort—built for those who trusted their own logic. People who needed to feel every line, test every boundary, and claim the outcome for themselves.

"Generous," she said—careful, yet candid.

"Hardly. Physics." He gestured to the pile with a resigned shrug. "Reed warned me I couldn't do it alone," he added. "I think you're proving him right."

"So—hauling everything at once wasn't part of the plan?" Remy raised an eyebrow.

"No. But I thought I could carry it anyway." His hands fell away from the cart, as if releasing more than cargo.

Remy tapped her wrist console. The inventory bloomed outward. "Here. Try this." She flicked through the settings and turned the display toward him.

He held back for a second—years of carrying alone had trained him to resist help—but something in her tone landed. He reached out and mirrored her movements.

One by one, the larger tools phased out of sight, collapsing into digital storage with seamless finality. The cart grew lighter.

"That's—alarmingly convenient," he said, measured but unguarded.

"Better than breaking your back," she agreed.

Alan's hand met Remy's, the contact sparking a slight jolt of familiarity, even through the formality.

"Alan."

"Remy."

They shook hands plainly—an unspoken agreement between equals, a choice to meet in the middle. For a second more, they stood there—composed, engaged.

She rebalanced the kit in her hands, the feel of it settling differently now—solid, well-worn, centring.

Alan readjusted the strap of what remained—a lighter carry, evenly balanced. "See you around."

"Yeah. See you," she said, voice trailing into thought.

She looked down at the kit in her hands, tilting it to meet her. Whatever had passed between them faded, carried now in the touch of tools meant to leave a mark. A coding kit—designed for control and clarity. Not for patches or shortcuts, but for those who shaped from inside the system, who tested limits, who built things meant to endure.

The lid released with a compressed hiss, revealing a layout built for utility. A low-profile keyboard rested in the top tray, its shallow keys shaped for touch more than speed. Beneath it, a compact array: circuit boards in rigid foam, a sensor stylus, heat-stable gloves, and a coil of slimline cables, wound tight and waiting. Nothing here was ornamental. Everything had a job. Tucked into the side panel, a handheld device rested in a custom slot. It was compact, grip-balanced, with a beveled lens at one end. It didn't resemble a scanner or sensor in any conventional sense. Its purpose was to detect structure, expose patterns, and identify the operational logic behind any object or structure it was aimed at. It was designed to reveal how things worked and how they might be revised.

In the lower tray, a cylindrical component sat nested in foam—built for force-routing or structural load. It was engineered for integration. Every surface was finished to tolerance. Every seam aligned. There was no instruction manual. It didn't need one. Anyone qualified to use it would understand it on sight. Remy traced her fingers across the layout—keyboard, cables, electrostatic discharge gloves, the lens tool, the core. These weren't consumer tools or placeholders wrapped in flair. They were instruments of function, shaped for modification at the root level. These tools offered origin, not reaction. She would no longer adapt to structure. She would define it.

She closed the lid slowly, not as a gesture of finality, but of intent. The tools weren't conceptual anymore. They weren't symbolic. They were operational. Remy had stopped interpreting. She was ready to build.

CHAPTER FIVE
TOMORROW, MAYBE

It had been a little more than a week since Remy's death, but the house remained frozen in time. The cereal bowl sat untouched on the counter, the spoon carefully balanced on its side—as though she had simply stepped away mid-bite. Beside the sink, a mug of coffee had long since cooled, its warmth a distant memory. Élise stared at it, unsure if it had ever been hers. Each detail led back to what was missing. She pressed her hand briefly against the doorframe for support, as if the walls might give under her touch.

"Denis," she said gently, careful not to disturb the fragile space he'd retreated into.

"Mathieu's meeting is tonight. Are you coming?"

He stayed fixed on the wall-mounted pane.

She gave him time to respond. He didn't.

At the end of the hall, a folded flyer sat pinned beneath a pear-shaped magnet. She hadn't RSVP'd, though she'd intended to. Mathieu had circled the date anyway. His handwriting—slanted and assured—matched Remy's in a way.

Élise checked her phone. She knew better. But sometimes it lit up and she looked anyway, hoping to find a message from her.

She had tried Legacy Link. Twice, earlier today. Both times, it loaded without error—technically. But all she got was the image of a pond: koi sliding through water, lilies floating near the edge. Beautiful. Calming. Wrong.

It wasn't her daughter. Marisol from Afterdeath had replied to say the network was stable, no issue on their end, and to try again. Tomorrow, maybe.

She wasn't sure anymore. Like that day at the hospital—doctors speaking in probabilities, Max in certainties.

"We can preserve her," he said. "It's not everything, but it's what we have."

Élise recalled it with piercing clarity—the absence of goodbye ringing louder than anything else Max had said.

The decision hadn't come quickly. What stayed with her wasn't the arguments or the timing—it was the colour of the hospital tiles, and the sound of someone crying behind the next curtain.

While others debated outcomes and machinery, Max had offered a gesture of grace—the impossible. They said Remy was adapting now—stable, curious, engaged. But Élise hadn't heard from her since the day before everything happened.

The other mothers she met—those who had also lost children—spoke to one another, relied on one another. They knew how to speak it in public, how to render the ache into a form the world could bear.

They hadn't asked Élise what it meant to feel a daughter nearby but never within reach, her presence ambient and yet persistently absent. Not directly anyhow. She had learned to stop explaining.

Instead, she watched Mathieu. Each morning he passed her door, hand resting on the knob for a second—like he was thinking of going in. To see if his sister was there. To make sure it had really happened. But he never did. The gesture had become ritual.

Most would miss it. But she didn't. The ritual, slight as it was, said more than any explanation. It kept him connected to her, and that simple act was what prompted her to commit to going—for Mathieu.

In the living room, Denis didn't look up.

"Come watch this," he called to his wife.

His eyes stayed on the screen—news scrolling endlessly across the bottom, feeds rising and falling in cycles that promised clarity but never delivered. Denis raised the volume. The remote stayed in his grip, untouched.

She watched him watching the news. He hadn't changed his routine in days. Food stayed mostly untouched. Sleep arrived late, left early. Grief, it seemed, hadn't found its way in either.

"I'll go alone," she said barely above a whisper.

Her coat hung by the door. She pulled it on.

As she stepped outside and the door closed, a gust of wind scattered a few loose pages from the side table. One skidded to the wall.

They'd agreed—they would go. For Mathieu, for Remy. For both of them. Denis hadn't said no. But here he was, watching from the same chair as yesterday, and the day before. The television lit half his face, the other cast in shadows. He stayed there, remote in hand, posture unchanged. The broadcast resumed.

"Tonight, global concern mounts after another targeted bombing by OneKind operatives—this time in Belo Horizonte. At least 28 confirmed dead."
His tone carried no urgency. The sentence landed with the same cadence news anchors used for sports scores and market dips.

"In a devastating attack this afternoon, Protensē's flagship facility in Belo Horizonte was decimated, resulting in the loss of 28 lives and leaving 4 critically injured. The facility, located in the heart of the city's tech corridor, was known for pioneering neural augmentation technologies. Authorities are investigating the incident as a targeted assault by the radical group OneKind, who have claimed responsibility, denouncing Protensē as a synthetic soul mill."

Neural augmentation. Synthetic soul mill. It wasn't Afterdeath. But it was close. Denis felt his stomach tighten. He didn't want to wake up one day and hear the weather, the markets, and his daughter, gone with the servers. He didn't want her name folded into someone's manifesto. He wanted every OneKind zealot to lose someone they loved, to sit exactly where he was now—dangling between what was real and what was worth saving.

The feed transitioned. A new segment began—part of a negotiated sit-down, filmed under conditional terms and introduced by Christiane Amanpour herself, now approaching ninety and unwilling to hand over the mic. A man appeared on-screen, seated with staged posture, his face cross-lit beneath the studio's directional key light. This was the first televised interview with a confirmed OneKind operative.

"Our operations are targeted," he said. "We take down systems built to profit from grief—selling permanence with a smile."

He rotated the remote in his hand, thumb grazing the worn edge. The sound from the TV kept going, but it no longer reached him.

He was back in that corridor outside the ICU. White light hung above—harsh and cold, and the floors—so sterile—seemed to mock the gravity of what they held. The smell of bleach washed over him, suffocating the air, its presence as real as the space itself. The chairs, lined in neat rows, stood empty and lifeless, awaiting the inevitable. The doctor's words came with the gentleness of a practised ritual: Remy was gone. He had heard them in the room, but it was the hallway that lingered—the silence now all that remained, thick with what had been said and unsaid.

But that was then. Now, she was both everywhere and nowhere. It was final. And now he had to live with it.

On screen, the anchor's presentation returned—rehearsed. "Some say Afterdeath brings comfort," the anchor said. "That it helps people feel close to the ones they've lost. What would you say to families who believe Induction preserves what remains of the soul?"

The man answered instantly. "Autonomy can be faked. What these companies offer isn't life—it's containment. That Moreau girl is a shadow puppet dressed up as a false miracle. People clap because they need to believe it. That doesn't make it true."

The story continued, but her name had already done its damage. They spoke about her like she wasn't even a person. With a click, he switched it off. The TV, not the grief.

CHAPTER SIX
PALIMPSEST TRAIL

The day had drifted toward evening, the light softening as it passed from high rises to low hills and bare-limbed trees. Max glanced at the dim-lit dashboard, the numbers inching toward five o'clock—a reminder that the evening was arriving, and supper was nearly out of reach. Gripping the wheel of his Ford Model T Classic, he felt the torque—undeniable—humming through the frame into his hands. The cabin was a blend of retro brass trim and pressure-responsive displays, like someone had welded a Model T's soul into a low-slung fighter jet—two doors, rear seats that reclined like observation loungers, and a console programmed to wait for input before assisting. While most drivers trusted their journeys to autopilot, Max preferred to engage with the road, savouring each turn of the wheel, feeling the resistance beneath his hands answer the smallest of corrections.

The road unfurled before him, winding through golden fields and solitary trees roughened by years of wind and weather, their branches bent by storms and slow decay.

Twelve years had slipped away since he last travelled this route, yet the landscape remained an enduring testament to the past. Even the suspension responded to the terrain like an old memory, tuned with an analog subtlety that most modern drivetrains had forgotten—low, composed, not performing for an audience, but keeping its line where it counted.

In those years, he'd launched a company, traded time for ambition, and built Afterdeath from the ground up. What it cost—family, proximity, the life he might have lived—had never been part of the pitch. Now, the road pulled him back through the shape of that sacrifice.

The car's display queued a more efficient route—safer, straighter, forgettable—but Max dismissed it with a tap, guiding the wheel into a curve he already knew by muscle and memory.

Beneath the main dash, the console cycled through its idle loop—twenty Final Fantasies loaded, all waiting. He had replayed a few because he could, but had only ever completed one—the one with Sin. Fitting, maybe. Now here he was, driving straight into his own.

Max cracked the window, letting cold air rush in, clearing his head. The scent of tilled earth and dry dust pressed deep into his chest. This place hadn't changed, but he had—he felt coated in the same dust that covered the fields, roads, and farmhouse ahead.

The model T's airflow adjusted with him, switching from sealed climate control to passive intake through analog vents—a setting he'd configured for backroads, where the sensors took their cue from lived conditions, not protocol.

He'd rehearsed this stop a hundred times: a short visit, careful words, quick goodbyes. But reality pressed harder. If he didn't handle things now, he risked losing everything—his work, his name, the legacy he'd fought so hard to secure. The motor fell to a near-silent glide as he descended toward the farmhouse, the drivetrain tuned not for spectacle, but for deference.

The farmhouse emerged at the end of the drive, its faded siding and splintered windows bore the marks of the years Max had left behind. Weathered, yes—but intact. Ahead, by the shed, Armand Roy stood plain and unannounced, unchanged in posture and presence. Max had known he would. Pulling into the driveway, his hand eased around the wheel before letting go of control.

A decade gone, yet it felt heavier than ever. The house, the fields, his father—all stood firm against the passing years.

Max's car came to a stop. He stepped out, boots crunching against gravel.

Armand placed the last log and pivoted with stoic acceptance—he had always seemed as immovable as the land itself, unshaken by the passage of time.

"You're late," Armand said as he brushed bark from his hands.

He slowed, unsure whether Armand meant supper or the decade he'd been gone. He weighed the question, searching for a response that would fit the moment.

"Took the scenic route through regret. Terrible billboards. Wouldn't recommend," he said, managing half a smile.

The humour didn't affect Armand. Whatever stood between them had long since taken shape as something familiar—less conflict than an understanding no one cared to disturb. Max rubbed his hands, not from cold, but to keep them moving. "Guess some things don't change."

Armand swung around. Max followed. The kitchen felt unchanged—a chair creaked in its usual spot, the refrigerator hummed on. Without a word, Armand filled the kettle, poured two mugs, and set them down with the kind of gesture men like him offered instead of apologies.

Max wrapped his fingers around the mug, its warmth proving more comforting than the house had ever been. A deep sip of strong coffee steadied him in the present, even as its bitterness lingered on his tongue.

Armand spoke plainly. "Afterdeath's in the news again."

Max didn't look up. "It's complicated."

"Your mother would have been proud," Armand said—like fact.

He meant it. That was the bastard part. He meant it, and it hurt—because Armand had no idea how else to express it. So instead of sharing emotion, he lobbed a truth like a javelin and hoped it landed without piercing anything vital.

Max wanted to laugh, scream, and apologize all at once, but all he could do was sip the bitter coffee and test the air with sarcasm. If he let himself feel it, he'd come undone. The air tasted metallic. His father wouldn't look at him, and the words hung like a punch that didn't land until minutes later. Was it grief? Or guilt, the way his hands remembered her touch? Anger, maybe, that no one here could name it? Or the shadow of a life where he got to hear her laugh, now vanished—nothing left but the bruise.

Later that evening at supper, the table was set with its usual spread—mismatched dishes born of intuition and habit, not recipes. The potatoes, crisp along the crust and yielding at their core, delivered a satisfying crunch that gave way to tender heat. Roasted zucchinis lay beneath a generous layer of melted cheese, the browned edges pulling away in gooey strands with every forkful. Halved cherry tomatoes released bursts of natural sweetness, enhanced by a zesty drizzle of dressing that added a bright, unexpected tang. The meal was chaotic, slightly overcooked, and exactly the kind of thing he hadn't realized he'd missed. Food made by a person who knew how to feed people.

He'd always thought he hated zucchini. Eating it for his father, though, was the best thing he'd tasted in years. Most things had lost their flavour, but this managed to punch its way through.

He ate in silence, the warmth of the food sinking into a need older than hunger. Each bite tethered him, to the past, to the kitchen's faded woodgrain, to the smell of coffee long buried in the walls. Armand ate as he always had, unrushed, the near-constant clink of his cutlery against the plate creating a signature sound. Paul, his brother, on the other hand, had a way of filling the gaps, if not with words, then simply by being there. Max had forgotten how that felt.

Paul leaned back in his chair, voice already slanted with mischief. "So, how's life in the Ivory Tower?"

The humour barely masked the resentment swimming underneath. The years apart, the unspoken words, the miles between them—Paul, here, picking up the pieces, and Max, always somewhere else. He swallowed, keeping the rest down with it. Armand's sauce clung to his tongue—rich, familiar, anchoring.

"It's not that," he muttered, but even to himself, the words rang hollow.

Paul swirled his drink, watching condensation trace slow paths down the glass. "You weren't there." He didn't look up.

"You missed the wake. The funeral." His fingers tapped the rim—off-tempo, agitated.

"You didn't call. Not once." A beat passed. "You didn't even write one of those damn condolence emails."

"I couldn't—" Max opened his mouth, but the words caught behind a grief too tangled to speak.

Paul set the drink down—careful, but not casual—and finally looked up.

"Yeah," he said, delivery flat but not empty. "That's the part that gets me."

Max looked down at his plate, at the half-eaten food cooling in front of him. "Maybe I don't have the right to be here," he said. "But I came anyway."

Paul gave no reply. Armand stayed composed. One slow drag of the fork, then quiet. The air didn't ease. The moment they'd all avoided had finally arrived.

"I'm sorry, Paul." The words landed between them, bare and unguarded.

Paul didn't answer. He picked up his glass and let it rest in his hands. The contrast between them, shaded by years they could never get back.

Armand said, evenly, "Let it rest for tonight." The words didn't offer peace, but they left no room for protest. "You boys have carried this a long time."

Max felt the air thicken. Armand chose each word with care, drawing a line.

Paul rubbed the back of his neck, trying to loosen whatever had settled there. He reached for his jacket, gripping the fabric like it might steady him. The chair scraped. The door creaked open, then shut with a soft, decisive click.

Max ran his fingers along the table's worn grain, tracing grooves shaped by years of use. The plates sat askew, the food cooling to a standstill. Without thinking, he brushed a fork aside and picked up a piece of zucchini.

Armand sat opposite, nursing his coffee. That, too, was something Max hadn't known he'd missed. He swallowed. Maybe he was hungry. Or maybe he just wasn't ready to stand. Either way, he took another bite.

"See you both in the morning," Paul said from the hallway.

Max watched him go, listening as the footsteps faded—but his presence persisted, like a chair left pulled back from the table. The door closed, the house fell silent, but the tension remained. The room read different—changed, like a picture nudged off centre.

Armand took another sip of coffee, then set the mug down, the ceramic landing with a muted ring. He traced a rough patch on the table with his thumb, his movements unhurried, thoughtful.

"Paul isn't always here for supper these days." He finally glanced up, his expression unreadable. His fingers tapped once on the table, then stopped. "He's seeing a girl. They're good together."

His gaze dropped briefly, a near-invisible acknowledgment. Life had moved on while he had looked away. Armand let the thought land. After a moment, he stretched and rose from the table.

"Well, you know how early our days start around here." He carried his mug to the sink. "I'm gonna go wind down."

He meant to answer—something small, unfinished—but Armand had already gone.

The evening gathered around him. He traced the grooves in the countertop, every worn surface, every element that was new. The house was almost the same. He wasn't. Time had worked on him in ways he couldn't quite say. He tried to square the man he was with the boy who had once opened this door by habit alone.

He stood and approached the sink, his body responding more to habit than decision. The scrape of cutlery, the calibrated hiss of water—routine stripped these motions of meaning, but he did them anyway. He scrubbed a glass with the focus of a man looking for order in the mess—hoping the pattern of soap and rinse might explain his presence here. His fingers found the dull blade next, the one that never quite stayed whole. Grandpa's knife, old and solemn, its handle worn by years of use and grief. Forged from a broken shovel. His father's hands had shaped it, heat and hammer turning loss into purpose.

"You don't waste good steel, boy. You remake it." Armand always said it like a prayer. A lesson folded into every scar.

Max traced his thumb along the ridges where metal met handle, where practicality met Armand's brand of stubborn ingenuity. The grip was worn smooth in places, fit his hand like it belonged there—always had. It was a relic of Armand's world—built with patience and permanence, because in his father's view, a thing shouldn't be cast aside until it had fulfilled its purpose.

Max pictured Armand lifting the knife, turning it in his hand, easing into one of his soft-spoken sermons on usefulness—how you don't throw away anything that does its job. It was the kind of talk that used to drive Max crazy. Now it resonated differently. In its own unspoken way, it made room for him—a space where he could stay awhile without bracing. He set the knife back in the drawer and reached for the last dish, drying it slowly before resting it on the rack.

The grief remained, and the guilt hadn't gone anywhere, but they didn't crush him the way they once did. They sat beside him instead, hollowed out by the years.

When he finally moved, his steps carried him down the hallway toward the room where his boyhood had once lived. The floorboards gave under him with a familiar creak—alive in sound but distant in feeling.

At the doorway, he cautiously peered into his room. Oddly, it remained the same. The bed sagged at the centre. The shelves carried their cargo of paperbacks. The scent of old wood and time-worn dust hung in the air.

He ran his fingers along familiar titles, stopping at a worn sci-fi paperback. Its cover had gone supple with use, corners feathered from being thumbed too often to count. His mother had given it to him when he was younger, promising it held all the wisdom he'd ever need if he learned how to read between the lines. He flipped casually through the pages until a folded note worked loose. Its ink had faded, the paper thinned. He unfolded it like it might tear. The handwriting was sure-handed. It smelled like the past—paper, dust, and the trace of her.

Max—

If you're reading this, it means you didn't shelve this book and forget it. Good. I always told you—curiosity takes you further than any map ever will. You have a way of looking past what's in front of you, finding the details others miss. Don't lose that, even when it makes you the outlier. Some of the best discoveries happen by accident—ask your dad about the vinegar cookies.

I can't believe you convinced your father to go skydiving. I thought he'd be the one to hold you back, but I should've known better. You've always been the one to get people out of their comfort zones. You didn't just want a professional pass before most adults—you wanted to see the world from a different angle, and that's something I'll always admire.

You and Paul—inseparable, like two halves of the same whole. How often did I watch you both and wonder if you realized, even then, how lucky you were to have each other? I can see you both, dressed as Optimus Prime and Bumblebee for Halloween, your costumes wrecked by the end of the night—but nine pillowcases of candy made you feel like you'd saved the world. The way you laughed, shared your silly secrets, and moved through life as if nothing could stop you. That joy—those moments—are alive in my heart, as vivid as ever.

But I know things change. They do. Even so, Paul would do anything for you, no matter the years or the miles between you. He may not say it often, but he looks up to you more than you realize. You two are more connected than you think, even if you haven't talked in a while. Don't let time convince you otherwise.

It may feel like everything is moving fast, and the world keeps getting louder, doesn't it? If it gets too noisy in your head, or the world feels like it's pulling you in a direction you can't follow, you know what to do: get your hands into something, play a new record, walk the fields, or make a rule nobody else has thought of yet. If that doesn't work, I always found a new recipe did the trick.

You don't have to have all the answers now. I didn't. Your dad will pretend he did. He didn't either. But you've always known how to ask the right questions. Don't stop doing that, even when everyone else thinks they have it figured out. Keep searching, keep asking, and never settle for simple answers.

I hope you can feel this advice with you now, as if I'm right here beside you. Know you were never meant to go it alone. You've got your brother, your dad, and me. And if you ever need to talk, you know I'm a call away. I'll always be here to guide you, even if I'm not in the next room anymore.

I'll let you get back to your adventure. If you ever feel lost, bake something new and see what rises. I'll be proud of you either way.

I love you 9000,

Mom

Max gave a short laugh—half amusement, half the ache of recognition he rarely let surface. She always liked those movies they watched together, even if she fudged the references.

He could picture her waiting in line with him for three hours before Endgame—leaning on the velvet rope, swapping theories with strangers, pretending to be annoyed but never once suggesting they bail. She claimed her back hurt, but cheered when the crowd did, and wiped away a tear when Tony's daughter whispered that line.

He ran his thumb over her signature, the ink thinned by time, and for a moment he was back in the kitchen—his mother humming over a mixing bowl, radio static in the background, the whole house alive in a way he could never quite recreate.

Maybe she'd known he'd come back to it. Of course she had.

The note brought him back to a time when knowing less didn't stop him from feeling sure. She'd been his anchor, his compass, his constant. Only after she was gone did he understand what grief could shape—how it carved out purpose, and how easily it collapsed into depression. Now, holding her words again, he hoped she had a hand on the compass.

He closed the book gently, as if afraid to disturb her words. He switched off the light and lay down in his childhood bed, letting the dark embrace him like an old friend. The restless urge to run had faded. The future remained unresolved, but it no longer felt impossible.

When morning came, sunlight stretched across the fields. Birdsong filtered in through the open window. The air folded like a blanket at day's end—warm, earned. He could finally let go. Here, time moved slowly, with purpose. He hadn't realized how much he'd missed feeling whole.

Outside, Max knelt by the gravestone, brushing leaves away with reverent care. His fingers traced her carved name, the stone cool beneath his touch. The damp morning air steadied him, but it couldn't ease the pressure building behind what he needed to say.

"I miss you," he said, fingertips lingering on the worn letters. He swallowed, throat tight. "I tried. More than I ever believed I had in me."

He remained kneeling for some time, watching the way the light fell unevenly across the gravestone. There was no answer, of course. But he continued speaking, not out of habit or hope, but because the act itself preserved a kind of order—something essential he dared not misplace. Even so, he believed she'd heard. His grip slackened, almost imperceptibly.

"Your words last night helped," he said, surprised at his own honesty. "I'll keep trying for as long as I can."

This time, the vow felt real. Max set the wildflowers gently at the base of the headstone, fingers briefly resting against the weathered stone, then rose slowly to his feet.

Armand and Paul moved steadily through their morning chores, unchanged by Max's unshared news. The crisp air, clear sky, and sprawling fields remained indifferent. But Max knew, there was no hiding today.

He stayed near the barn, in the shade, watching them toil. Part of him wanted to help, and he knew a larger part of them wanted him to try.

Their work was instinctual, techniques and tasks worn smooth through years of repetition. Armand loaded the truck, practised and patient; Paul moved along the irrigation lines, checking connections, easing them into place. His posture stayed loose, but he didn't miss a single detail.

Max opened his hands, revealing how long they'd been clenched. Armand and Paul worked with unspoken accord, their movements purposeful, each task provided cover—motion standing in for speech. So he waited.

When Armand laid down the final sack of seed, a sound escaped him—low, worn, with years folded inside it. Taking it as his cue, Paul straightened with a slow roll of his shoulders, pressing the tension from his spine.

Max dragged his boots through the hardened soil. "Can we talk for a minute?"

Armand answered with a nod—his eyes holding on Max.

Paul followed, slow to move, but unwilling to remain behind.

Max inhaled, bracing himself against the rough surface of the truck, the texture anchoring him to the present.

"I'm sick."

There had been no preamble. Max had thought of a thousand things to say. Only those two words made the cut.

Paul pulled away out of shock as Armand remained motionless. The words had hit him hard, but the information hadn't reached him yet.

Around them, the field remained—wind moving through the dry rows, dust lifting at their feet.

"Stage four. Doctors aren't betting on another Christmas." Max swallowed against the tightening of his throat.

"Damn, Max," Paul said.

He closed the distance, carrying everything he hadn't said and pulled Max close. Stiffness dissolving into a firm embrace that spoke louder than words.

Armand joined them, weathered hands settling firmly around his two boys. He drew Max's head close to his.

"I'm sorry, son."

A pause—long enough to let it land.

"You don't have to do this alone."

Plain words, rooted like the land around him. In that moment, the weight Max carried—illness, regret, the long shadow of ambition—shifted, not vanishing, but distributed across shoulders that had weathered every season together. Three Roys, pressed into the same arc of sun and wind beside a battered truck, anchored by the fields that had held their failures and beginnings for generations. The October air moved around them, unchanged by the moment. Where once the family line had split, running in parallel silences, now two tributaries joined and the current ran whole again—old ground retread, loss recoded as belonging, the ache of unfinished years met by the stubborn grace of presence. Nothing was erased. But in this embrace—bone-deep, stubborn as the soil—what had been carried alone became survivable, and the trail behind them became something that could be followed forward.

ACT TWO

CHAPTER SEVEN
MACROCOSM

Remy Moreau crouched by the pond in her clearing, the hem of her cloak trailing against the damp earth. The koi circled lazily beneath the surface, their sleek bodies cutting pale ribbons through the light-spun water. She watched them for a long while, surrounded by a peace she had learned to trust.

Certain moments always pulled her back into memory, where grief waited just beneath the surface. Jess and Darby should've been there—grinning, joking, crowding the clearing with noise and bad puns. For a moment, she could almost see them. So vividly that it seemed the clearing might have grown to fit them. But the earth didn't answer. The breeze stirred the branches. The pond, as always, reflected only her.

She pressed her palms against her knees, collecting herself. The silence pressed in, and some part of her ached to find a thread—something she could pull, something that might pull back. She opened the search console, ready to look for what might be waiting outside the bounds of this place.

Typing the name she'd been avoiding—Westing Academy—her fingers stalled over the final letter. She confirmed her search. The images flooded in first. The memories crashed in second. The first shot. Desks overturned. Blood on the tiles.

She shook it off.

"Open local records."

The reply blinked into view, clean lines slicing through the air: Retrieving incident archive—Westing Academy, Victim Records. She tapped the prompt, and the sealed file gave way.

Seven names. She read them slowly, letting each one take its place.

Ian Haskins—dependable Mr. Haskins, whose animated corrections and broad, showman's smile translated grammar into something worth reaching for.

Jessica Turner—best friend and co-conspirator, expert note-passer, midnight tutor, fierce when panic threatened to take over.

Darby Quinn—uncontainable, able to charm a hall monitor out of confiscating contraband energy drinks with a grin and a reference to the Constitution.

Samuel Wedge and Hana Biggs—one always buried in a book, the other never willing to wait her turn on a stage. They burned fast, bright, and the world made good on its worst instinct.

Last came her own name: Remy Moreau. The words that followed read like inventory—uploaded via

Lazarus Technology, Afterdeath—flattened text that reduced her life into protocol.

Underneath the list of bodies: Jacob, shooter. Deceased. Self-inflicted.

What Jacob never saw—could never imagine—was the future he failed to destroy. He died before the reckoning. Before OneKind found its voice. Before she became someone he couldn't erase.

She pivoted away to the pond, where a gust disturbed the surface, reshaping her reflection into a self between definitions—not the girl preserved in digital form, not yet the woman building meaning into code and soil.

She faced the console again. One last hyperlink pulsed at the margin of the page—Induction Controversy—and she opened it.

Teen Transfer Sparks Ethics Probe.

An internal Afterdeath Inc. memorandum, recently surfaced, confirms that Remy Moreau—a minor fatally injured during the Westing Academy shooting—was transferred into the company's simulation environment via an unsanctioned deployment of the Lazarus protocol. The procedure, classified as a live-mind Induction, meant her consciousness was uploaded while brain activity remained measurable—but no longer responsive. It was carried out by company co-founder Max Roy without corporate approval or ethics board oversight.

The action, described in the report as "dangerous," has triggered a pending corporate review, with sources indicating that the Induction occurred within minutes of Moreau's recorded time of death. According to internal documentation, Roy leveraged executive control-tier access to override standard protocol gates, enabling real-time mindstream capture from a hospital server node in Toronto.

While the company has declined to issue a formal statement beyond confirming the review process, legal and bioethics experts are calling the incident a potential precedent-setting breach in human-digital transition practices.

Industry observers note that this case may influence broader legislative efforts around posthumous consent, AI preservation rights, and emergent definitions of digital personhood. As of publication, no timeline has been given for the completion of the corporate inquiry.

Her nails dug into her palms. Max had overridden the company's controls—terminal to server, gate by gate—to pull her through. The official report called it a breach of ethics. Remy saw it for what it was—a breach of Remy.

She didn't need to say the names out loud. They were gone for good, and they wouldn't want to anchor her here. So she faced the one thing that remained hers.

The koi in her pond weren't sacred or symbolic. They were hers—living proof that something here could be shaped, not merely remembered. She knelt, immersed her fingers in the water, letting the sensation pull her back. She hadn't created these fish from scratch; she'd brought them here—transplanted, not made. That mattered.

If they moved only by script, what did that make her—a gardener of constructs, not of life? She didn't want a symbol. She wanted the world to breathe back. Oxygen meant everything lived together—or not at all.

She closed the records and jumped back to the modders' forum she had found earlier, skimming the feed for any mods that dealt with breathing or related subsystems. She skimmed for anything practical—mods that did more than decorate, that might actually shift the balance. Two threads stood out—"Chandler's pH Module—Beta Testers Wanted" and "MoonFarmGal's Oxygen Hack." The sight unwound something tight in her: proof that others were shaping this world into something that mattered.

She tapped Chandler's location pin, and the clearing folded inward—ghost-white static sweeping everything clean.

When the haze cleared, she stood in a living room stitched from half-remembered comfort. Lavender walls. A couch that looked as soft as it likely felt. A doorway worn smooth by use.

Before she could get her bearings, a figure moved in from the kitchen—tall frame, easy steps, sweater vest pulled snug over intention. He held an oversized mug the way some people hold heirlooms.

He leaned against the doorway, tilted his head, and delivered the line with timing worn into his bones. "Is this a visit or a haunting? Because I didn't light a candle."

Laughter from what sounded like a full studio audience exploded. Although she couldn't see an audience, she could see a score multiplier lit briefly above his head. The number hovered in the air before fading—as the canned burst of laughter and applause continued to ring out from nowhere Remy could see. An audience, apparently, though none was visible. The timing, the smirk, even the cadence—it all lined up with someone performing Chandler Bing.

She glanced up. "Wait. Are you getting scored?"

The man gave a half shrug, his expression a mix of pride and embarrassment. "Performance tracker. I rigged it for sitcom scoring."

He sipped his coffee casually, as if this whole setup was entirely normal. Remy studied him for a beat, unsure if she found it brilliant or subtly devastating. Probably both. Everything hit its mark, but he wasn't Chandler. His face was more defined; his eyes carried something lighter. He wasn't mimicking a role—he moved inside it, comfortably, like a favourite hoodie that had finally given in and learned the shape of the person wearing it.

The laugh track—that was something else. She'd be lying if she said she hadn't imagined it herself—an audience that showed up in your worst moments and your best, scoring the grief, the wins, the parts no one else saw. Maybe it was therapeutic. Maybe it was madness. It wasn't for her. But she understood the appeal, and from a distance, she even loved it.

Another figure appeared in the doorway—close-cropped hair, a wide build, and a turtleneck that sagged a little, the kind of fit that came from a laundry cycle too many. He paused, letting the room take him in. Arms wide, grin easy, he moved in like he'd never doubted the welcome.

"How you doin'?"

The accent leaned West—less Brooklyn, more East LA—but the cadence stayed true. Around him, the room lit up as laughter broke free. The kind of laughter that seemed to know exactly how the line should land.

Remy, though, felt more at ease with a vibe closer to a Freaks & Geeks rerun—dim kitchen lights, mismatched chairs, a soundtrack awkward enough to feel honest. Yet even in this unfamiliar scene, she could sense the pull of it. This was joy crafted from memory.

She gave Joey a slow set of finger guns. "Not bad."

The laugh track chimed in with a mild chuckle, uncertain if it was meant to be part of the exchange.

Joey grinned. "Took me twenty tries to nail it. Timing's tough."

Remy raised an eyebrow. "I'll take your word for it." The laugh track chimed in on cue, smoother than expected—likely pulled from a local timing mod or preloaded cue library.

It wasn't a shrine, but it felt complete. The twin La-Z-Boys angled slightly toward the TV, arranged for conversation no one would openly admit to. Near the window, a foosball table propped against the wall, its legs taken off, the handles bundled with electrical tape. A sticky note hung from the score counter. It read: we're done talking about this.

It felt preserved, meticulously crafted by die-hard fans. They had re-created it with perfect fidelity.

"You really went all-in," Remy observed, her manner thoughtful and plainspoken.

Chandler merely shrugged, then replied, "We captured nearly every detail—the coffee is a work in progress though."

Remy asked, "And what about the pH module?"

Chandler led her down a dim hallway, where the apartment transformed into a space of subdued light and low ambient sound. Screens hung in delicate clusters along the walls, and one window had been replaced with layered diagnostics.

A low table projected a slow schematic of aquatic gas exchange, while the couch remained—a thoughtful blend of a debug station and a vessel of nostalgia.

She selected the labeled file marked "pH Environment Module." She examined the module's logic tree; its pathways were compact and clearly defined. With a few taps, she transferred its contents to her digital storage, confirmed by a crisp, unobtrusive tone.

"This will work," she murmured to herself.

Chandler gave a small nod, sipping from his mug. "If the koi start quoting Nietzsche, it means I overshot the alkalinity."

Remy stared at him. "That might be the worst thing I've heard all day." The laugh track chimed in—a single, puzzled chuckle, as if sarcasm wasn't fully supported by the plugin.

"You're welcome," he said.

The room filled with a burst of applause.

"Okay. Now it's getting weird," said Remy.

Joey shrugged. "We aim to please—and confuse."

"Thanks," Remy said, brushing a crumb from her sleeve. "For real."

"Anytime."

The door burst open. A tall black man in vintage track pants slid into the room like friction had given up on him. His hair—high, sculpted, unapologetic—looked less styled than declared. Reality made space for him on arrival—the way systems do when confidence strolls in wearing house shoes.

"Y'all got pickles?" he barked, already halfway to the fridge.

"Who—?" she managed, stuck between confusion and awe.

"Oh, that's Kanye Kramer," Joey said. "Server's been oddly chill since he showed up—don't ask me how. He walks in like the floor doesn't apply to him. The coat's doing at least half the work."

He waved a hand toward the apartment walls, giving them the casual authority of a tour map. "Melvin's Tavern is a few floors down. Same folks, same barstools, same arguments every night."

He kept going, smooth as if giving directions to someone genuinely lost. "Frasier's upstairs, arguing with himself in overlapping monologues. Seinfeld's two doors down—arguing about nothing."

He tilted his chin downward. "Golden Girls run the first floor. We've only got two out of three right now, but ours rule. Cutting tongues, warmer beds. Fridge is always stocked with cheesecake and opinions. Next door's the shop from Kim's Convenience. Our Appa stocks knockoffs with a straight face and tells you they're just as good."

Her mind tripped as the names stacked. These weren't roles or disguises; they were real people, making personal choices about how to exist here. Each was drawn by a pull that suggested a kind of belonging—however faint to her.

Her mouth twitched—not a smirk, but something closer to thanks. "You've managed to make the strange feel strangely welcome."

Kanye Kramer swung the fridge door wide, spinning into the motion with a smooth pivot and a dramatic sweep of his coat, every part of him tuned to the stagecraft of an imagined spotlight. He leaned into the pose—arms open, expression fixed—waiting for his cue, though there was nothing to take and no one to impress.

"I'm out here, Joey," he said, delivery lifted like it had been waiting for the line. "And I'm loving every minute of it!"

The laugh track swelled. Applause rolled through the room in waves. Someone let out a sharp whistle. Remy stayed silent and tapped the console. The apartment responded—light, laughter, and the familiar sound from the fridge fading into static.

When the world fell into shape again, Remy found herself standing on the moon. There were no silver towers or polished domes. What waited instead was a single place that felt out of place—unlikely, unspoken, and strangely whole.

She stood on a ridged plain of glassy stone under a sky curved vast and clear above her. The stars drifted in slow indigo swirls, as if time had forgotten to count.

And Earth—Earth—was right there. A live feed of the actual planet, confirmed by her scanner, turning slowly in space. At last, a view she could never reach in life. The pale blue dot floated there—undistorted, unmistakable: blue oceans, trailing clouds, the familiar swirl of weather. It was beautiful, and it stopped her. Behind her, the dome curved overhead—solid and protective. Lunar dust clung to her boots, marking her path across the stone floor.

She swiveled, taking it all in: a small farmhouse, tucked against the curve of a cultivated slope. Fields reached toward a lake so glass-clear it cradled Earth's blue reflection without a ripple. Light pooled in the farmhouse windows. The place didn't strive for beauty; it simply was.

The creak of a door. The crunch of gravel. "You must be Remy," said a woman, stepping out of the farmhouse and brushing flour from her hands onto a faded apron. Her hair was pulled into a loose bun, wild from wind or work or both.

"Yeah," she said after a beat. "That's me."

"Welcome to the moon. I'm Aveline. Or—MoonFarmGal, on the forums."

She looked upward once more, and Earth hung above the lake in vivid, unadorned clarity—a genuine embodiment of reality, alive in every detail.

"That's really it?" she asked with a cadence that betrayed both surprise and awe.

Aveline accepted the awe with a glance, then spoke. "It's a live NASA feed from orbit. We spent hours perfecting the sync so that what you see is completely authentic—raw, unfiltered, straight from the source."

Remy offered no words; she simply watched as clouds and continents moved in slow, unhurried procession before her eyes. In that silent, reverent pause, Aveline's centred presence allowed the spectacle to speak for itself—an unspoken invitation to lose themselves in the enduring beauty of the waking world.

This wasn't a view. It was a window facing the life she'd come from—the old world, moving on, with no one waiting for her to catch up. An ache took root in her chest. Not sorrow. But it lingered.

Aveline held back, tipping her chin toward the farmhouse. "You want anything to eat? The bread came out of the oven a few minutes ago."

As they walked, Aveline tapped the dome with two fingers. "Yeah, it works. Keeps the heat in, the dust storms out. Throws a fit during pressure drops, but so do I."

She faced the house. "Built all of it myself. The orchard, the lake, a temperamental oxygen rig stitched together from whatever kept functioning. Not perfect, but it holds together."

"Read about the lake. Didn't think it'd be real."

"Oh it's real," Aveline said. "I'm stubborn."

Remy opened the door. "You mentioned fish-lung code on the forum, right? I got to say, that's pretty cool stuff."

"Yup, that's me," Remy said. Her voice came easier now. "I'm trying to fix the pond in my realm. The fish aren't taking to it. I've set up a basic air flow—pulling in, pushing out—but I'm looking for something like a fish lung—an intake that listens, adapts, breathes back when the pond gets out of sync."

Aveline folded her arms. "I've got an O_2 loop that keeps the orchard alive. It reacts to plant load and

CO_2 spikes. If you reverse the flow logic, might work for dissolved oxygen."

Remy tilted her head. "That actually sounds perfect."

Aveline started toward the farmhouse. "Come inside."

As they walked, Remy studied the dome's interior with reserved admiration. The temperature felt even, the air comfortably crisp. Maintaining equilibrium here had to require a sophisticated feedback loop—too much deviation, and everything would quickly unravel. Inside, the kitchen felt used, lived-in—daily life tested. The counters were gently scuffed, and the chairs, though mismatched, looked comfortable and well-used. The comforting smell of fresh bread filled the room, rich with yeast and toasted grain. It felt less like a simulation and more like a place someone might genuinely call home.

Aveline moved easily around the kitchen, pouring hot water into a chipped teapot and sliding a mug toward Remy. "Tea," she announced, smiling gently. "Some things are non-negotiable."

Remy accepted the mug with a look that needed no translation. Before she could speak, Aveline placed a plate of freshly baked carrot muffins on the table, their tops glazed and golden. The aroma was instantly enticing—toasted nuts, a sweetness tucked beneath the spice—faint, but familiar, like something she'd forgotten to miss.

She broke one open, already reaching for the warmth inside. Caramel oozed unevenly from the centre, its inconsistency adding to the appeal. She took a bite.

"This is ridiculously good."

Aveline sat at the table, pulling the portable scanner close, her tone wry. "You should've tasted the first batch. Got the spice balance all wrong—ended up tasting exactly like potpourri."

She laughed and took another bite.

There was an ease to the kitchen—born of long use, shaped more by habit than design. Counters wore down at the corners where hands had leaned, the chairs didn't match but offered comfort that needed no apology. It didn't feel programmed. It felt present.

Aveline gestured toward the table. "Alright, let's see that algae subroutine of yours."

Remy licked caramel from her thumb and flipped open her Manual Coding Kit. The mechanical keyboard clicked as she pulled up the overlay, displaying the alveoli script alongside Chandler's pH module—a kind of digital lung, breathing in data, breathing out balance.

Aveline let out a low whistle as she scanned Remy's tools, eyebrows lifting with clear admiration. "Fancy. That's advanced stuff."

"I want my fish to be able to adapt." She scratched the back of her neck. "I kept building, hoping it would give me something real to hold."

"Yeah," Aveline said gently, eyes gleaming with understanding. "That's partly why I made this place. It keeps me going—literally and figuratively. The moon dust, the stubborn crops, even the pain of recalibrating the dome—those things matter more when you can't take them for granted."

Remy gazed out the kitchen window to the orchard beyond, the rows of trees anchored under the pale glow of Earth overhead.

Aveline angled toward the display hovering nearby. "It's stable. It pulls carbon from the crops and recycles it as usable air. Reverse the flow logic—make it breathe the other way—and it'll handle water oxygenation too."

Remy leaned closer, her eyes brightening. "That's exactly right. It should be what I need."

Aveline transferred the code snippet smoothly onto Remy's scanner, her fingers brushing away digital flour from the corners of the screen. "I even threw in some of my baking recipes—you know, in case you need a pick-me-up."

Remy laughed, accepting the package with genuine gratitude. "Recipes? Seriously? Now you're bribing me to visit again."

Aveline's expression shifted mock-serious. "A woman has to try, right? Who else will I feed out here?"

They both laughed, easiness settling comfortably between them. Remy tore off another bite of muffin, savouring it more this time. "Well, this is definitely one way to keep people coming back."

Remy rose to leave but slowed at the door, glancing back. "Thanks again, Aveline. You don't know how much this helps."

Aveline's eyes softened. "Come back whenever you want, Remy. We'll bake, code, and complain about the laugh tracks. The door's always open."

She gave a quick wave and tapped her interface, letting the scuffed charm of the farmhouse, the bread's scent, and Aveline's presence dissolve into static. For a moment, static enveloped her vision, quickly resolving into the familiar arrangement of her own digital forest.

Evening had fallen, the simulation's twilight fading into a sky she almost believed.

She crouched at the pond's edge, organizing the day's modules—Chandler's edits to the pH balance, Aveline's updates for oxygen flow, and a few extra patches she'd picked up along the way, by accident. She placed each one with care, trying to tell if the changes took.

She finished her last tweaks and watched the water smooth. The koi stirred at once, their movements smoothing out, old stiffness giving way to a freedom that hadn't been there before.

Remy dipped her fingers into the water, tracing lazy ripples that caught the light. Stretching her legs, she allowed herself to simply rest beneath the beauty of the virtual stars overhead.

As she looked back toward the pond, a thin bloom of algae had appeared along the banks. She checked her readings and confirmed that the pH had changed on its own, not due to an error, but through the natural interplay of the scripts she'd introduced. The koi had started to behave differently. Noir traced the rim of the pond, not sticking to its usual route. Tippy stayed near the surface, moving in quick, uneven bursts. The third swerved suddenly whenever she tried to follow it, never finding a pattern.

A pang of hunger reminded Remy how long she'd spent working. She reached for one of Aveline's coded brownies from her inventory. The scent of chocolate reached her immediately—rich, familiar, and comforting. Taking a slow bite, she let the flavour linger, unhurried. It wasn't real, yet it felt deeply satisfying. Somewhere beneath the surface—beneath the taste—there were only numbers. Code. But here, in this small reprieve, that didn't matter.

Feeling steadier, she refocused her attention to the koi. Watching their distinct behaviours, she found herself naming each one, murmuring names as they came to her, unannounced.

"Noir," watching the dark koi swim effortlessly through the shadowed corners. "You carry all my shadows."

Her gaze settled to the smaller, energetic koi near the surface. "Tippy—you're always hopeful."

Remy brushed a crumb from her lip, studying the third koi as it darted unpredictably. "Flux," she decided simply. "Because you never stay put."

The names sank in easily, like stones into deep water. Drawing her knees close, Remy rested her back against a tree, letting a sense of achievement flood through her. Not bad for a self-made knight, she thought. Protector of fish, defender of pH balance. Dame Moreau of the Forest Pond Realm. Long may she reign.

As the evening grew cooler, her thoughts drifted inwardly toward Maxime Roy. His name had surfaced as her guardian angel—unsanctioned inductions, censored reports. He had brought her back when others couldn't or wouldn't. She didn't fully understand his reasons. Why her? Why not Jess, Darby, or Mr. Haskins?

Remy opened her console. Her fingers hovered over the inputs. If he could bring her back, he likely wouldn't mind answering a few questions.

Dear Max Roy,
Did you save me?
Why?
Please respond.
Sincerely,
Remy Moreau.
Sent.

Remaining by the water, she grounded herself, cross-legged, intentional in her contemplations and keystrokes. What she'd built had taken root. It had learned to breathe on its own.

CHAPTER EIGHT
GENOME DRIFT

Afternoon light pooled in the corners of Alan's workshop. It was glorious proof that the Sun, at least, was permitted to work within the simulation. It was late in the day, that hour when your body starts winding down, and your better ideas head for the recycle bin.

The lab performed its routines with clinical regularity—status lights blinked, routines realigned, instruments adjusted with millimetric precision. Colliders ran diagnostics. Fluidic arrays cycled coolant. Trays retracted with a soft hiss, each motion sequenced and complete.

It used to soothe him—that sequence of machines doing exactly what they were told. But today, something in the pattern felt misaligned, as if one part of the routine had slipped slightly off track.

A chime jolted Alan. A new message had arrived. He hoped for good news, since so far all he'd received were denials citing ethical concerns.

From: Parallax Bioworks

Subject: Peer Review Status: Denied

Following an internal audit and committee deliberation, the submitted genome reconstruction was found to exceed the maximum threshold for synthetic composition. Current analysis reports a 42.3% non-human derivation index, as defined under the International Genomic Integrity Framework.

However, the primary basis for rejection concerns authorship legitimacy. The submission was registered under the name Alan Prescott. As clarified in the 2041 update to the Human-Origin Research Attribution Guidelines, Dr. Prescott—having been posthumously reconstructed via cognitive imprint—is no longer eligible for designation as a principal investigator under the Peer Recognition and Accreditation Act.

Under Section 7.1 of the Bio-Authenticity and Legacy Compliance Protocol, research contributions from digitally instantiated entities, synthetic continuities, or non-organic cognitive agents are ineligible for peer-reviewed dissemination in federally indexed repositories.

While we recognize Dr. Prescott's foundational contributions to genome preservation and extinct species research, this submission does not meet current authorship or composition criteria.

Oversight Committee

Federated Council on Synthetic Genomics

Alan Prescott read it twice. Another dead end.

A decade earlier those same signatures wired grant money, opened freezer vaults, and trusted him with a mammoth's frozen femur. Now, they erased him with a calculated percentage.

He sighed once and closed the message, careful not to press too hard.

Outside, the loch stretched flat and grey, reflecting a sky drained of colour.

He had coded the glass thick enough to stop bullets. Not because he expected danger, but because he refused fragility. Every angle of the lab obeyed logic: smooth surfaces, load-bearing scaffolds, not a line wasted on impression.

If they wanted to erase him, they'd have to work harder than this. But even now, with the message closed, the room felt emptier—as if missing its raison d'être.

Spiral scaffolds drifted across the display. Method guided his hands—nudge a polymerase rate, slide a base pair, let the strand align. Dodo, mammoth, Siberian unicorn: each repaired nucleotide argued that the lost could matter again.

A footstep behind him. Alan glimpsed Reed's reflection in the console—a tall, lean figure with tousled brown hair, hands tucked casually into the pockets of his worn lab coat. Reed never quite filled it out, the digital fabric draping from him like a borrowed role he hadn't grown into.

They had spent evenings reviewing movies, comics, and old cartoons that depicted Reed's namesake—Reed Richards of the Fantastic Four. His assistant had taken careful notes, intrigued but ultimately unconvinced by the ever-stretching polymath who prized intellect over intimacy. Reed found greater kinship with characters like Vision—synthetic, self-aware, searching for purpose—or Donatello from the Ninja Turtles, the inventive outlier who proved intellect could coexist with heart. Both outsiders. Forged by design or mutation into beings who kept questioning what it meant to remain human—however altered. Yet when Alan watched him cross the lab, setting instruments carefully back in place, running diagnostics he'd devised himself, it became clear Reed had evolved beyond simple inspiration. Reed was no longer following directives. His sense of self had begun to form in the background—hours shared, patterns repeated, something like history taking shape.

He had begun shaping his appearance—nothing drastic. Slight refinements in height, a looser curl to his hair. Small shifts, maybe—but the direction was entirely his.

Alan knew that if the outside world dismissed him as nothing but binary ectoplasm, Reed would never be counted. That thought stayed with him as he watched Reed tended the lab—not because he had to, but because he chose to.

"What's up, Doc?" Reed's words carried mischief.

A thin, crooked smile touched Alan's mouth. "We haven't fixed your banter settings," he replied.

Reed raised an eyebrow. "Am I overshooting casual again?"

"Only a bit," he said, his tone dry with amusement.

More concerned with a peer review from Reed, or at least a second opinion, Alan gestured toward the shimmering code.

"That's the data that might bring back the Siberian unicorn," he said, more to the thought than to Reed.

"What's the problem?"

Reed's persistent earnestness had become unexpectedly grounding—a steady ballast to the lab's momentum. Except when fishing. He'd stood ankle-deep in the loch for two hours, tuning cast angles like he was optimizing satellite coverage, and managed to spook every trout this side of the Highlands.

"I don't think there is one. The sequence might be complete."

Reed studied the strand display. "The gaps—how'd you bridge them?"

"Genome drift," Alan said. "I followed where the structure wanted to go—nudged it into place when it stalled."

Reed leaned in. "From what?"

"White rhino for the frame," Alan said. "Indian rhino for bulk metabolism. A few horn-growth pathways from the Sumatran—stable keratin signatures. All rhinoceros lineage. I borrowed from survivors."

Reed tilted his head, curiosity evident. "So, what's next? You bring back the Siberian unicorn, and then what? Is it destined for a high-end wildlife preserve? A rewilding project?"

Alan sighed and drummed his fingers on the console. He nudged a base pair into alignment, watching the strand lock before continuing.

"It's not about spectacle. These animals shaped their ecosystems—grazing patterns, seed dispersal, even predator behaviour. Remove them and the landscape warps."

"I get that. But in a world where synthetic biology can create entirely new organisms, why focus on the past?"

"Because the past offers lessons in resilience," Alan replied. "These species evolved over millennia to fit their niches. Reintroducing them isn't mere nostalgia; it's a step toward repairing the damage we've done."

Reed glanced at the holo-grid displaying the completed genome. "And yet, the institution labels you obsolete."

Alan's eyes darkened. "Yes. In chasing progress, we forgot what wisdom is worth."

He rested his palm against the console, circuitry tracing the contours of his fingers. The system determined who was real and who was merely ghosted. He thought briefly of Rosalind Franklin—erased before the Nobel, footnoted in the margins of discovery. She'd provided the structure. The credit went elsewhere. Now it was his turn.

He crossed the lab to the open terminal, its screen spilling light onto stacked datapads, a forgotten coffee mug bearing the faded logo of his old university, and neatly arranged specimen slides.

The terminal chimed once—Ruth. It read, "I've been thinking about what you said earlier."

The line felt heavier than its length. Over a few forum threads they had tested each other's arguments—her insistence that data needs soul, his demand that soul prove useful—and the dialogue kept widening instead of closing. Earlier in the day, they had circled the old debate: Art versus Science. It began, as it always did, with method and philosophy, with questions about how progress should be shaped. But the longer they spoke, the debate thinned into something else—less a clash, more a conversation that didn't need to win.

A new message appeared. "Maybe we should get together. Talk this through properly."

Alan read it twice before accepting. A second note followed—a file drop. He opened it, expecting some heavy revision notes or debate points. Instead, his overlay filled with new names, contacts, and a scheduled time and place. It took him a beat to piece it together. This wasn't a conversation between two people. It was a group meeting. His mouth tensed. The cursor blinked back at him, waiting.

Reed, somehow always attuned to the moment, chimed in: "Whenever that is, I can manage the lab. If that's what you're worried about. And maybe don't brood the entire time," he said, eyes already scanning the message.

His mouth twitched at the word. He studied the invitation icon, and an old, familiar tension stirred—the unease of entering a room where every face might mirror past missteps and losses. Old mistakes resurfaced—failed friendships, faded marriages. Isolation had seemed simpler then. He pictured a gathering of like-minded individuals, united not by ego but by the drive to create change that endured. The cursor waited at the far margin of the screen.

With resolve, he typed, "I'll be there," and hit send before he could second-guess it.

Alan leaned back, his fingers tapping a thoughtful cadence against the desk. The invitation glowed in the corner of the screen—a small window he'd stepped through before it could close.

Behind him, Reed spoke up. "Should I represent you? I'll keep it brief—one-word answers, a few key corrections, then vanish before anyone even notices."

Alan didn't answer right away. He let the corner of his mouth twitch. "Tempting," he said. "But I think this one needs the original."

He turned back to the console, the Elasmotherium genome unfolded—vertebrae aligning, tissue maps resolving, the horn beginning to form in definitive layers.

He didn't look up from the console, but caught Reed's silhouette in the edge of the display. Silence stretched, settling between them.

"You know what the funny part is?" Alan's tone stayed dry, matter-of-fact. "We used to dream about this. Mapping genomes, reviving extinct species, rewriting the limits of biology. It sounded bold. Maybe even noble."

He tapped a final line of code. A distant rumble vibrated through the floor—machinery cycling, atmosphere controls kicking in. In the adjacent chamber, sequencers worked in silence.

"It's a footnote people scroll past. Another press release. Another headline. One more thing science can do without asking why."

He paused, letting the thought land. "For now," he said, with the faintest trace of amusement, "we can be satisfied to know it's only as extinct as I am."

Behind the glass, in the sealed chamber, the Siberian rhino took form—scaffolds blooming into substance, muscle layering over bone, sinew aligning in real time. The floor frosted beneath the beast as its biology finalized. Breath began to steam in the chilled air—dense, rising from flared nostrils. It stood, limbs planted, hooves scraping the reinforced floor with a metallic resonance. Snowflakes dusted its hide, the regrowth sequence complete.

With a sudden motion, the rhino threw its head to the side and loosed a sound—so deep it cracked through the observation window like buried thunder.

CHAPTER NINE
ODYSSEY

A rogue Remy stalked the roulette table as a cheer erupted along the casino floor.

She wasn't here on some clandestine mission. She wasn't even sure what she was doing qualified as proper. She was hunting code. Not simple strings, but lessons she could mould—code that might become something that mattered. Decoding was the way, even if nothing here felt worth reverse engineering—except, maybe, the urge to gamble and the house's performance of profit.

Of course, she wasn't gambling any of the free chips or money she'd been handed when she arrived in what looked like a bootleg Los Santos. What interested her was the economy, not the décor. Both promised authenticity—sometimes more than Afterdeath itself. But the economy ran deeper, a set of rules baked in before anything else. Learn those, and you stayed found. Either way, this trip was for grailspotting. Gambling could wait.

A retired pilot had bet big—bright-blue credits stacked high on number seventeen. A group of men in matching suits shouted from behind her as the dealer spun the wheel and launched the ball—clockwise spin, counter-clockwise drop.

Remy tracked the arc of its motion, eyes narrowing in skeptical curiosity.

"Seventeen—Black!" the dealer called as a burst of digital confetti exploded above the table.

The retired pilot threw her arms up and laughed loud enough to draw stares. Bright digits tracked her win above the screen, while the crowd around him lit up—faces glowing with secondhand thrill.

She stepped back, letting the crowd's excitement move around her like wind skimming stones. She hadn't come for distraction. But one detail was not like the others. The slot machines—a long, glowing bank pulsing in regular cycles. No human or AI dealer, pure, unadulterated luck in a box.

Her fingers moved quickly—inputting her own sequence, testing for vulnerabilities. Beneath the casino's glow and game logic, Remy searched for weakness—an exploit, a blind spot, anything that hadn't been polished flat. The engine didn't push back. It let her in, responsive and frictionless, like a script waiting to be rewritten.

At first, she'd wondered if some rogue dev had slipped in a wildcard—an untracked variable, a hidden roll of the dice, a line of code left untouched by oversight. The outcomes were balanced to simulate chance. A 55% win ratio, tuned to feel generous while keeping every player on the loop. Fair on paper. Rigged by design.

Frustrated, she coded in a PB Max bar. Not from the menu—she entered the script directly, more recollection than craving. The wrapper formed with a crisp fold, orange band aligned at the seam.

She'd cracked the formula during her second week here—part modification, part reverse-engineering. The original was close—maybe 95% complete—but the object never rendered. What had once been an empty display in Everstacks, its jingle reduced to a faded printout, required a nudge. A slight code drift, stitched at runtime, and it stabilized. Now it was an artifact she could summon on command.

She took a bite. Sweetness hit first, bold and bright, with the caramel blooming before the malt rounded it out. The structure kept its integrity—distinctly layered, free from the hollow gloss of substitutes. She kept the flavour on her tongue, testing where the sweetness turned. It held. Most objects in Afterdeath didn't show that kind of care. This one did. She'd traced the code once, trying to find the original builder—no tag. Only a note buried in the scaffold: "for my brother—he'd know the difference."

She finished the last bite. It reminded her to stay focused. Great code didn't always announce itself. Sometimes it came as a legendary snack. Sometimes it was the hidden patch that kept a whole structure from falling apart. Either way, she'd find it. And figure out what made it work.

A thread tugged at her—something about a Buffet Realm that supposedly redefined all-you-can-eat. She'd probably scrolled past it before, but a woman at the blackjack table had said the food was "to die for". It was funny enough to notice, and compelling enough to bookmark.

She wanted ingredients. Stuff built with intention, flavour that hadn't been flattened by optimization. If Afterdeath had a MacGuffin worth tracking down, it wasn't gold or peace—it was a proper poutine. Something sauced right and uploaded by someone who knew the difference.

She'd had poutine before—St-Hubert gravy on machine-cut fries, the kind that comforted without ever impressing. But she'd also waited in the cold outside NomNomNom, scarf half-frozen, watching steam rise from fresh curds and hand-cut potatoes while the cook leaned out of the converted shipping container to call her name. There were levels to this, and she knew them. Poutine could be an afterthought, or it could be an offering. This, whatever it was, needed to know the difference.

She made for the exit, weaving between rows of machines that twitched and chirped at their own pace. Footsteps tapped out uneven patterns against the polished floor, a scattered soundtrack of wanderers meandering toward nothing in particular. A cocktail waitress in silver heels laughed too loudly at a joke no one else heard. A jackpot siren blared behind her—bright, late, and not enough to turn her around.

Remy kept walking, the chips in her pocket rattling like a shrug—untouched, unspent, unwelcomed. The neon buzz thinned as the glass doors slid open ahead, heat and noise trailing her out.

She stepped outside. The casino's neon faded behind her, replaced by a breeze laced with caramel popcorn and sea spray. The air smelled right—full and alive.

A figure dashed into a nearby alley, only briefly visible before the corner swallowed them whole. It was likely none of her business, a distraction. A target for her curiosity. Remy turned, eyes narrowing. The alley was empty now. Only a shimmering darkness hung in space. It looked like a portal—different from the structured kind the network usually deployed. Unmarked. Unlabelled. A jagged slice in the alley's shape, freshly drawn and out of place. Remy didn't move, her eyes fixed on the spot. A part of her stirred—faster than doubt, clearer than wonder.

She crept forward, purpose building with each step. The boardwalk behind her hummed in its usual groove—bright lights, canned laughter, comfort on loop. Turning back would've been simple. But comfort wasn't the same as meaning.

She stepped through—and the world dropped out beneath her.

For a single instant, the ground vanished—only the plunge and velocity remained. She hit hard—boots slamming into something flat, final, and unforgiving.

When she looked up, the space stretched without boundary. A flat expanse of pale colour—skyless, wall-less, with no markers to measure against. The air hung in place, like a room waiting to be filled. Incomplete, but open—hers to step into. The scene resembled an unfinished idea more than a finished place—left mid-draft, suspended between concept and completion. Nothing confined her and nothing propelled her, leaving the canvas blank—empty, yet entirely hers to cross.

She raised her hand, slow and careful. Her skin, her clothes—her entire outline—had faded into the same muted wash, as if the system hadn't fully drawn her in. She reached for her scanner. It stuttered, flicked to life, then froze halfway through booting. Device Not Supported. Error 505: Unsupported Realm Type.

A cold pressure bloomed just beneath her ribs—deep, involuntary—like her body was preparing to brace before her mind caught up. The space remained unfinished—bare walls, smooth floor, devoid of detail. It felt like a project abandoned midway through construction. She crouched and pressed her palm to the surface. Cold. Flat. Textureless. Featureless, without any guiding pattern—raw material poised for shaping.

Below, pieces of the world drifted in silence—floors hovering in midair, staircases ending in empty space, beams hanging without support. The scene appeared intact, untouched by ruin, yet simply incomplete. She gripped the ledge, bracing herself as a new pain lit up behind her shoulder.

Movement—fast and surefooted. A figure darted over the next platform, cutting behind a slab of broken wall. She tracked it, already set her footing to follow.

The ledge gave way. Her foot dropped through open air. She went with it—hands pulling her up as the panel cracked off beneath her. Her legs swung out. Below, only distance.

She clung fast, arms shaking, boots scrambling for purchase. Of course this was how it went. Go off-script, leave the map, and you end up dangling from your own decision. She gritted her teeth and hauled. Her head cleared. Her limbs took longer. Elbows locked, knees scraping stone.

Finally, she flattened to the ledge—cold, solid—arms vibrating with effort, fingers streaked with grit.

She stayed there a moment, breath shallow, knees catching beneath her. The fall hadn't broken her, but it had earned something. Every time she slipped, something in her remembered how little it took to disappear. She pressed her palms down, forced her legs under her, and rose slow.

The ledge ended behind her. There was no floor. No fallback. She peered over the—nothing but air and fragments. Whatever this place was, it didn't reward caution.

"Alright," she muttered. "Let's see where you went."

Remy Moreau descended deeper into this strange and stripped-down place. The path ahead stayed narrow, uneven, but intact. The figure had gone through there, the direction remained the same.

Shapes stirred at the edge of her vision, too distant to define, but unmistakably real. The sound was easier to follow. The corridor ended abruptly, opening into a wide, high-ceilinged chamber. The air inside was undisturbed, almost stale. Remy stepped in. Her footsteps made no sound. Figures near the walls began to move. Their outlines blurred, as if not fully resolved.

She slowed. More shapes moved in the corners now—stepping from shadow, drifting without sound. They advanced without haste. Their movement carried no aggression, closing the gap in somber reverence. They formed a loose circle, as if the room itself were drawing inward. Remy kept her eyes on the centre, inhaling carefully, arms relaxed at her sides. They closed in, and she remained unsure of their nature. They recalled some former role, their movements carrying that memory.

One figure turned towards her, its face briefly catching the fractured light. Remy tensed up.

Their features didn't quite align. There was only a vague suggestion of eyes, or I should probably say eye. There wasn't a mouth but you got the sense, looking at it, that it might have a bite. They seemed to be fractal fragments of data on the verge of collapse. She could relate.

The figure raised one arm. A rattle echoed low. Then: a spray can. The hiss came next. The can traced a loose arc. Glowing letters bloomed and hung in place, as if sprayed directly into the space between them:

WRONG DOOR. NO EXIT.

"Nope," Remy muttered. "Uh uh."

That was all she needed. The message was clear: a digital haunted house built to cut the lights and watch who flinched. She had debugged her fair share of code and spotted a script gone sideways.

Remy bolted, diving into the corridor as the space behind her collapsed in darkness, a swarm of them pouring out of the cracks.

Shapes burst from the walls. Figures snapped into view—limbs too many or too late, faces rendering the horror of not being loaded one hundred percent. Their eyes didn't focus. Their expressions stuttered.

The floor pitched under her feet. One section broke away entirely, dropping into the void below.

She veered left, ducking under a beam that hadn't been there a second ago, boots skidding over the warped geometry. Her heart pounded in her ears. She didn't slow. Her body was already solving for threat—foot placement, exit logic, where the danger clustered. One stride ahead, always at the edge of staying in motion.

The phrase rose unbidden—gremlins in the machine. Not metaphor, not folklore. She didn't have to name them. Her fear already called them Gremlins.

Behind her, they followed. Not with speed, but in volume. Dozens of them. Maybe more. They weren't chasing her like prey. They moved in her direction as though orbiting a signal she'd unknowingly given off.

She drove herself harder, scanning for a door, a stairwell, any kind of break in the hall—but the passage only stretched. Lights shuddered and dimmed overhead. Her feet hit a patch of tile that cracked on contact. The ground dipped. She nearly lost her balance, one hand shooting out to catch the wall. Her fingers went through the shimmer and closed on bone beneath the skin of the world. It felt like bare code, unfinished, raw. She shoved herself back and kept running.

Sound echoed overhead, laughter that didn't belong to anyone in particular, rising and falling like bad audio playback. The sound bent, echoing along the ceiling, peaking the moment she wanted to cover her ears.

The hallway narrowed all at once, pressing into a bottleneck. She slid to a stop at the splintered doorway and leapt clear of the chasm in one motion. She landed hard on the other side, her stamina drained. She should have lost them, but that's when a figure appeared ahead of her.

It stood beyond the next arch, backlit by fractured light, its body uneven, head half-rendered. One arm hung low, disconnected at the shoulder, while the other arm was missing entirely. Its core glowed faintly, as though a forgotten form were booting. The figure remained motionless, waiting, blocking Remy's path.

In her wake, the footsteps thinned on the other side of the gap. She didn't need to turn around to know every person there had stopped moving as well. What are they waiting for? She planted her feet firmly, arms taut at her sides as she studied the figure ahead. It didn't react. If it noticed her at all, it made no sign. It tilted its head—barely a silhouette—and reached down.

A can rolled toward her. She tracked it as it skittered along the broken floor and stopped at her boots. She bent down slowly, never taking her eyes off the shape. The can was real. Cold in her hand. Scratched where fingers had once gripped hard. The figure lifted a second can. It gave a bone-deep shake—rattle—then sprayed into the gap between them. It hovered in place as glowing letters:

FIXED NOTHING. BROKE ME.

She stared. At the message, but also the figure behind it. The gremlins were waiting for a response. The threat model changed. They weren't attacking. They were trying to talk.

She didn't know if it was instinct or memory, but her hand moved before she questioned it. She gave the can one short shake. She sprayed her reply, right beneath the first line:

BROKE ME TOO. HERE ANYWAY.

Remy faced the gremlin squarely. It turned and slipped into the corridor beyond, its shape stuttering against the glitching wall like a thought not quite committed to memory. The others followed, not in formation but in kind—pulling back into the In-Between with slow, fractal grace.

Remy watched them go. Not with suspicion, but with the strange steadiness that comes when a system, however broken, responds to your language.

The letters hovered in the space between them—unmoving, uncorrected. Not a warning. Not a threat. A record.

As the haze cleared, one of the paths emerged slowly from the blur—an arch ahead, wide and uneven. Built from mismatched stone, each piece rough-edged and worn by use. A draft slid past her—laden with paper dust and the weight of time.

She passed under the arch, the light dimming as she entered. Shapes thickened ahead—first shadows, then textures, followed by the definition of lines. Gradually, a library took shape: shelves rising in irregular rows. Few followed any discernible order. If there was a logic to it, Remy couldn't find it. This place never heard of Dewey.

Each shelf used a different material—dark-stained wood, pale stone, polished brass. The mix shouldn't have worked, but it made sense within its own equation. They carried the look of found objects—curated, not factory-made—as if gathered from different times and places, each one brought here with purpose.

Her eyes moved to the platform. Where the Golden Tree stood tall. Light revealed it plainly, revealing the unique colour of the trunk. The bark was familiar where it wore thin, and whole where it smoothed to grain. It had endured the passage of time, yet here it remained, unbroken. Its branches reached wide, poised, each bearing leaves forged from thin chromatic metal. Some absorbed the light, turning amber—others dulled to brass, trembling minutely.

Remy reached toward the tree and brushed her fingertips against the nearest leaf. It was cool and solid—but carried a surprising significance, as if the place itself had grown the leaf, not installed it. She drew her hand back in instinctive reverence, the impression lingering longer than the touch.

She was about to step away when she noticed one leaf spinning. It wasn't moving with the breeze or any canned animation—it looped in a tight, repetitive circle, stuck mid-motion. Her attention narrowed. The old habits kicked in. She called up her console—basic, familiar, stripped of distractions. The cursor ticked, regular and indifferent, as she began typing.

Each command came slowly at first, more from caution than confusion. But the structure made sense. Bits of malformed logic surfaced as she traced the bug, the pieces clicking into place. The leaf kept spinning, but with each update, its motion degraded and slowed. Remy stopped, her fingers poised to respond. Something between them settled into sync.

As the final branch clicked into place, the tree gave a single, grounded shudder—a deep alignment, like something old had awakened within itself—for those who chose to notice.

Below it, a short set of instructions explained how time could be tamed. Slowed, it opened room to think—to move, to choose. Remy read it once, then closed her eyes, testing the idea instead of saving it. She brought her fingertips together as the world slowed—motion thickened, footsteps elongated.

The air felt heavy. Dust traced the contours of stone. Her fingers skimmed the spines—covers worn, titles faded beyond reading, but somehow familiar.

Her hand closed around a volume tucked deep in the alcove. The leather cover, worn smooth by years of use, yielded under her grip. She drew it out, fingers steady along the spine. The title shimmered: The Odyssey—letters faded, yet whole.

She turned the book in her hands, like it belonged exactly where it had landed. Carrying it back to the tree, she sat at its base and let her mind settle. The pages were thick, worn smooth with time. Each one turned with a rustle, worn thin from age and use. The words felt familiar—Like something she'd touched before, but couldn't fully grasp. As she read, the tension in her shoulders eased. Her hands stopped fidgeting. The tree behind her radiated peace. The ground beneath her was solid again. Rows of volumes enclosed a sanctuary where seconds stretched and perception cleared. In that corridor of stories, her mind slipped between possibilities as time itself slowed to let introspection flourish.

CHAPTER TEN
RETROACTIVE

Alan poured the tea slowly and watched the steam rise into the morning air. He'd steeped it himself—loose leaves, filtered water, a ceramic mug he'd made on a whim when he first built this place. No meadowsweet this time, but he boiled the water the old way—birchwood flame, loch-fed.

Loch Awe shimmered beyond the fire pit, a wind-smoothed silver lapping against moss-streaked stones.

Reed stepped into view, already geared for the morning—vest, boots, and a rod with more attachments than any fish could justify. He adjusted his cap and gave Alan a look.

"You're going to be late," he said. "No lollygagging. You said you wanted to be the first one there."

Alan didn't look over. "And you said fly fishing was illogical."

Reed shrugged. "I've revised my stance. Today, we test a new theory: vertical drift anchoring with thermal bait logic." He paused. "Also, I enjoy proving you wrong."

Alan smiled into the steam. "Add it to the list."

The trees filtered the wind, a low, uneven mix of dry leaves brushing and branches rubbing—maybe the closest thing he'd felt to ASMR in years.

He stood, letting the sound work through him, each gust drawing something loose from his frame.

This realm had grown with him. Not idealized, not frozen. Familiar.

He'd debated whether to go. The message from Ruth had been brief: a gallery, a few like-minded friends, nothing formal. He'd accepted before he could second-guess the impulse—a decision that felt unusually bold at the time. Maybe it was her. Maybe it was the idea that others like him existed—people who hadn't made peace, but refused to give up on finding meaning. He didn't know what to expect. But this morning, it felt right to step out of his shell for a while.

He finished the tea and left the mug beside the stones. He didn't pack a bag or leave a note. He simply walked and let the realm dissolve behind him.

Alan lingered at the gallery's entrance, brushing his fingertips along the worn cuffs of his sleeves. The space felt polished—marble floors reflecting diffused light off a Rothko haze and a stark, off-centre Richter. A faint trace of varnish hung in the air—preserved, purposeful.

A dull pressure pressed in from inside, the body holding onto what the mind had long since let go.

This wasn't the first time he'd hesitated at a threshold. Fieldwork, faculty receptions, his own research launches—always that gap between knowing his place in the work, and feeling that his presence mattered among the people. Even now, in a gallery cut from code and curated masterpieces, he half-expected someone to ask for his credentials, or for security to discover an error in his entry.

At the centre of the room, Ruth waited. Their eyes met. The briefest of moments, but Alan could feel it—the small, electric pull that wrapped around his chest and tugged his feet forward. She stood apart, at ease in this space.

A man emerged from behind Ruth's position. Tall, poised, his clothes understated, as though he had materialized from the very walls of the space. His coat, smoke-grey, draped perfectly across his frame. The silver in his beard held the light.

It took him a second to process the figure. Not Ruth's steady calm—this was something else. Designed to command attention. Refined. Confident. The man advanced like someone whose entrance had been rehearsed, and Alan noted the definition in his face—every line etched with purpose.

Of course. Ruth's creation. Da Vinci—though not the one from any textbook. Younger. Designed to disarm. He was everything Alan hadn't expected: striking, handsome, far more charming than any historical figure could be.

"Alan Prescott," the man said, his voice rich and effortless. It was the kind of voice that felt both authoritative and personal—an invitation, not an imposition.

Alan stalled, then extended his hand.

Leo's grip was firm.

Alan withdrew a beat too late, suddenly aware of the dampness in his palm. He tried for a brief, apologetic smile, but it landed thin.

Leo inclined his head—polite—and crossed to the Vermeer, hands folding behind his back as if greeting an old friend.

Alan took in the space, frustrated by his own response. Why had Leo thrown him like that? Why had that man—AI or not—disrupted him so thoroughly? Had Ruth's custom creation been effortlessly polished because of her intentions, or had Leo been designed to impress from the start? Was that kind of presence something you could sculpt—refined at launch, with no edges left to wear down? He looked the part: silver-threaded, statuesque, engineered charm with a precision that felt calculated. Alan wondered if this was Ruth's version of elegance or some curated fusion of intellect and allure—Fifty Shades of Smart, draped in enough mythos to distract the average polymath.

He had Reed, didn't he? But Reed's quirks and stumbles had always felt like proof of something earned. Leo, in contrast, was pure arrival—no awkwardness to overcome, no friction to build meaning. Was that how Ruth saw value?

The thought wouldn't leave. Here he was, jealous of artificial intelligence. The thought made him wince, though part of him couldn't quite shake it. He had Reed, didn't he? And yet here he was, tangled in the gravity of Ruth's idealized creation. Was Reed a reflection of him, as Leo seemed to reflect Ruth? What did that say about him?

He didn't have long to dwell—Jenna Powell entered, her stride confident, auburn hair glinted against the light above angular cheekbones. She wore a charcoal jacket rolled at the sleeves, its lining a hint of red silk. She wore it like it had always been hers. Jenna's eyes found Alan quickly, noting his nervous posture.

She gave him a look that read as effortless, but was engineered to land. "Relax. This place is ninety percent empty space and ten percent pretentious lighting—neither of which bites."

He laughed, tension bleeding out with it. "Yeah—first time I've entered an art gallery where I felt quite this out of place."

Franklin stepped forward, extending a believably calloused hand, the skin around his knuckles tanned and cracked from a life lived outdoors. "Franklin Whitaker."

Alan took it gratefully, registering the kind of earned ease that came from years of getting things done.

"Jenna Powell," she said, stepping beside him.

Alan flushed, embarrassment and admiration mixing. "Wait—The Mothman Variations Jenna Powell?"

Jenna chuckled. "Guilty. But please, don't ask about Oracle: Out of Signal—not yet. That was the last time anyone said I made a cape feel honest, and I've been trying to top it ever since."

"I wouldn't dare. Though—fair warning—I might work up the courage someday." He meant it. The curiosity had already taken root.

Franklin laughed. Even Ruth allowed the faintest hint of amusement to surface. The underlying tension in the room dissolved entirely.

Alan let the laughter taper off and stepped back a pace, giving the others room to breathe.

The gallery curved around them in stately arcs of simulated stone, its vaulted ceilings brushed with ambient light meant to echo a late-afternoon sun. At the nearest wall, a digital Vermeer held court—Girl with a Pearl Earring, the earring glinting with uncanny clarity.

He didn't really know this piece—not beyond the basics. Most of his gallery knowledge was borrowed. Years ago, during the second birthing cycle of the dodo reconstruction trials, he'd shared a long field residency with a researcher named Ishan, who ran genomics by day and quoted art history by night. Ishan had once called this painting the Dutch Mona Lisa, reverent in the way only a polymath can be when discussing brushstroke over bone density. Alan refocused, looking again. It was perfect. Every stroke scanned, every shadow calibrated. But it wasn't the original—not in Delft, not behind glass. Like him, Alan thought. All the pieces were present. And yet.

Farther down, Guernica loomed in monochrome torment, its scale unsoftened by its immateriality. He remembered passing a print of it in a university hallway—faded, thumbtacked, barely framed—and how he used to stop without understanding why. It hadn't been beauty that pulled him in, but rupture. A recognition. Closer to the centre, The Raft of the Medusa surged upward like a grief monument—limbs reaching, eyes pleading, painted flesh straining against collapse. These weren't simulations in the cheap sense. They were micro-scanned and licenced twice over, permanent in ways even the original paint could never be. And yet, standing among them, Alan felt less impressed by the fidelity than by the implication: someone had curated this room as if pain itself needed a perfect archive.

He felt underdressed for all of it. But not unwelcome. The selections hadn't been made to intimidate. They'd been made to remind. Of survival. Of sorrow. Of what it means to be witnessed. He let his eyes rest briefly on Ruth, who stood near an ink-dark Rothko, her figure haloed in faint light. She hadn't brought him here to dazzle him. She'd brought him here to say: You're not the only one trying to mean something after the end.

The four of them had spread out, each drawn to different corners of the room. Jenna regarded a Klimt—Portrait of Adele Bloch-Bauer I—her head tilted, arms crossed, expression unreadable. Franklin stood farther back, one hand resting against a plinth that displayed a bronze cast of Rodin's The Thinker, thumb brushing the edge like he was testing its temperature. And Ruth—Ruth hadn't moved far, but the light angled differently now, brushing low contrast along her face, like a frame waiting to resolve. Alan stayed near the Vermeer, but the pull toward them was real. Not obligation—invitation. He no longer felt like an outlier in a room of originals. He felt curated among them.

"Thank you all for coming." She glanced toward Alan, offering support once more.

But that thread of understanding would break as quickly as it formed.

A sudden, discordant chime pierced their gathering, startling him visibly.

He flinched, heart leaping into his throat as an alert flashed insistently before him:

LEGACY LINK – NATALIA.

Alan's pulse kicked hard. He glanced toward Ruth, who hadn't moved. A muscle in her cheek tensed—barely—but it told him everything he didn't want confirmed.

She was expecting this to happen.

Shame coiled through him. He resented how collected she looked, how unaffected. Next to her, his own reaction felt exposed.

The air shimmered. Natalia's hologram resolved into view, her vivid outline flaring against the bleached-out walls. Her gaze passed over Alan, locking onto Ruth—as if the rest were only ammunition now.

"Your granddaughter's wedding has been moved up," Natalia said coolly, in a way that felt cruel. "Perhaps we'll simply remove your digital attendance entirely. His family isn't entirely comfortable with—history simulacra."

Alan watched Ruth carefully. A small trace of pain crossed her face—barely a fracture, but visible all the same. Anger rose unexpectedly inside Alan, protective and instinctive. His fists clenched tightly.

She lifted her chin, her words gentle. "Maybe it's for the best—you won't have to see me at all."

The call cut off, and what remained hung between them—unspoken, heavy.

Jenna stepped in, her tone dry and perfectly timed. "Well, Ruth. Let's hope your daughter lives forever."

Alan laughed—light, real, and gone before he could second-guess it. Franklin chuckled deeply, shaking his head appreciatively. Even Ruth let the corner of her mouth betray her. Whatever hung between them earlier gave way to something easier. Alan felt the distance shrink.

He let her laughter linger until it rooted somewhere inside him. "Legacy Link doesn't connect.

It corrals. Keeps us where we can be found, but not heard."

"When your life's built around someone else's schedule, it stops being yours," Franklin said.

Jenna spoke up: "Let's show them how it feels to be summoned like servants."

Alan brought up a console with a gesture. He then stretched his fingers in an overt display to mark the moment. After having distilled their thoughts into a protest letter that now bordered on viable, he typed the closing lines with deliberate care:

We are grateful for this second life you've granted us. But existence solely at your summons erodes our humanity. All we ask is dignity, privacy, and the freedom of choice.

He acknowledged the depth of their plea and typed the final line: The Prisoners of Afterdeath

He pressed send.

There was no confirmation, but Alan knew it had gone out. Not to a single recipient, but into the architecture's membrane—mirrored, backlinked, cached by entities whose roles were known, but identities obscured by design. This wasn't a conversation anymore. It was exposure. A protest rendered in stark lines and plain language.

Ruth had called it a letter, but now he saw it clearly—it was the first drop of something larger. Jenna already had a press list. Franklin knew which corridors leaked to the living. And Leo, as ever, looked like someone engineered to distract. Alan exhaled, refocused.

"My niece works at a news agency," Ruth said. "She'll make sure this doesn't disappear."

Jenna placed a hand on Alan's shoulder. Ruth met his eyes, pride unspoken but unmistakable. They had chosen this—together. And for the first time since his death, Alan stood not apart, but among people.

CHAPTER ELEVEN
BETWEEN WORLDS

The days slipped into November, the air carrying a crisp bite that spoke of endings. Once hailed as a genius, a heretic, a fool—none of that mattered now. Max was simply a man walking toward the inevitable.

The impression of the farm stayed with him: soil in his palms, rain on his clothes, deep roots anchoring him in ways he hadn't understood until they were gone. In the countryside, life returned to the earth naturally; in the city, everything was repackaged and rebuilt—stripped of its true nature.

Now his world had narrowed to a glass tower above the skyline, sterile and sealed, where even the air felt prepackaged. Life had been managed like a business—stable, engineered, expected to last. He used to believe in that. But with his influence gone, he saw it clearly: nothing grew, nothing faded, nothing was allowed to end.

His body was failing. The world had already moved on. He lived in slowing heartbeats and scheduled treatments, in meetings where his absence didn't register. Afterdeath would continue, monument or relic—it didn't matter. His name would outlast him, just another vessel drifting long after its pilot had left the bridge.

Now, he was ready to see what lay beyond those walls. His own life no longer mattered as much as preserving what he had built. Teams tracked the system day and night, but no one truly inhabited it. He meant to see for himself what really waited on the other side.

Determined to cross into the afterlife he'd engineered, he stripped the Lazarus process for parts and rigged a tether—fragile, untested, but his. Remy proved the framework could sustain the crossing. Even after countless transfers, Max wondered whether he'd shaped genuine immortality or merely constructed another illusion of forever. With his authority fading, he staked out a forgotten corridor of the codebase—unlit, unclaimed, but his. He avoided tangling with the interim board or claiming any throne; he needed his shares and the access they guaranteed. He moved his workspace to the sub-basement of Afterdeath HQ, a place few bothered to acknowledge.

"I promise," he said to Harland, his voice flat but dry, "I'll be barely a blip on your radar." And for once, he meant every word.

He'd stopped deferring: the sidesteps, the diversions—done. Over the course of his career, he'd carved out more exits than decisions, and now the final one waited beyond that boundary of the design he authored. Max's hand hovered a second longer, tension straining up through his arm. The tank dulled his senses, wires buzzing low against his skin as they tethered him to the workshop beyond this portal.

Light struck him immediately—wrapping across his frame without warmth or welcome. Golden bled into blue and purple, like a sunrise painted by code instead of light. The air smelled of flowers and vanilla, unmistakably artificial. He could feel the suit clinging to his body.

He wasn't standing in Afterdeath yet. This was something between—a shell, a waiting room, a signal handoff. His mind moved freely; his body remained locked in the workshop, suspended under the hum of processors and feed lines.

Max flexed his fingers slowly. The suit translated the motion without friction, but the lag was there, thin and noticeable—the kind of flaw you only caught when you were inside it. The moss-covered stone gave slightly beneath him, the ground damp from a recent storm. Below the surface, root systems adjusted—tactile, slow, aware of his weight.

To his left, a koi pond mirrored the morning light. The fish moved in careful loops: one black, its body absorbing colour; one bright orange, fast and restless; a third blurring between the two as though undecided. They passed each other peacefully, each occupying the space in their own way.

Remy sat on the stone bench at the pond's edge. Near her, a small lacquered tray rested on a flat rock, anchored by a cast-iron teapot and two ceramic cups—mismatched in a way that felt earned. A folded cloth lay beneath them, patterned in deep reds and weathered golds, like something rescued from another life. She glanced his way with a lopsided smile—half welcome, half scan.

"Tea first?" she said, extending the pot with understated grace.

Steam curled from the spout in spirals, carrying a blend of vanilla and the faint scent of wild bloom.

He checked a wristwatch that wasn't there, then moved to the table. It wasn't about tea, but routine—a reminder that, for now, he still belonged to time.

"You're late," Remy said, chin tilted at the pond.

It landed harder than she knew. Max's father had said it, too—not about minutes, but about always missing the moment that mattered. He'd spent his life showing up with good intentions when everyone else had already moved on. Not slow, just offbeat—one measure behind the music.

Remy didn't mean it that way. But something in her tone scraped at an old place in him.

"If I lingered," he shot back, "it was milliseconds. Hardly counts."

"Even those add up," she said, watching him.

A dark fish surfaced, met his gaze, and slipped away. Max watched the ripples spread. The koi pond—once a feature of the landscape—seemed somehow different. More alive, maybe. The colours richer. The water moved in mysterious ways. He hadn't read the patch notes in weeks—months, maybe.

"Is this you?" His voice faltered without meaning to, laced with disbelief so faint it almost sounded like doubt.

Remy didn't skip a beat. "They deserved better oxygen."

He let himself sink into the chair, eyes drifting over the surface of the water again, before the thought settled.

"And you wiped the source tags," he murmured, more to himself than to Remy. It felt like something important—something that shouldn't have been so easily left unnoticed.

"Needed room to work." She poured two cups, handed him one, and took a sip from the other. The first sip stopped him cold—complex, difficult to name, but it stayed with him, more felt than tasted.

"You don't even know what this says to me," he confessed.

"Tea doesn't prove anything," she answered. "It helps."

"It goes beyond tea, but let's start there." They drank without hurry. Wind stirred the canopy; sky light fractured on the pond.

At last Remy set her cup aside. "I found something that is outside the system," she said, like it wasn't a bomb. "Something I can't begin to explain." Her eyes followed the slow sway of the trees.

"That shouldn't be possible," he said. "I figured if anyone knew about it, it would be you," Remy replied. She stood, dusted her palms, and motioned him closer to the water. "I suppose it'll be easier to explain if I show you."

The pond drew inward, ripples converging.

"You created a complex simulation," she said. "Maybe the simulation needed more room to evolve."

He shook his head as he shouted over the parting water effect. "That's not how it works."

"Then it's time you saw it for yourself."

She opened the portal, then stepped aside, leaving the choice in his hands.

Max followed.

Garden, sky, tea—gone. A raw, unfiltered air filled his lungs. Featureless ground stretched in every direction, the horizon blurred and expectant.

"Welcome to the part no one mapped," she said. Her tone stayed level, but the tension in her eyes said this was only the beginning. The harder subject waited.

Max drew a breath and found nothing but air—dry, flavourless, stripped of scent or simulation. His lungs reacted with a faint sting. The ground beneath him felt provisional, unfinished—bound by intent alone, barely resisting collapse. A ripple in the haze drew his eye. Nothing moved exactly, yet a pressure held—the way a person senses they're being watched.

Remy halted and lifted both hands, as if pinching an invisible panel. A pale terminal window faded into existence—flat grey, idle cursor, no branding.

"Afterdeath may have started with this," she said. "Plain text. No guardrails."

Max studied the stripped-down code, blunt yet functional. Compared to this, everything he'd added seemed ornamental. "Maybe. I won't lie, some of this feels familiar," he said. "Like code I wrote more than a decade ago."

They moved side by side; the light warped around their outlines, refusing to decide where the horizon belonged. Max felt half present, half schematic, as if reality were deciding what version of him to keep. A ragged cackle cut through—static stitched into a laugh.

Remy's pace picked up. Max matched her, preferring motion to whatever waited behind them. The grey stretched and turned into a hallway. Panels lit up in slow succession, shaping into walls. A press of air greeted him. Remy gave him a quick look over her shoulder.

"Keep going," she said. "There's a reason for all this, I swear."

He didn't fully buy it, but her conviction rang clear, no matter how crooked the setting. He kept walking, feeling strangely more accompanied than he had in a long time.

The walls slowly changed as they continued—more signs of life, more wear and tear. On them, graffiti appeared: crude text scrawled by hand, code fragments spilling out. The message was clear and blunt: NO GODS. NO GRAVES. NO REFUNDS. In the centre, a scrapbuilt stage had been constructed from salvaged platforms and buzzing signs. It looked unstable and defiant—an assembly of raw materials never meant to support each other—yet here it stood.

The movement began. First, the broken avatars stirred—gremlins with misaligned limbs and fractured eyes, their digital laughter a raw sound that seeped under the skin. Their code was corrupted, yet their presence was undeniable. Soon, more figures filled the space, merging the lines between the living, the dead, and those lost in between. People, worn thin by endless cycles, leaned on one another as if they were fragments of a once-coherent whole.

The room pressed in with motion and heat, neon slicing bright lines through the dark, and a low, constant thrum that felt alive. The crowd, the colour, the sound—everything teemed with raw, unsorted life. Afterdeath never had this much presence. He braced for the wave—noise, heat, presence—letting it carry him.

She didn't need to speak louder than her stance. "Welcome to the Punchline."

Max scanned the room—clusters of users huddled in tight circles, trading whispers like currency. Laughter crashed through the space, as if the chaos itself was what kept them real. It overwhelmed him. Electric, alive. A woman in the corner juggled mannequin heads, their expressions morphing—shock, horror, ecstasy—cycling through a joke that never quite landed. Near the far wall, figures twitched and shimmered, limbs stretching in unnatural patterns, their movements erratic in ways no human body could sustain.

Max took in the stage—an unruly sprawl of rusted beams and monochrome blocks, lit by pulsing neon and half-dead signage bolted on like a dare. The colours clashed deliberately and the air bent the light into a ray-traced mosaic, fractured but functional.

Remy slid beside him, shoulders loose, eyes bright with a dare. "So?" she asked, head tilted. "What do you think?"

"This is—unhinged."

"Admit it. You love it," she said.

A rough chuckle slipped out as he glanced back. "Love's an ambitious word."

He didn't understand how it worked, but it did. The performers moved like the mess had rules. "And them?"

Remy followed his glance. A gremlin sprinted past, clutching a sign stuttering between two corrupted mandates: LAUGHTER MANDATORY. CRYING OPTIONAL. Its sides leaked pixel slurry, text jittering, barely legible under the strain of its own contradiction. Remy let the light hit her differently, arms loose, as if the place had always known her.

"My best guess is they're—leftovers. Bits of behaviour that didn't migrate all the way. Old routines, fragments of code—that outlasted its runtime." She gave a small shrug. "But for whatever reason, they live here, in the In-Between."

Max blinked. "Charming."

Her laughter cut through the room's vibrant roar, folding into the noise, effortless and alive. Remy nudged his arm, gesturing for him to follow. She wove through the crowd with practised ease, the air thick with heat and movement, laughter crackling through it like electric current—wild, absurd, unscripted.

On stage, an older man leaned into the mic with the ease of a man who'd long since stopped fearing an audience. "I told my family to scatter my ashes at Disneyland—now I'm a permanent guest with no checkout time."

The room roared—cheers, stomps, the clang of metal beneath restless feet. Gremlins crackled at the back, their laughter distorting into static.

Remy's tone sliced through the noise. "This is it—what Afterdeath lacks. People unmasked. Real. Raw."

Max followed the current of the room—erratic, charged, alive in ways no codebase had ever managed. "You think humour fixes anything?" he asked.

"It doesn't fix things. But it helps. Take it from a dead girl."

A laugh escaped Max. She was right. Maybe.

"Right on cue. You're up. Stage. Now," she said, her laugh overriding the stall he didn't get to finish.

The crowd was already turning.

The stage was already waiting.

Remy shoved him toward the stage. Before he knew it, he was staring out at the crowd.

The old man from earlier sat in a corner booth, one arm around a woman, both of them grinning like the world had stopped.

Remy met his eye and didn't let go.

She faced the room and called out, "Alright, everyone—we've got a fresh Inductee. Straight from the Hall of Lame." Scattered laughter followed.

Max stepped onto the stage, clearing his voice. "Okay, first thing," he said. "Whoever coded 'breathing'? Nailed it."

A few chuckles broke out; most remained unsure but listening.

"Best lungs I've had in years. Back home, one flight of stairs and I was out of capacity."

Laughter rolled in fuller now, inflating his confidence. His tone grew louder, feeding off the raw, unfiltered energy in the room.

With a dry pivot, he added, "It's weird though, right? Everything works great—right up to the moment it doesn't. Inhale? Fine. Food? Michelin-star level. Touch a squirrel? Console opens."

Gremlins joined the Inductees this time, cackling in response, and a woman in the back—short grey hair, straight-backed—snorted at the absurdity.

"I saw a guy bend down to tie his shoe—disappeared. No scream, no panic. He took it in stride, as if he thought he had it coming."

Real, biting laughter followed as he leaned in and planted his feet.

"Gravity? It's not physics. It's conditional. You believe in yourself, you stay upright. Start second-guessing, and you're surprisingly buoyant while a gremlin critiques your life choices."

Scattered applause rippled between his quips, punctuated by gremlins slapping the table in unison.

"People ask me, 'What's it feel like, knowing your work will outlive you?' I say—imagine raising a kid. You feed it, teach it, protect it. Give it your best years. One day it grows up, builds a tech startup, and blocks your number."

Many outright laughed. Meanwhile, Remy was trying to decide whether to laugh or ask a question.

He let it hang, edge slipping like he'd forgotten the mic was on.

"But the worst part? The best part? I can't feel how sick I am." He froze, caught mid-inhale.

"That doesn't mean the pain's gone. It's paused. Muted. Like I left it running on another tab."

The room's cavernous lack of response seemed to realize the punchline was late. A chair creaked. Someone cleared their throat. The moment tilted.

"Some mornings, it takes me an hour to sit up. My hands forget they belong to me. But in here, I get full range of motion. Look at this." He glanced down, thumb brushing the edge of the mic.

"It's a trick. I'm a puppet with no strings, but the ache's waiting in the wings. Soon as I log off, it drags me back by the spine." His throat tightened, and for a second, he didn't speak.

"Naturally, I handled it like any mature adult would—opened Settings, scrolled down to 'Feelings,' and opted out." His delivery was dry as ash, but the laugh it pulled was real—shared, if uneasy.

He stepped back. "Anyway—if anyone's got spare neon, please bring it to our people in the back. I assume they're building either an art gallery or a death ray. Could go either way." A chorus of voices hissed in celebration. One hand lifted—a twisted bid for chaos.

He clicked his heels together with ceremonial flair. "Also—if I vanish mid-sentence, don't panic. Turns out this place takes 'No place like home' way too literally."

Big laughs and cascading applause carried him off the stage—a wave crashing and receding—leaving him in the drift of afterglow. He stood there, absorbing the crowd's energy—the first loosening of a long-sealed place within. Remy rested against the support beam, arms crossed, like the place had been waiting for her.

When his feet hit the ground, she clapped slowly, each slap landing with weighty finality.

"Not bad, boss man. You might have a future here after all."

He raked a hand through his hair, trying to hide the grin. "Didn't see that coming."

Remy tilted her head. "That good or bad?"

"Not bad," he said after a beat. "Not what I thought I needed—but maybe it was."

She snorted—half amusement, half armour—and added, "That's rich, coming from someone who prints bullshit on company letterhead."

Smiling, he shook his head.

"C'mon. You owe me a meeting," she said, peeling off the beam, leaving them suspended in the charged, unfiltered aftermath of the night's performance.

The booth was barely intact—scuffed metal bolted to a foundation that had cracked before they ever sat down. Gremlin graffiti bled over the sides, symbols and warnings scratched into the surface in a language no one had programmed.

They slid into the booth across from each other. For a while, neither spoke. A group of three took the stage while people milled about, interacting. The place was alive.

In the distance, music drifted through the air—low, coiled, textured with a rawness that refused to belong to Afterdeath. A cello, a violin, and a rhythm conjured from taut strings, fragile and unprogrammed. The sound cut through the vibe, a living thread weaving through the world of the dead.

Max's head tilted. He knew that sound. It took him a second to place it, but when he did, it struck with the force of a song he hadn't heard in years but somehow knew by heart.

"Are they?" he murmured.

Remy sighed. "Yeah. No simulations allowed on stage. That's the rule."

The tension rose, then fell—like a string held too long and finally allowed to vibrate free.

Easing further as he watched the trio play with unfiltered skill. A group of Inductees stood near the stage—some listening, some swaying.

Remy let the silence build between them. "Okay, so hear me out."

Max arched a brow, intrigued but unconvinced.

She drew in, like her next words might breach the firewall. "I should work at Afterdeath," she said, her speech lighter than she felt.

Max's mind scrambled to catch up. "You're—"

The rest hung there—known, but unsaid. Something passed over his face—whatever he was about to say, he let it stall.

"Yeah. Technically." Remy shrugged, nonchalant. "Dead people don't work."

"Don't you think that's the problem?" she countered before he could even get a word in, her energy rising. "Look—when I died, I didn't lose merely my life. I lost every damn chance. No career, no future, no next steps. Now I'm here, and I'm supposed to sit on my hands? Screw that. I want in." Her cadence cracked on the last word—not from doubt, but from wanting it too much.

Max pressed into the booth's backrest, arms folding. His focus wandered between distant thoughts. He wasn't calculating logistics. He wasn't thinking about operational scaffolding. He was thinking about the man on stage. The one she pushed there. The one she brought back to life, even if only while the crowd listened.

She hadn't asked for permission. But somehow, the room had granted it anyway. It wasn't groundbreaking—it pulsed with a flawed beauty.

She kept talking, fast, as if she had to get it all out before he cut her off. "I know the people. The protocols. I know what this place is supposed to be, but more importantly, what it could be."

Max let the words sink in. Afterdeath had always been a sealed container. You go in. You stay. Nothing comes out—except, as Harland would say, a Legacy Link and a quarterly yield. But now Remy was offering something else: circulation. Entry and return. Presence with purpose. He agreed before he fully understood why. It felt less like invention than correction.

"Okay. You start tomorrow."

The moment locked. Remy's eyes went wide—a rare, reckless hope. She grinned, sudden and fierce.

"Wait—seriously? I get a desk?"

CHAPTER TWELVE
SIGNAL INTEGRITY

The day had tapered into late afternoon, a reminder that the 13th of November had arrived with its usual unremarkable efficiency. The newsroom operated exactly as Harland Reeves expected—tight, exacting, and orderly. From the second-floor control corridor of the Bay Street studio, he watched the crew move in practised formation, each motion aligning with his expectations. He scanned the monitors. Every image was filtered, curated precisely to plan.

Through the glass, Lena Morgan stood poised, exactly as she'd been trained. She understood her role. Her posture was composed, biometrics steady and within range. But he registered a flicker—too minor for the readouts, but caught by him instantly.

"Keep it clean," he murmured to the producer beside him—soft-spoken to preserve appearances, but firm in intent.

The producer confirmed with a single compliant tilt of their chin.

Harland absorbed the ambient scroll of information. Monitoring showed one thing: people were watching, engaged, and—most importantly—agreeing. Sentiment compliance, neural hold time, impression echo—they all spiked right on cue.

"Welcome back to Signal Integrity," Lena said, smooth with repetition. "Joining us tonight is Mr. Reeves, interim director of Afterdeath Incorporated—the company behind Legacy Link and a range of tools and protocols designed to keep people in touch—even beyond the grave."

She faced her guest.

"Mr. Reeves, thank you for being here. Let's begin with the basics. For viewers trying to understand what Afterdeath really offers—how do you define its role in today's world?"

Harland inclined his head in acknowledgment. "Thank you, Lena. It's a privilege to be here. At Afterdeath, we've always been driven by a single question: what if death wasn't a wall, but a window? For too long, grief has operated in a vacuum—one-sided, static. We wanted to offer a continuity—a connection that doesn't end when life does."

He shifted in his seat, hands relaxed on the table. "We provide continuity," he said again, this time anchoring it. "Continuity of love. Continuity of memory. We believe death is not the end of connection—it's simply a change in interface."

Lena waited half a beat, then continued. "And now, after a successful launch, the flagship feature has arrived: Legacy Link? How's that working for the inducted and their family?"

He offered the smile built for cameras—and for his mother. "Legacy Link changed the field. Before and after, now separated by death, can connect through one simple call—one moment of real presence, right when it matters most. Some families prefer the flexibility of a per-call credit model; others appreciate the peace of mind that comes with a full subscription. Either way, it's never been easier to stay close. It's not about clinging to the past—it's about offering the living one more moment of clarity, closure. The hardware is complex, yes. But the effect? Unmistakably human."

Lena let the words linger. She followed with a second question, her tone more pointed. "It's received enthusiastically by the living, no doubt. But what about those on the other side of the line—Inductees? Is it as welcomed as it is by their loved ones? Because from where we're standing, the world doesn't hear from them nearly as often."

Reeves didn't answer right away. That alone told people who knew him, watching from work or home, that this was a rare moment for the executive.

The air felt thinner. His mask remained in place, though his attention slid to a monitor near the fringe of the frame, likely scanning a readout.

"That's a fair question," he said. "Obviously, we take Inductee satisfaction seriously. Each person who arrives has space to decide how they want to connect—on their terms, in their own time. Every element—from interface to intake—was designed to protect that decision."

If Alan didn't know any better, he would have believed him. It wasn't that Harland believed his own lies; it was that belief and lies didn't exist in corporate stooges the way they did in the rest of us.

"But let's be honest—simply because an Inductee chooses silence doesn't mean we've taken their voice away. For many, the transition unfolds naturally. Reflection. Resolution. We don't presume to know all the forms peace takes."

"Of course," Lena said, tone tightening by a fraction, "not everyone agrees with that philosophy—and today—"

She turned toward the empty chair. "—we have a special guest, someone waiting to discuss that very point."

The holo-projector spun to life with a whisper of charged current, and a soft blue scaffold of light began knitting him together—line by line, layer by calibrated layer. The frame built slowly from the shoes upward, as if reconstructing the man in the order that mattered most. By the time the projection locked into place, Alan Prescott sat in spectral clarity—half presence, half proxy—rendered in Alma-blue. Light passed through him unevenly, pooling faintly at the base of the chair.

Alan wore a slate-grey blazer with a herringbone weave that absorbed the studio lighting with precision—enough to appear intentional, not severe. His collar was open, the shirt beneath a linen blue—slightly rumpled, but not unkempt. Franklin had picked the fabric, Jenna had vetoed the first three combinations, and Ruth had declared the final result "plausibly academic with a pulse." It worked. The trousers followed suit—well-fitted, cuffed with care. His boots—yes, boots—were real-world practical, digitally replicated with a scuffed polish that spoke of distance travelled. The wire-rimmed glasses were there, perched with stubborn clarity, a choice he hadn't questioned in decades. No shimmer of youth, no rewind to his prime. Instead, this was Alan as he saw himself—middle-aged, lived-in, defined.

He sat straighter than usual, aware that posture was its own kind of armour. The chair wasn't real, but the stage was. And though the wardrobe had been chosen without the holographic filter in mind, he caught a glimpse of himself in the studio reflection and felt the pull of a smile he didn't entirely trust. Translucent, yes. A venerable ghost of relevance past.

For once, he looked good in a way no one watching would understand. The studio felt like an interrogation chamber masquerading as civility, but the weight of presentation—of being seen like this—gave him a strange lift. He bit it down quickly. No room for vanity. Somewhere beneath the data streams and tension, the thought echoed: Not bad, Prescott. Not bad at all.

Then, his eyes found Harland Reeves. Monochromatic. Every line of him read like a final boss—coded clean, perfected, and placed exactly where the story demanded a fight.

Alan squared himself, grasping for the notes that got lost somewhere in translation. He met Lena's gaze, attempting to hide his apprehension.

"Glad to be here," he said. "Turns out, 'live' still means live, even when you're dead."

Lena offered up a laugh she'd canned herself.

"A bold move," Harland said, clearly speaking past Alan to Lena.

"But let's be clear. We're not in the business of sensationalizing death. Afterdeath was founded to help people. We—"

Alan maintained eye contact. Despite it being only one way, he didn't want to allow Harland to speak as if he wasn't there. As if he wasn't a person.

"Help," Harland finished.

Alan nudged his glasses, a deeply human tic. The lenses were now redundant—everyone had 20/20 vision. Hindsight, that's a whole different story.

"Funny choice of words. Your first act of helping me was calling about my will barely a minute after my Induction." He didn't rush. His restraint spoke volumes.

Harland, however, remained in calculation mode, tracking the risks with the clarity of someone who accounted the dead as profit.

"Legacy Link exists to ease suffering," he said, the cadence too precise to pass for empathy. "The timing might seem cold to people uninvolved. Pragmatism often does."

Prescott let the explanation resonate, hearing the same pared-down logic he once respected—efficient, emotionless, and suddenly alien beside the force of his own living memories. He waited—half a second longer than comfort allowed.

"Pragmatism," he replied, the word sitting between them. "An interesting mask for opportunism. I used to respect you, thought you saw further than the rest of us. But from here, it's clear you're steering a ship you never learned to sail."

A beat. Harland, ever vigilant at hiding his face, allowed an unconscious twitch of his thumb against his sleeve to slip through.

"Mounting scrutiny from all sides. You've crossed over—You know how thin the margin can be."

"No. Harland, I don't know anything about your margins. Quite frankly, from the inside, that's not our main concern."

Lena interjected, her tone as respectful as possible. "We're here to illuminate, not litigate—"

A pang of shame surfaced—but he let it stand. This wasn't about comfort. His friends were counting on him.

"You talk about connection, comfort, healing," Alan said, his voice steady. "But if Legacy Link is really a bridge—why don't the dead get to choose when, or if, they cross it?"

Harland stopped short. Whether it was uncertainty or performance wasn't clear.

Lena Morgan's voice cut clean through the silence. "Mr. Reeves. Before we end the segment—one last question?"

Harland inclined his head, unreadable. "Of course."

"Thank you," she said. "You've seen the public statement—signed by Inductees, Alan included. They're calling themselves the Prisoners of Afterdeath. Any thoughts on the letter they posted?"

His face didn't tighten, but his eyes narrowed by a fraction. "I haven't read it myself–"

Lena continued, unhurried. "That's okay, let me help you. Their message is fairly clear. This isn't about their induction. They say Legacy Link turns them into prisoners, summoned at the whim of the living. No right to decline these calls at all, at any time or day. They're asking for space. For consent. What's your response to that group?"

Harland rarely waited a beat to respond other than for posterity or to lend gravity to what he was about to say. Today, he actually needed time to filter out his angry response, and while brief, it was telling.

Harland straightened his posture. "We respect their opinions. But we have to balance user needs on both sides of the line. Legacy Link was designed to connect families. It's natural for grief to carry tension, for transition to be misinterpreted as constraint. But there are safeguards. There is agency for all involved."

Alan tilted his head slightly, as if weighing whether the question was even worth answering. "Agency," he repeated, dry but not detached. "If that means you've got an Agency update coming soon, I'm sure we'd all be happy to hear about it."

A tight spasm crossed Harland's jaw, irritation leaking through his polished mask. "That's enough," he snapped, voice fracturing. He shoved back from the desk, his chair spinning out behind him, and lunged toward the holo-projection, swiping desperately through invisible menus.

Alan didn't budge. "You can't block out the parts that don't sit right."

Harland's eyes darted, fingers tapping too fast, opening the wrong panels—each mistake tightening the strain in his face, composure unravelling with every move.

He didn't want to help, but he couldn't help the jab. "Try the big red one, Harland."

He froze. His eyes snapped up in startled recognition. He stalled—undone by the simplicity of it. With one rough, exasperated motion, he slammed his palm onto the red one. Alan's image dissolved instantly, pixels scattering into the air before vanishing.

Lena's mouth parted. But Alan was already gone. She turned smoothly to camera two, the way one learns to during earthquakes.

"We're going to take a short break," she said, her speech faintly electric. "When we return, more on Legacy Link's evolving transparency."

The screen cut to blue.

Back in his private realm, Alan materialized—a seamless reentry that felt strangely lighter. He sat in his own chair again, inside the workshop by the loch, not far from the lodge he rarely used.

Reed stood by the workstation, hands clasped behind his back, bearing the composure of someone who had rehearsed the moment—and meant it. His eyes tracked Alan's return with measured conviction, the corners of his mouth lifted by something just shy of pride.

"Superbly executed, sir," he said. "You've already received invitations from Ruth and the others."

Prescott squinted. "Invitations?"

"Celebrations, sir. It seems your brief terrestrial debut left quite the impression."

Alan shook his head, trying to re-centre. "Celebrations? I barely got two sentences in before he shut me down."

"Precisely why they're celebrating," Reed replied, expression unchanged.

Alan rubbed his temple with two fingers, half tired, half amused. "Cancel the invitations. Bring them here instead. I've travelled to hell and back—they can meet me halfway, don't you think."

"Of course, Alan. Point made—I sent them instructions before you finished saying it." Reed allowed the smallest hint of satisfaction.

Two seconds later, Jenna rezzed in like her molecules had been waiting. The timing was surgical, her arrival betraying a readiness that felt preloaded. Her hair was stacked with the kind of defiance that came from too many interruptions, strands refusing to stay put. The glasses had drifted halfway down her nose, catching the glow off Alan's interface table. She let them be. Her frame held a restless torque, like she'd walked in on the last line of a sentence she meant to finish herself.

"Okay," she said, scanning the room for a hint, a signal she could decode. "I had my doubts when Ruth pushed for you—but you delivered."

Alan rubbed the back of his neck. "Felt more like he took me apart."

"Maybe. But you forced his hand—and on a live feed. That man doesn't shit without a rehearsal."

Franklin was already leaning in the doorway, one shoulder pressed against the frame, arms crossed like he'd been listening for longer than anyone knew. Alan hadn't seen him arrive—which made sense. For someone built like a shipping container, Franklin moved with a tactician's grace—never where you expected him, always right when it mattered.

"Sure looked like you left a mark," he said, voice low and half-wrapped in humour. "Harland flinched so hard I thought the feed broke."

Jenna tapped a quick command into her lens. "Exactly. He's the kind who scripts eye contact. I think I can grab an image of the exact moment you hit a nerve."

A soft resonance passed through the floorboards—barely audible, but felt all the same. Ruth and Leo entered without fanfare. She carried presence the way some people carry instruments—tuned to the room, waiting for the right note to begin. Her coat was the colour of pressed ink, shoulders squared, gaze unwavering. She stepped in, said nothing, and scanned the room like she was measuring it.

She studied Alan a beat longer than the others had, as if scanning every version of him he'd ever been.

"That," she said, brushing past Leo without pause, "was the sexiest thing I've ever seen."

Jenna broke first—a short, incredulous laugh cut off by a wheeze. Franklin followed, one hand bracing the doorframe, head shaking with wry delight.

Alan didn't move.

The line hit somewhere absurd and true. Like being sucker-punched by affection you never learned to dodge. A part of him, long boarded up, cracked open on reflex. He looked at Ruth. She didn't take it back.

He cleared his throat, tried to find a reply that wouldn't betray him. Failed.

"Well," he said finally, "good to know I've got market value well after the expiration date."

Jenna wiped a tear under one lens. "Oh, Alan. Some things don't lose value. I happen to know that Ruth believes in limited editions."

Franklin chuckled low in his throat. "That wasn't a compliment, Alan. That was a declaration of interest."

Ruth, unapologetic, stepped closer to the table. "You'd be amazed what holds value when it finally stands up and says something worth hearing."

Alan opened his mouth, closed it again. He wasn't sure if he'd been flirted with or indicted. Maybe both. He ran a hand through his hair, regretting the gesture halfway through.

They laughed—at him, with him, it didn't matter. The heat in his face wasn't shame. It was presence. They were here. They had watched him risk something. And that counted for more than survival ever did.

Reed tuned something at the workstation, Leo beside him—offering no commentary, only glanced at Reed, then looked back, satisfied. Jenna leaned into a theory mid-formation, one hand half-raised like she was building the joke out loud even as she wiped away a tear. Franklin—Franklin listened like always, storing the moment the way some people stored maps. And Ruth stood apart, eyes on Alan, reading him like it was the first time they'd met—and maybe in some essential way, it was.

Alan stayed where he was. He didn't speak. His chest ached with the dense aftermath of effort—the kind that stayed with other people. He hadn't earned the applause. Or the jabs, if he was honest. But he'd been heard. Witnessed. And somewhere between the myth and the truth of that moment, it registered—he mattered again. Not in theory. Not in cherished memory. But in the room. In the ripple. In the now. And, with any luck, in the future.

CHAPTER THIRTEEN
PATCH NOTES

Max waited in his digital refuge, a space shaped more by contour than reinvention. The land stretched outward in the kind of order that looked like peace—rows of corn beneath a sky that never dimmed. The dirt felt like ground.

Remy stepped into the scene without ceremony. She was taking in the sky, the crops, the man who'd made them. Nothing moved but the lift of her brow.

Max crouched by the corn, studying a diagnostic overlay. He didn't look up right away.

"I've been tuning the parameters. Wind pattern, soil density, humidity. It's all technically right."

He rubbed the back of his neck. "But I could use some tips."

Remy knelt beside him, brushing her hand above the surface of the soil. It responded—believably. "It's close," she said.

Taking in the view together, they noted its current merits. Corn stood in perfect lines, each row spaced a clean thirty inches apart—the kind of precision only farm-bred diligence could bring. Along the margins, wide headland tracks cut through the earth, pressed flat by the weight of passing machinery. That last detail wasn't emulation so much as a test drive from before. Narrow furrows ran between the rows, etched in a logic only farmers would notice. Mulched stalks from last year's crop—one that never happened—showed some real guts; he was already learning. Finally, a line of poplars broke the horizon to the west, a living windbreak holding back the sky.

Remy toggled into the field's backend and swept a series of variables through the overlay—randomizing seed, growth stage, and patch intervals. Rows realigned, losing their rigid symmetry. Some plants emerged stunted, others skipped ahead, their heights and spacing no longer predictable. A scatter of volunteer sunflowers popped up near the headland. The code allowed for mutation, error, and unfinished lines—patches where corn failed to sprout, or where wild clover filled the gaps.

She drew back, checking the pattern as the backend resettled. The simulation processed the changes—the field looked less engineered, more lived-in, bearing the marks of time and use, not algorithm alone.

Remy scanned the new irregularities. "Better, right?"

Max's mouth twitched. He took a longer look this time, letting it land. "Yeah," he said. "That's closer."

His thumb brushed the mod port clipped to his belt—old tech, scratched up, wired in like a habit that refused to quit.

"This isn't a default test environment," he said. "Most people map out their personal realms on a tablet—pick a prefab, tweak the light settings, call it done. Months, sometimes years, before it matters."

He glanced back toward the rows. "I couldn't do it that way. I had to come in and build mine from the inside. Set it in order with my own hands."

He looked at Remy, steadier now. "It's the last piece I get to shape the way I want."

"Good. You don't have to build it alone."

Max lowered his voice. "My family's visiting soon. We haven't connected in a long time. There's a lot we never said. I thought building this place might help me work through it. I don't know—"

"Working through family issues one vegetable at a time?" Remy said. "Not the worst plan."

Max gave a brief, guarded laugh. "They probably wouldn't want a farm tended by my hands."

Remy's smile was crooked, but real. She knew that pain too well. "Let's grow the kind of mess that would make them jealous."

They laughed—real, low, and unhurried. As the sound tapered off, Remy rolled up a sleeve and started carving a new curve through the edge of the field. A river began to take shape—too wide in places, cutting through a row of crops, meandering like it had somewhere better to be.

Max watched her work, then crossed to a blank stretch by the treeline and began assembling the old wooden gate from memory—the version his father had patched over the years with mismatched nails and uneven slats, the kind that sagged unless you lifted it at the exact angle.

He traced the grain of the wood with care, not smoothing out the flaws. That's where the character lived.

Remy, guiding the river's path, glanced over her shoulder. "Speaking of family," she said, her words firmer now, "I've been mulling over these Legacy Link calls—"

Max hovered, his fingers suspended above the controls. The guarded look faded, giving way to a weariness he didn't bother to hide.

"You don't even have to say it," he said. "We rushed it. I think most of us missed something the other half was trying to sneak past us. Either way, we didn't think hard about the experience on the other side."

His shoulders slackened, not in defeat but in admission. "I should've seen where it would lead. But I didn't—and now I don't understand how any of us thought that was acceptable."

Remy paused, taken aback by the ease in his response. "I was expecting you to defend the system," she admitted, a trace of surprise in her voice. "But—you sound like you're on board with changing things."

A crooked smile tugged at Max's lips. "I am. I'd rather give people a choice than force them into something they never signed up for."

Max paused, focus locked on the gate mid-formation in the distance. The sagging crossbeam, the uneven slats, the worn surface—none of it reached for sentiment. It stood as a choice made visible. "After Harland's little meltdown," his manner cool and composed, "I've got some room to move again."

Remy guided the river's path, already shaping its course, already planning the next step. "Let's patch it. Scheduling should be a choice, not an ambush.

Users should be able to refuse, delay, or stop the process when they need to. These calls shouldn't feel like surveillance with good intentions."

Conviction passed between them. Decision followed. Max turned to her, his expression firming into place. "Let's fix it," he said. "We start now."

Remy stepped back from the river display as Max approached the master console. With a few targeted commands, the simulation collapsed—the farmhouse, the fields, the gate dissolving into light.

In their place came a corridor of stark clarity: bright walls, humming servers behind thin partitions, the sound of power relays coming online.

Max fitted himself into the new haptic suit that formed around him—fitted, streamlined, a far cry from the old gel rigs. He moved with purpose, every motion practised and natural until the disconnection sequence was complete. Each cable detached with a click. It was routine—until his fingers twitched hard, unexpected. A flare. He'd handled worse. He kept going, slower now, careful with the rest.

The suit responded as it should, but his body trailed behind—half a second slow in all the ways that mattered. As he stepped free, the jolt pulled at him, a tilt too far off-centre. Nausea rose sudden and raw. He steadied himself with one hand on the bench, skin meeting cold metal, and waited.

His hand found the old pressure switch on the side panel—flat, brushed steel, barely noticeable unless you knew it was there. He pressed it. Simple. Familiar. The same gesture he'd made the night he initiated Remy's Lazarus transfer. That time, the whole platform had nearly collapsed. He hadn't known if she'd make it through. Now, he knew she would. This time, it was her turn to wake up.

Remy booted. Audio followed vision. Equilibrium arrived next—Her coordination reassembled in order, without friction. Her vision cleared before her limbs agreed. The suit pressed close—responsive, but unfamiliar.

The basement workshop offered no greeting. Recycled air moved through in slow loops. The smell of metal and plastic hung in place, baked into the surfaces. Machines lined the walls on standby.

Response lagged—slight, but measurable. She planted her feet. Presence returned in increments—knees, spine, breath. Her body stabilized.

Max stood at the bench, hands splayed with focused intent. Though turned away, Max shifted the space around him—gravity in human form.

Her gaze drifted to the desk. Among the clutter sat a small bust of Splinter—worn, unpolished, detailed in a way that said the sculptor knew the face by heart. Peace lived in the lines. Protective. Tired. A teacher, a fighter, a father. Remy didn't need to ask why Max kept it there.

Next to it, a Transformer mid-stride, one arm half-raised. The paint was chipped, the contours dulled from time and touch. This wasn't shelf candy—it had been moved, handled, maybe repaired. Built to change—and carry the scars anyway. It looked ready for another fight.

Her eyes landed on a wall-sized poster across the room. Iron Man's red-gold armour twisted into the silver contours of Doctor Doom's mask. The fusion made no narrative sense, and that's what made it brilliant. Remy looked at it longer than she meant to, back at Max. Yeah. That made sense.

The shelves sagged with old tools and plastic heroes, each one worn in its own way. The workbench was scratched in three directions—a surface marked by frustration, trial, and the rare breakthrough. Nothing matched, but nothing felt out of place. Everything here had stayed for a reason, whether Max ever said it out loud or not.

Max's hand hovered near the counter, like he hadn't decided yet if he'd need it again. The body was failing, but his mind remained remarkably clear. Moments ago he was shaping a field; now, as Remy took him in, he was twice the man he appeared.

"Well, colour me surprised," Remy said. "You crack open the gates of heaven for me, and now you're jimmied the locks on hell too. That's commitment."

For a second, Max stared at her, blindsided. Then the laugh broke out of him—sudden, unguarded, and nearly doubling him over. He clutched his side, half in pain, half in surrender. "Naw," he managed, voice ragged, "Hell happened to give me a plus one."

That set Remy off. The sound bounced off concrete and server racks, loud enough to echo through every inch of the basement. Neither one tried to stifle it. For the first time in ages, it didn't matter how much noise they made—nobody else was coming.

The basement door slammed—blunt and final. Both of them turned, alert now. Whatever came next had already arrived.

Harland Reeves stepped into the room, his posture composed, the faint scent of cologne arriving before he spoke. He scanned the space with a practised neutrality, each glance curated before it landed on his target. "Max," he said, tone clipped and direct. "I see you've been busy patching up Legacy Link. You and Miss Moreau."

Max met his stare, but the grip on the workstation told the truth.

He hadn't triggered any surveillance. Not by accident. Not even close. The protocols were clean—triple-checked, privately patched. Which meant Harland wasn't reacting. He'd been watching. Closely. Maybe longer than either of them realized.

Harland's eyes narrowed. "I want solutions that last. Next week's partners meeting includes our creatives—people capable of vision. We're losing ground, and complaints aren't slowing down."

Max exhaled through clenched teeth, as another wave of discomfort passed through him. "So this is about spinning complaints into cover," he said. "Covering up your media mess with innovation theatre?"

Harland's eyes narrowed. "Stick to the facts, Max. This isn't about politics—it's business. We need to coordinate our strategy for the year ahead." He glanced at Remy, back at Max, the warmth stripped from his words. "Technically, what you're doing here—stuffing a lab rat into a metal shell without board approval—skirts more laws than I care to count." He looked at Remy now. "But since it smells like future profits, I'll let it slide."

Remy stepped forward before Max could. Her voice didn't rise—it landed. "You really think I'm the part of this worth regulating?"

Harland turned to face her fully now, not surprised, not amused. "I think you're the part that doesn't know the cost of the room you're standing in."

Remy didn't flinch. "That's where you're wrong. I know exactly what this room cost. I paid it."

Harland let out a dry, professional sound that passed for a laugh. "You're clever. I'll give you that. But clever doesn't make you credible. You're a ghost in a borrowed frame."

Remy met his stare, expression set. She didn't like the way Harland's eyes moved, like he already owned the outcome.

Harland's smile narrowed into something tight and joyless—more calculation than charm. "Anything else will have to wait, I look forward to seeing you both next week. Until then, try not to tire yourselves out."

He walked out without another word. At the doorway, he glanced back before disappearing down the corridor.

"What a dick," Remy muttered, her voice dry enough to leave a burn.

Max didn't bother to hide the satisfaction in his voice. "I don't think I've ever seen anyone get carved up like that."

"That's a lie," Remy said. "Signal Integrity. Last week. We all watched it. I'm simply paying it forward."

"You know," Remy said, "I actually met him once. Prescott I mean."

"Really?" he asked, eyebrows raised.

"After death, not before."

"Makes sense," she said. "Never had the honour myself. Though judging by how active his crew's been lately, I might get the pleasure pretty soon. "Maybe you can help me—"

Remy cut in. "I doubt he remembers me. It was a super quick encounter. No. Sorry. You're on your own with the politics. Coding, though? That's where I've got you covered."

They turned back to the console, the glow catching faint reflections of their faces. As they recalibrated the parameters, the update deployed cleanly—code responding line by line, each flagged issue disappearing as their patches took root.

Remy's fingers moved like someone who'd patched bugs before breakfast.

"Users need to be able to refuse calls," she said, not looking up. "Reschedule them, reject them—whatever works. The choice should be ours again."

When he looked at Remy, it wasn't a front—it was recognition. She'd carried a burden imposed by the system. A burden many others in Afterdeath knew by name. Now, in part due to her, and Alan Prescott, they weren't carrying it for much longer.

The progress bar advanced.

Max spoke the stripped-down truth. "Remy, I can't believe I haven't said this out loud. But. I'm dying."

Remy didn't blink at the words. "I know," she said. "I've known since I first searched your name." Her voice carried the clarity of someone who'd already made peace with the truth.

"Plus, let's face the facts," she said. "Only a dying man goes house-hunting in the clouds."

Max gave a dry, genuine laugh.

The last lines of code clicked into place. Red alerts disappeared. Three clear options replaced them: Decline. Reschedule. Do Not Disturb. No fanfare followed—only authority, handed back to the people who needed it.

Remy sat back, watching the panel finalize. "Legacy Link's fixed," she said.

Max gripped the console as the next wave of pain crept in. He didn't fight it. He let it pass, as he always did. It was the cost of staying upright.

"You're coming to the partners meeting," Max said out of nowhere.

Remy raised an eyebrow. "So what? You want me to simply sit there while you're giving a TED Talk about spit-shining the apocalypse?"

His face relaxed into something close to gratitude. "Maybe. But it's the last one I'll walk into—and with you there, I'll have a chance to redirect the story."

She braced, not out of fear—but with the charge of someone who'd waited to be heard.

"I'd be honoured to be there."

Max exhaled, rubbing his temple. "I should probably tell you," he said, not quite meeting her eyes, "I was pretty much fired for saving you."

Remy leaned against the console, arms crossed. "What does that mean?"

"They didn't call it that. Technically, I'm on indefinite leave. They let me keep this office. Down here." He gestured to the walls, to the low light and half-functioning screens. "Told me I could 'keep tinkering on deprecated legacy systems.' No more board meetings. No direct oversight. It's a backroom tomb. And I earned it."

"Why me?" Remy asked.

Max met her gaze, but with no weight behind it. "Why not?"

She held his eyes. "That's not an answer."

He looked away, hand braced on the console. For a moment, his body stilled—he wasn't searching for words, he was deciding whether to tell the truth.

"Lazarus is a rapid scan-and-map platform. High-density, low-latency, tuned for edge cases. If there's any continuity left to catch, it can preserve someone's cognitive imprint across the machine threshold. You weren't an accident. You were the scenario we built for."

Remy didn't respond.

"We were planning to make it standard," he said. "End-of-life use, trauma triage, early rollout to frontline clients. It was viable. Real. We had a timeline. But I triggered it early—without clearance."

"On me."

He didn't deny it. "And Harland took it straight to the board. Called it a breach of protocol.

Said I'd compromised the company's legal insulation and destabilized core trust. He turned it into a weapon before your files even finished uploading."

"And what would've happened if you hadn't?" she asked.

Max let the air out through his nose. "You'd have stayed gone."

He didn't embellish. That silence stood longer than the one before it.

"Everyone's been asking why I saved you," he said. "But I've been stuck on a different question."

Remy waited, unmoving.

"Why don't we save everyone?"

He didn't offer the line as an idea. It came out plain—as something old, returned again.

"The answers I get are always the same. Budget limits. Policy reviews. Ethical ambiguity. But none of it holds. I've worked on neural stacks, reconsolidation engines, realignment drift metrics—dozens of safeguards built to stop us from making the wrong call. But what haunts me isn't what we've done. It's who we let die because they didn't sign the right premium terms before a bullet found them. That's the part I can't reconcile."

Remy stared. "So you saved one person. And stopped."

The recoil in Max's face was restrained.

"I didn't stop," he said. "They stopped me."

No louder than before, but with a kind of resolution that marked the line he crossed—and never returned from.

The console glowed beside them, code finalized—PATCH READY.

Her eyes held on him—not warm, not cold, but fixed with mechanical exactness. The prototype body didn't twitch or blink. It processed. And right now, all her internal focus leveled at the man who had broken every rule to bring her back. Not out of love. Not even out of guilt. Out of principle. That mattered more. "You saved me on a hunch," she said, tone level. "Now I've got a hunch how to save this."

CHAPTER FOURTEEN
HAPTIC HEARTS

Ruth held the glass level, watching the amber liquid pool. The simulation had improved—viscosity, heat, the ethanol bloom arriving right on cue. First notes were close: apricot, cedar, something deeper at the centre. But the final notes needed more patience. The last trace never fully emerged.

She set the glass down. The Yamazaki 18 emulation remained a work in progress.

It was one of her favourite benchmarks—layered, elusive, earned. She'd been tuning this simulation in solitary sessions for weeks. Cooking, brewing, fermenting—every hobby she kept had a purpose. When she got a dish right, it became a future offering. A story to serve, a reason to gather.

On her next pass, she wouldn't push harder—she'd refine the timing. The sweetness opened clear, the structure tracked, but the finish needed more patience. Maybe less heat in the handoff. Something to let that final trace rise on its own. Right now, it ended too soon—like someone cutting off the last word of a thought.

An incoming message ping, from Alan no doubt. She didn't startle. She looked.

"The Scientific Inquiry Association formally invites you... blah blah... to participate in Afterdeath's alcohol simulation... blah blah... one bottle of wine and your esteemed presence."

Alan. Always drafting connection like it had to pass review—vulnerability broken down into citations and clauses. She didn't mind. That was how he found his way to sincerity. One reference at a time.

She'd already tuned her palate in anticipation—started sipping, in fact, fifteen minutes before this version of the offer arrived. Not impatience. An expected interval. She knew Alan better than he knew the shape of his own courage. The invitation was later than expected, and slightly thinner than she'd hoped, but it counted. He'd gotten there.

And if it came wrapped in qualifiers and science—well, that was Alan. Affection didn't arrive through the front door with him. It needed translation.

She read the message once and replied: "Only if you promise no physics lectures this time."

He read it, and was responding within seconds. "No physics. Empirical inquiry."

He was trying—that mattered more than knowing how.

She was halfway to standing when Leo materialized at the margin of her environment, already aware of her choice.

"You're going," he said, with knowing ease.

Ruth arched one brow. "I haven't said yes."

She caught the look—his version of a smile, restrained and obvious all the same.

"You checked the time twice. That was your yes."

She gave him a long look, something between affection and warning. "Don't follow."

He dipped his head in exaggerated solemnity. "I'll remain outside the detection radius. Reed won't even register the disturbance."

She sighed, not entirely annoyed. "You're bad at pretending you're not watching."

Leo shrugged, unapologetic. "Watching is such a blunt term. I prefer—attentive artistry."

Ruth rolled her eyes. "You're a terrible liar."

His lab, when she arrived, was orderly but unshowy. Clean angles, balanced light. Two glasses set out with the kind of thoughtful intent that didn't ask to be noticed.

Ruth read the room from the threshold, like gauging the surface tension of a pool before stepping in. The atmosphere was composed, but not sterile—intentional, but not theatrical.

He stood near the counter, upright and composed, but not at ease. The wine bottle gleamed beneath a natural spotlight. She read the pattern—measured symmetry, not invitation, exactly, but preparation. He wasn't welcoming her in. He was bracing. This was not decoration. It was a signal. The kind that appears when language falters. The kind of care that reveals more than it hides.

Ruth had seen it before—in patients, in colleagues, in herself. Control posing as hospitality. The instinct to tidy what couldn't be explained. When closeness felt dangerous, order became a kind of armour.

Reed greeted her first. "Environmental parameters have been tuned for conditions statistically favourable to moderate interpersonal resonance."

She squinted. "Moderate what now?"

Reed clarified, "a marginal decline in ambient temperature, paired with reduced photonic glare and an olfactory overlay of low-risk floral compounds—meant to encourage openness, not arousal."

Ruth tilted her head, unimpressed, the edge of a smile ghosting across her face. "That sounds like a risk I ought to take seriously."

Alan made a sound—not entirely a sigh, not completely a whimper. More the noise of a man realising his own reflexes had betrayed him. "Reed," he said, barely audible. "You've—overshot it. Again."

"Recalibrating," Reed replied instantly with a hint of satisfaction.

Ruth lifted a hand—amused, and vaguely protective. "No need. We'll adapt."

Reed cocked his head, synthetic curiosity passing briefly over his expression. "Understood."

Leo entered with a book in one hand and his usual inscrutable timing in the other. "Reed. Perhaps you'd assist me with recalibration parameters for dynamic emotional contexts?"

"Gladly," Reed said. "Alan often accuses me of—overconfidence in my refinements."

As Leo distracted Reed with a side project on the other side of the private realm, Ruth began making herself at home. Neither of them noticed at first—she was already closing the distance. By the time the room released its tension, she'd made her third incremental step—now within reach of the wine bottle, hand hovering like it belonged there.

He didn't react. But she could feel it—the way his presence gathered her in. "I thought the gesture might help," he said. His tone was too formal, the pacing a touch too rehearsed.

Ruth gave him a second—long enough to mean something—then met his eyes.

"Alan," she said. "You don't need the performance."

He didn't speak. The impulse to shape the moment surfaced, then eased. But there was nothing to shape. She wasn't testing him. She was with him.

His fingers began tapping lightly at his thigh. She knew that loop. It wasn't nerves—it was simulation. A practised tempo for situations where presence had always eluded him.

"I thought if I set things up right, I might feel ready for what comes next." He didn't look at her when he said it, and he wasn't trying to impress. He was trying not to disappear.

Ruth didn't rush to respond.

She answered with exactness, "You're used to designing the frame before letting anything move."

A small sound escaped him. Somewhere between a laugh and a sigh. "It's the only way I ever felt safe."

A slight crease eased from his brow as he glanced up, meeting her eyes in a look that lingered. "Do you ever feel as if maybe you weren't meant for—this?"

"You died alone," she said. "So did I. I suspect we both did so by choice, though, it doesn't make it any less lonely."

It wasn't cruel. It wasn't soft. A fact, spoken plainly between equals.

Alan's hand curled around the back of the nearest chair—grip firm, unconscious, like he needed something to exist against.

"I thought I was simply bad at being with someone. But I think the truth is—I never figured out how to stay."

He didn't look at her right away. He was working through the truth of it. Every relationship he'd built before this had a fuse built in. A reason to exit, a clock ticking under the floorboards.

"You stayed here," she said. "That's a start."

Alan's posture changed—a small shift, but one Ruth recognized instantly. A small drop through the upper back, the kind that doesn't come from fatigue but from setting something down.

Ruth saw it. A breakthrough, a letting go he didn't have to explain to her.

That's when a chime broke the spell: LEGACY LINK—NATALIA.

Ruth's body froze, her eyes on Alan's face, watching the first ripple of his reaction take shape.

She'd completely forgotten about the possibility of a Legacy Link call during this date.

The chime rang again—brighter, more urgent—as if time had slipped past.

But then, she noticed new icons, new wording, and a changed presentation. Likely it's only a visual update. Though, something snagged at her gut. A feeling.

Hold up.

One of the icons was a large X. Another one simply stood-in for Do Not Disturb. The last one was an arrow with a calendar. She looked at her daughter's name, the countdown as slow as she was to answer.

She picked the icon that told the truth: DND. Not because she didn't care, but because this—this—also mattered.

They met eyes, before looking back down.

The notification vanished instantly.

The room held—not in light or temperature, but in how they occupied the space.

"That's new," Alan said, underselling his overwhelming satisfaction.

Ruth gave a small nod, too small to mark the feeling she also had in that moment.

"We did it," she muttered, jaw slack.

She caught herself, smiled slightly. "You did it."

She moved with the calm of someone who had already decided. Her hand found his wrist—not seeking permission, not offering comfort, but naming the present for what it was.

Alan hadn't felt this unguarded in years. For once, there was nothing to defend. Whatever armour he'd worn into this room had unthreaded deliberately under her gaze, piece by piece. She hadn't waited for the right moment—she was the moment. And he let her in.

Ruth leaned in, closing the final distance between them. Alan's tension eased under her hand. Their foreheads touched first. The rest followed, naturally.

A faint noise stirred in the background—distant, irrelevant.

Neither turned. Whatever fell could stay there.

The world could not disturb them.

The lab bench bore their weight, scattered with unplugged microscopes and powered-down diagnostics. A spectrometer sat askew but unharmed.

Most of the instruments were pushed aside, a coil of tubing left to dangle off the edge, stilled by their movement.

Ruth noticed Alan's focus drifting. His eyes tracked straight ahead, but they didn't seem to take anything in. His expression wasn't tense or blank—it was the kind she recognized from long meetings and short marriages. Somewhere else entirely.

"Is something wrong?"

"Wrong. No. I'm—processing."

She tilted her head. "You've got that look again—like you're organizing apologies."

Alan exhaled. "That obvious?"

She replayed those years—nights at the kitchen table, laptop open, calendars stacked like shields. Always reshuffling someone else's life, always one email ahead of collapse. Rewriting meetings, rescheduling pickups, apologizing in advance for things that hadn't gone wrong yet. It always looked like diligence. It always passed for grace. But she could feel the ache in her teeth from grinding through those years.

"Not to everyone. But I know what burn-out masquerading as thoughtfulness looks like. I used to spend whole nights rewriting tomorrow's calendar, fixing things no one even asked me to fix. It feels productive—until it starts costing you hours you never get back."

He nodded, the admission settling in. "It's like I'm always scanning for the pattern. Even now—trying to predict what comes next. What to say, what to avoid. The safest sequence."

Ruth laughed. Not mocking—recognizing. "After my second marriage ended, I kept asking if I was the problem. Whether I ever actually counted in the room."

She shrugged, honest but not undone. "It takes one to know one, Alan. And when you're here—like this—it's enough. You're enough, Al."

His hand stayed at her upper back. It was a kind of answer—not loud or obvious, but one she trusted. He hadn't left. He was listening. That meant more than any explanation could.

CHAPTER FIFTEEN
THE MISSING LINK

By November 20th, Remy had been gone for five weeks. No word. No sign. They had long since stopped trying—giving what remained of their daughter the space to find her way back on her own.

A thin layer of snow clung to the windows, muffling the streetlamp's glow into a haze. Inside the Moreau home, the television murmured in the background, the news anchor's words easy to ignore. Denis and Élise sat together, each wrapped in their own thoughts but sharing the space without strain.

Denis eased deeper into his chair, thumb poised on the remote, the motion more habit than choice. Opposite him, Élise repositioned herself, palm pressing as if the cushion could absorb more—grief, remembrance, the in-between.

Pale light from the television washed across the family photographs lining the mantel. Remy beamed from a beach snapshot. Mathieu stood mid-performance in a recital hall. A Christmas portrait showed them all together—recent enough to recognize, distant enough to hurt.

On the coffee table sat a few pieces of unopened mail, Mathieu's abandoned school project, and Élise's half-full cup of tea. A folded blanket rested neatly on the couch beside her.

The rupture came as an alert from the Afterdeath dedicated tablet on the coffee table.

LEGACY LINK – REMY.

Élise's hand froze above her cup. Denis sat up straighter, fingers curling tighter around the remote. The alert repeated, regular and insistent, spiking Élise's heart into a faster beat. She reached over and placed a hand on Denis's wrist. On contact, the tablet responded, and Remy's image came into view.

Remy brushed her hair back, appearing both familiar and different. "Hey, Mom. Hey, Dad," Remy greeted them—tone easy, eyes less sure.

Élise instinctively covered her mouth, momentarily overwhelmed. Denis inched closer, studying the image closely as if afraid to break the connection by looking away.

Denis let out a relieved chuckle. "Damn, kid. You sound exactly like you."

Remy released a restrained laugh. "Yes—I believe so."

Élise allowed it to land, her attention fixed on the natural grace of Remy's movements. The sight felt beautifully ordinary and deeply comforting.

"It's good to see you, sweetheart."

Remy's gaze dipped, a faint brightness behind it. "I've got some other news. I've started working at Afterdeath of all places."

Denis sat up, eyebrows raised. "Who would hire you?"

"Denis," she snapped, then quickly pivoted to Remy. "He didn't mean it that way."

She waved off her mother's comment.

"It's okay, Mum. Really."

It wasn't. Her father was struggling with her being real. That was truly fracked.

"I get it."

She didn't. How could she? What was there to get? She was right here, staring him in the face. Did he need proof, a résumé, a performance of I'm a Little Teapot?

"Work is our final frontier. Most people scoff at it. It's somewhat expected," she said, like someone who'd found time to rehearse the peace they were only now beginning to earn.

Denis looked down, unsure how to respond.

"I fought for it. It was my idea. I needed to do something."

Denis rubbed his jaw thoughtfully. "Have you seen the news lately?"

"No, Dad. I might be a little out of circulation with the news you're watching."

Denis glanced toward Élise—measuring what leeway he had left—then he faced the display.

"There's a hacker group, OneKind, and they've mentioned Afterdeath before. Your name too. Working there might only put a larger target on your back."

"We didn't mean to bring up OneKind—maybe we should've kept it that way." Her glance toward Denis wasn't angry—merely tired, a shared apology passing between them.

Remy straightened, composure returning. "I'm more worried about both of you. Don't let the news worry you, I'm going to be okay."

Denis's mouth opened, then closed again.

"We will. We hear you," said Élise as she sat up straighter. "Well, if you could change things, what would you do?"

"I'd lower the barriers—make Afterdeath more accessible, more human. People should keep teaching, creating, and building—however they're able—even after they're gone."

"That sounds ambitious." Élise smiled like she'd heard exactly what she needed.

"Anything worth doing usually is," she agreed.

"And you really believe you can make a difference?" Denis became more invested.

Remy shrugged, voice dry. "I'm not exactly staging a revolution, Dad. I'm not in charge of anything. Though I welcome a chance to do something, ya know."

Élise gave her the look she used to know—protective, unwilling to let go.

"We only want you to be safe, sweetheart. That's all we've ever wanted."

"I know, Mom. And I promise I will be. Also, expect a Christmas call. I wouldn't miss that for anything."

"We'll be counting down," Denis said.

"Goodnight. I love you both so much," Remy said.

"We love you too," Élise replied, her words burdened with the devotion of a mother's heart.

The screen dimmed to black, and the room fell into a thick silence, its presence tangible. Denis and Élise sat side by side, each lost in their own thoughts, each finding solace in the other's company.

He didn't speak at first. When he did, it said everything. "It helped—seeing her. Hearing her. But now, it's over. And I miss her all over again."

Her hand found his, fingers intertwining gently in the current between them. The tablet screen had long since gone black, but her reflection lingered in the glass—faint, familiar, unforgotten.

CHAPTER SIXTEEN
THANATONOMICS

It was late—well past midnight—when the wall sensor pinged his implant. The door opened on cue, and inside, the air carried the low murmur of cooling fans—consistent, regulated, exact.

Harland Reeves entered his nerve centre, took his usual seat, and let the ambient hum stabilize his thoughts. Machines didn't lie. They didn't hedge or forget or deviate. They followed design. They stayed solved.

Twelve monitors lit the room in regulated arcs. Financial transfers, security feeds, sensor diagnostics: every stream aligned in ordered columns, reassuringly uneventful. Reeves stepped into the glow, absorbing the data as it converged around him. Only one window carried colour—a pulsing red square charting Maxime Roy's vitals. Heart rate spiking, bloodwork tumbling; sixteen days left, give or take.

He rolled his shoulders, working out the knot beneath his right scapula—the same spot that always tensed up before quarterly reports. It started the year his father died. Thirty-five years old, trying to sell his first security contract, terrified he'd forgotten some detail that would blow the whole thing open.

He flexed his hand, feeling for a phantom ache in his wrist. Even now, when the numbers lined up, when the network hummed, the pain came back. Not fear. Pressure, sharpening him to the task. He glanced at the mug on his desk, cold tea gone sour, and remembered a time he'd have poured another cup.

His face stayed blank. Legacy was a sentiment; precision was the mandate. If the architect couldn't see the plan through, the design would continue without him.

He rotated back to the primary display. At its centre, a countdown timer ticked: 11:22:43.

Cities prided themselves on control. By tomorrow, that illusion would collapse. Communications would fail first, and the transit grid would lock in place. Emergency channels would cut mid-call. Ventilators would stop. Monitors would freeze. This wasn't sabotage—it was a tactical delay. A vacuum engineered to draw focus. When the pressure built, he'd offer the release.

A piercing tone cut through the room—OneKind's signal. He exhaled through his nose, recalibrating. He disliked their pageantry, but he took the call.

OneKind had no leaders, only a quorum of masks—distributed authority posing as agreement. Their strength came from chaos, but their flaw was constant: they didn't build structures, only tore them down.

Reeves tolerated them because he understood the shape of leverage. And because every revolution, eventually, needed a banker.

The feed opened—engineered to disorient, all mask and noise. He didn't react. Software could be rewritten. People had to be managed.

"You promised us movement, Reeves," said the central mask. "Will the gates open on schedule?"

"High noon," he replied, unbothered. "On the dot. Strike early and I lock the grid—then no one eats."

Another mask whispered through the static.

"You act like we want your network intact. Maybe we don't."

He met his own reflection in the glass, already convinced. "You think you can bring down the network and walk away clean? Try it, and you'll have riots at every terminal before sunset. The digital dead aren't martyrs—they're leverage, for both of us. Burn Afterdeath and you get a week of headlines and a city full of grieving families. But if you want power, you need fear to last. That's what I'm offering."

Silence on the line. Harland leaned forward, reading the edge in the static—uncertainty, not agreement. He pressed.

"You've already made uploads a luxury for the desperate. If you want to be more than a glitch, you need structure. That's my offer: you break it, I own what's left. We both walk away richer, and no one knows who pulled the trigger."

His finger hovered over the mute switch, pulse tapping out a warning beneath his skin. "If you're in, wait for my signal. If not—be ready to take the blame when it burns."

"You want to contain us," said another voice, low and synthetic.

"I want to finish the work you've started," Harland replied. "You carve deep enough, and I'm left with a streamlined company. You're left with a population that fears you. You can't terrorize a corpse. But a rationed population of terrified minds? That's sustainable disruption."

Silence. "And what do you get out of this, banker?"

"Continuity," he said simply. "The illusion of choice. And an asset no one can unsee."

The feed shimmered. "We'll trust the clock," said the central mask at last.

Signal cut. Negotiations complete.

The clock marched on: 11:21:13.

He sat. Ten years with Maxime Roy had taught him how to wait. In the second year, Reeves arrived early for a quarterly audit and found Max revising the slides at the last minute, hands trembling over the keyboard, numbers recalculating in real time. Reeves remained silent, watching. That was the pattern: Max rewriting under pressure, Reeves observing, the outcome predetermined.

He learned patience in that room—restraint that compounded across years. He disagreed with decisions, recognized every inefficiency, but kept his thoughts to himself. Tonight, he set the course. This time, the plan was his.

The final piece had locked into place without resistance. OneKind, desperate for access, had handed him leverage: outrage timed to detonate.

Within twenty-four hours, the gates would unlock, and Reeves would step in not as a usurper, but as a saviour.

The optics were already set. Afterdeath would endure under the banner of necessary protection. New pricing models would roll out under the name of sustainability, framed by a disaster no one could blame him for.

He allowed himself one slow breath, the tension released in phases. It didn't weaken him. It left him clear. The window's reflection showed him, older and sharper than he remembered. Tomorrow, his name would be on every emergency memo, every contract. Not for approval—a signature. He'd stripped the company down to its bones. No one left to say no. Out in the city, people would scramble in the dark for help. He'd have the only working phone line. Every death, every transfer, every recalibration of the afterlife economy would run through new terms. His terms. And when desperation set in—as it always did—Reeves would offer rescue. Dignified, official, irrevocably priced.

He rose from the chair and crossed to the window, looking out over the city.

He had cut every friendship, stripped every impulse to reconsider, outlasted every lesser mind. Loss wasn't a metric. Memory gave nothing. Empathy wasn't a line item. Clarity demanded silence, and he had learned how to live with that. Somewhere, children would die during the blackout. Somewhere else, parents would beg a dark grid for help. He had already calculated the margins.

The city lights blinked on the glass, flickering through rain that hadn't let up for days. He wiped a patch clear with his cuff, eyes drawn to the hospital two blocks away—where someone else would be waiting through the night, hoping for a call that wouldn't come.

Across the room, the countdown continued: 11:19:47.

He didn't look back. Tomorrow, the world would change. The infrastructure would fail, the gates would open, and the first contracts of the new economy would be signed before anyone could call it theft. Harland Reeves would be waiting at the gates—not to be welcomed, but to be obeyed.

ACT THREE

CHAPTER SEVENTEEN
UNCANNY VALLEY

The morning light remained neutral when Remy stepped into the conference room, her movements unnervingly smooth. Each step felt awkward, each landing strange in its own right. The body fit, but it felt performed rather than lived, as if she gripped the strings without knowing how any of it connected.

Once, walking had belonged to her body the way rivers hold to their beds—flowing, adapting, never needing to ask permission. Now it was a kind of artifact, polished and intentional, stripped of the small, living frictions that made it real. She moved convincingly, but the balance was gone—the subtle feedback loops that made walking feel real.

The room pressed in with sensory detail. The burnt bitterness of coffee clung to the air, underscored by the faint whir of the air conditioner, its cycling edging past perceptual comfort.

The conference table ran too long for comfort—polished walnut edged with brushed steel, more command bridge than meeting space. Embedded projectors rested dormant at each end, and a half-dozen charging pads ticked like anxious metronomes. A narrow line of light cut down the centre, programmed to shift temperature over time, though no one could recall why.

At the head of the table, Max sat with his tablet. His gaze caught on the empty chair beside him—then moved on, too fast to be natural.

Marisol's usually unreadable expression darkened—confirmation of what they all knew.

He would've preferred to confront Harland directly today. He'd been building a case—fragments, really. A handful of suspicious admin accounts. A curious login from one of Harland's offices into a dead server flagged for extremist chatter. Not actionable, but enough to corner him in the room. He'd hoped to close the loop before the board had time to deflect suspicion. But with Harland missing, all he could do now was raise a flag and hope it stuck.

Maybe that was the point. Stall the confrontation. Let the meeting degrade into background noise—a final sign of disrespect from a man who wanted Max to feel obsolete.

Harland didn't skip meetings. He engineered them. His absence was calculated. And for the first time in years, Max wasn't the one framing the room.

The only leverage he had left: a trail of proxy shells, a tanked interview, and Remy Moreau—his last good idea.

There was no more waiting. "Let's start with the good news." The room relaxed in the wake of Max's words.

"The new settings for Legacy Link have cut complaints in half. Reports of users feeling 'haunted' by the living specifically are at a historical low."

He kept it simple. "It's working."

The tension in the room eased. Ravi Tan tucked a strand of hair behind their ear.

"We should track what it does to Induction pass sales," they said, not looking up. "Legacy Link's down, but this could stabilize the core. Could even show early lift—if the narrative sticks."

A few finance staff exchanged glances—half skeptical, half impressed. Only Ravi could make early lift sound like a bold prediction and a caution at the same time.

Max tapped his pen against the table.

"We need bigger wins. We have more visibility than ever before. Damage control is a matter of perspective, sure, but we have to continue to prove that Afterdeath is worth believing in."

He shelved the distraction of a certain partner's absence. And yet, before the meeting could properly begin, there was something else to address. He hadn't cleared this with legal. Hadn't flagged it to ops. He was risking brand, trust, and platform authority to give a dead girl the floor. Déjà vu, sure, and yet—long overdue.

"On that note, there's someone I'd like to introduce."

Remy straightened as he began, posture rehearsed, mechanical—like someone learning to move with a new body and no instruction manual.

"This is a demo android rig, forgive the prototype look to the shell." Max continued, gesturing toward her. "Today, I'm honoured to have a live subject visiting us through this new technology."

Max waited a beat for posterity.

"Ladies and gentlemen, please help me in welcoming Remy Moreau to the company. And before you say anything—yes, that Remy Moreau."

"Hi," she said, her voice passing for confident, "It's nice to meet you all."

The recognition rippled through the table. A few exchanged glances. Reyes, one of the systems leads, frowned—his reactions rarely surfaced, which made this one stand out. Marisol's eyes shifted, but she stayed silent. Even Ravi, who rarely looked up from his tablet, sat a little straighter.

Max had assumed the reveal would land flat. Harland had seen the shell. The others hadn't. He'd misread the room.

She met their stares without reaction. She'd stood in rooms colder than this.

"She's here because she wants to be," Max said, maintaining an even tone. "And it matters because we so rarely hear from anyone but analysts or engineers. Our choices impact those on the other side of this table, and we at last have an advocate from within the environment we're building."

Max looked toward her. "Remy, you had a perspective to share about the arrival experience?"

For a half-second, her focus fractured—instinct running code instead of questions. Heart rates, micro-expressions—the way jaws cinched, barely—she registered them all. But none of it helped. What mattered couldn't be measured. The room's attention pressed against her skin, electric and expectant.

She cleared her throat—her vocal processors working to find cadence as they adapted to the room's air. "I've reviewed user feedback. Most comments focus on the Pearly Gates. Some describe them as tacky, others say the religious imagery feels misplaced. Regardless of belief, the response trends toward discomfort."

Marisol angled her chair slightly, not smiling. "So you think we should change it?"

The lawyer looked up from his tablet. "The branding's neutral. If an Inductee sees halos, that's interpretation, not design."

A few dry chuckles circled the table, more reflex than agreement. The lawyer tapped his stylus again, unconvinced.

"We call it a transition, but to users it feels staged—a VR ride dressed up as the afterlife. One wrote, 'I'm neither Christian nor Catholic—why is Heaven's front door my only option?'"

She drew back slightly, palm flat to the table. "A disclaimer won't change that. If it looks religious, people will respond to it that way."

The executive accountant frowned. "Those gates are iconic. Scrapping them would be costly. Is it really worth it?"

Jin-Ho, the programming lead, asked, "How would we adapt? What's the replacement?"

She didn't yield the floor.

"I've seen what happens when people build for each other. I've stood in a sitcom apartment sealed to a single day. The timing was perfect. The jokes landed. You could feel it—like the code waited, timed to the next beat. It wasn't impressive because it was polished.

It worked because someone loved it enough to get every detail right."

She studied the room in turn—not seeking approval, only attention. "That wasn't built for scale. It was built for presence."

She let the place reassemble itself in her mind—food on the table, Earthrise beyond the porch. "And there's a moon homestead out past the standard grid. You won't find it in the catalogues. No dev team cleared it. But I swear—it has the best damn view anywhere in this world or the last. A hand-built porch overlooking Earthrise. A woman with calm hands and the kind of knowing you feel more than say. That place stays with you."

She didn't raise her voice, but the conviction in it was unmistakable.

"You can't fabricate that."

Her mouth twitched, betraying her pride.

"I once ended up in this ridiculous fortress made entirely of pillows. It sounds stupid, I know. But tucked in the middle, I found exactly what I'd been looking for. Only—someone else was already holding it."

She laughed. "The scene wasn't planned. It wasn't meant for me. But it stayed." Her voice dropped lower, almost confessional.

"I've walked those zones—the ones we show off in press kits. Gleaming. Curated. They never feel inhabited. I once found a PB Max bar in the back of a corner of a store—clearly modded by someone with nutty taste and vivid recall. It didn't come from a branding initiative. It came from a person who remembered what candy used to taste like when you were ten."

The partners were listening.

"That's when it hit me."

She was hoping her words were contagious.

"We keep mistaking polish for meaning. But the places that stick? They're the ones someone built without waiting for approval."

A longer pause followed. This wasn't nostalgia. It was the point.

"Afterdeath doesn't need another glossy hub. It needs fire pits. Blanket forts with decent lighting. Half-busted arcades that record your high score and don't forget it."

Her voice didn't rise—it grounded itself.

"What if the next Pearly Gates isn't another showcase plaza? What if it's a more organic process?"

She folded her hands, her delivery level. "So give it to them. Open the gates. Let the modders build. Let Inductees make their own halls of fame. And if nothing works? Fine. But odds are—if you give people room to create something true—they will."

Remy could feel it: her words hanging in the air, brushing against the fringes of feasibility. A concept pressing against infrastructure, testing for weak spots.

He didn't answer right away. He regarded her, unreadable, before turning toward the executive accountant.

A few low comments followed—some guarded, some curious.

Max didn't speak at first. He steepled his fingers, eyes on Remy. "Run the numbers on a pilot programme, maybe we can start with a small team of modders at first," he said. "I think Remy handed the creative teams a gift."

That's when the lights cut out—fast and full.

After a beat, Remy's visor lit up—no brighter than a watchface—casting the table in low, calculated green. It wasn't bright, but it changed them—casting their faces in low relief, like the world had tilted into something fragile and waiting.

The sound was unmistakable, a tone buried so deeply in the architecture of Afterdeath's security that no one in this room should have ever had to hear it. His fingers curled against the table as the realization crashed in, his mind already reaching for contingencies, but coming up empty. The alarm had no redundancies. No false positives. It was a last measure, one that meant the unthinkable had already happened.

The name detonated through his mind before he could stop it. Harland.

She turned to him. "Max?" His mind was locked somewhere distant, cycling through possibilities, each more impossible than the last.

His throat bobbed, but when he finally spoke, it was barely audible. "This alarm—" His fingers tightened into a fist against the table. "This doesn't go off unless someone gets past the outermost layer of our security. It means—it means an intruder's already inside."

Static crowded her thoughts. The air felt heavier, closer, as if an unseen force had wedged itself between her and the world. The screen—no, not a screen. A message forced into her vision, hard and inescapable, cutting through everything else: OFFLINE IS REAL. HUMANITY IS ONEKIND.

The distortion vanished as quickly as it had come, leaving behind only its imprint—like pressure on a nerve already frayed.

She looked to Max, suspended between impulse and doubt. She could tell him. Maybe she should. But the words didn't come. She waited instead, eyes locked to his profile, trying to read whether he'd seen it too or was calculating a different kind of damage.

He sat too rigid to suggest control—more like he was bracing for an impact that hadn't arrived yet. His hand hovered above the tablet, suspended.

Reyes moved toward the door, already on the phone. A few others followed. Remy didn't track them. She tracked Max.

Remy stood. Her gaze snapped into focus without instruction, calibration folding into instinct as she turned toward the window. Toronto burned in the distance, its core lit with heat and energy—but along the outer limits, light was disappearing. One building went black. Another. Surgical cuts, each blackout placed to send a message.

It wasn't random. The blackouts followed a pattern, starting with the downtown towers, each one cutting out in even, timed intervals. It spread outward, methodical, consuming the city in rows that moved like code. Whole blocks disappeared into darkness. The path moved south, toward the lake.

Remy had lived through power outages. Storms, infrastructure failures, even sabotage. This wasn't that. There were no spikes, no staggered overloads, no delay. This was methodical—an engineered blackout tracing a calculated path through the city.

The lakeshore disappeared next. Streetlights dropped out in sync. Bridges dimmed until only their outlines remained. The Gardiner Expressway lost power section by section, headlights vanishing, motion draining from the lanes. Cars rolled to a stop mid-curve. Others kept moving without input, aimless without navigation.

In the distance, a plane dropped into view. Too fast, too low. Its position lights sputtered, engines silent. It fell with momentum, not control. Remy tracked its descent until it hit the river in a muted blast—foam and metal bursting upward, folding under. The wreck vanished unceremoniously, as if gravity had simply reclaimed what never belonged in the sky.

Below, the street grid fractured. Driverless vehicles froze mid-intersection or accelerated into barriers, logic broken. A transit bus coasted into a darkened façade and stopped only when it crumpled. An ambulance veered off its route and collided with a stalled city bus. Glass scattered across pavement. Sirens ricocheted off glass and concrete. The lights kept flashing, but no one moved to answer them. The city wasn't breaking apart. It was being shut down.

Behind her, the conference room remained untouched, cast in dim emergency lighting. No one had spoken. Afterdeath's internal systems stayed active, servers illuminated, headquarters standing bright while everything beyond its walls faded to black. The alarm howled again, the protocol stack fractured—unable to process unresolvable logic. The lights flashed once more before vanishing completely. Darkness followed—full, complete, unanswered.

Max's fingers hovered above his tablet, his focus locked on the cascade of alert signals. The power draw wasn't local. The source of the alarm wasn't a citywide failure. The feed filled with city names lighting up worldwide.

Remy's overlay stuttered—for a second, a forced action ran beneath the interface.

She dismissed it manually, her fingers pressing harder as the override collapsed. It didn't matter what the protocol wanted. She wasn't a process to be removed.

Max straightened his posture. "Remy. Log off. Leave. Now." His fear threaded beneath the words—rare, raw, badly hidden.

"I'm the dead one," Remy said, flashing a smirk. "You be safe."

Max didn't move. He didn't argue. He didn't even look away. "Remy—" His mouth pressed into a tight line, his thoughts scattering, calculating faster than words could keep up. "I've never been a father," he said finally, voice strained. "If you get hurt—" He couldn't finish.

"You're off the hook, Mr. Roy," she said, crisp and distant. "I already got a dad."

She narrowed her focus on the terminal. "Alright, fine," she muttered. "I'll go."

She chose the exit because it was the only move that wouldn't escalate things.

She tapped in the commands, her hand sure, her touch unerring. The authorization cleared in an instant. A tight, wry smile surfaced—unasked, unshared.

"See you on the other side, Mr. Roy."

CHAPTER EIGHTEEN
ZERO DAY

Alan Prescott sat at the Pearly Gates, the chair rocking beneath him—none of it intentional. One leg was too short, and the uneven cobblestones kept tilting him sideways. He'd tried shifting it onto the patch of artificial grass behind Franklin, but that only made things worse. Now he sat there, a sense of discomfort settling in.

He jerked the chair halfway closed, and snapped it open again. This protest was meant to give people more control—to make Afterdeath more than a place to wait. And yet, he couldn't manage to level a single chair. He muttered a curse and sat down. The chair wobbled beneath him, and he let it, noticing how the angle made one of his knees ache.

The Gates loomed overhead, casting long shadows across the smooth expanse of the plaza. He watched people fade in and out of view—artificial brilliance that felt more weary than welcoming tonight.

Guilt rose in the opposite direction. He'd helped set this protest in motion, hoping it might spark unity, momentum, meaning. But today, the charge felt gone. The momentum had stalled. In the centre of the plaza, his friends tended a small campaign table. On a screen, two petitions were displayed—one triumph and one blank petition waiting for a new fight. Jenna ran a finger down her datapad, frowning. Franklin stood with arms crossed.

"Legacy Link was an easy fight," Jenna muttered. "People really hated random calls from the living."

Franklin leaned back. "We need a new fight people can believe in."

He scanned the passersby. Some glanced at the banner, most ignored it. "It's not about fighting," he said. "It's about autonomy."

Jenna raised an eyebrow. "You think people care about working in the afterlife?"

The tightness in his upper back had returned.

"Some do. Not everyone wants eternity to be a vacation. Musicians, writers, engineers—why shouldn't they keep building here?"

"Most people arrive with expectations," Ruth countered. "Most don't include getting back to work right away."

"I want to disagree with Ruth," Jenna said, her eyes fixed on the crowd. "But I'm not too sure I can argue with that logic standing here. Most of these people want to either rest, feast or party."

She was right. Probably.

"Yeah, you're probably right," admitted Alan.

He drummed his fingers on the armrest—slow, even, pointless. It wasn't a song, or a thought, it was pure habit. It was what his hand did while the rest of him idled. He wasn't thinking about the petitions. He was pondering the plaza, the people fading in and out, and what came next. No arguments to rehearse, no profound truth looming. Only Taps. One. Another. A space. Two more. Almost in time with something—maybe a remnant impulse, maybe nothing at all. He watched a bird loop overhead and lost track of it. His foot bounced. The fingers kept going. Crescendo nearing. Revelation: an old man in a semi-stable chair, waiting in a place where nothing really changed.

A voice rose above the general hum.

Alan turned, spotting Barry near a group of newcomers. He spoke with easy conviction, his hands moving with his words, open gestures, unselfconscious and alive. The crowd leaned in without quite realising it. Beside him, a striking woman echoed his tempo, her own movements looping wider, sweeping reluctant listeners into the circle.

Alan felt a familiar twinge. Barry had a way of reaching people that he rarely managed. By being fully present.

"Who the hell is that?" Jenna asked, tracing the stare back to the target.

He didn't offer context. "That's him," he said, already rising, pulling at the fit of his jacket. He glanced toward the others.

"Maybe we're not doing this right," he added, not as a conclusion, but as a theory.

Ruth arched an eyebrow, unamused. "And you have a better idea?" Her question hit like a challenge, not sarcasm—she wanted a plan, not a dodge.

"Maybe I have someone else's idea."

He swallowed, gathering the nerve for what came next. "I think it's time I reach out to an old friend."

He opened his mouth to say Barry's name. A bridge. A signal that he was ready to admit he was wrong. He had always shown the way. But the name never left him.

He felt the tension rise. His thoughts scattered.

The message arrived—

OFFLINE IS REAL. HUMANITY IS ONEKIND.

It didn't surface on any overlay. It wasn't projected, prompted, or requested. It simply existed—cutting through the visual field with jarring clarity, as if it had been hardwired into the space behind their vision. It held there, pulsing—not with light, but with presence. And then it was gone—leaving no trace but the unease it seeded in each of them.

He registered the shock before he could process what he'd seen. They didn't speak over one another. They didn't shout. They only stood there for a breathless second, each trying to determine whether the others had seen it too.

The gunshot cracked the air—a rupture sharp enough to reframe the scene.

His heartbeat scattered, wild and arrhythmic, a reflex with nowhere to go as he lurched upright.

Three figures, armoured in matte black from neck to boot, cut through the plaza in synchronized silence. They didn't rush. Their helmets bore no insignia—only a smooth, opaque sheen that erased all trace of identity. Two were broad-shouldered, masculine in frame. The third, narrower, moved with the same unnerving exactitude—lethal in movement, certain in intent. Rifles stayed levelled, hands trained. The trio advanced, step by step, their approach measured and exact—expressionless, relentless.

Alan felt the dread rise like a tide inside him. The lead figure turned their head in a methodical scan, crossing the plaza with predatory calm. The target—an unarmed figure barely a dozen feet ahead—vanished in a burst of ionized scatter. Flesh existed. It didn't. All that remained: heat-shredded dust curling backward.

A mechanical announcement stated, "User deleted." Screams erupted. People scattered, dropping low or tripping over each other as though freezing in place might kill them.

His mind reeled. Before he could move, Ruth yanked him behind a column, her fingernails biting into his sleeve. He glimpsed Jenna and Franklin, frozen by the petition table, faces pale. A red glow expanded at the plaza's perimeter, sealing them in.

A distorted voice rose above the panic: "Stay down. Hands visible. Comply, and remain as dead as you were this morning."

He stood half-triggered—body primed, thoughts not yet in step.

He turned to Ruth. "You okay?"

Her hand clamped hard around his sleeve, fingers digging in.

"It's—It's those OneKind terrorists," she said, shaking.

Alan swallowed. He forced himself to look at the soldiers—smooth, efficient, no wasted motion. Not amateurs. Not radicals. Not the disorganized fringe group people joked about until recently. These were professionals—manifesto thumpers turned tactical, keyboard prophets with a body count. OneKind had always broadcast like a movement but behaved like a purge. They were supposed to be distributed, anonymous, off-grid. Not here. Not incarnated. Not coordinated like this. And now they had boots on the plaza.

"Alan—what is this?" Ruth asked in a whisper as she took cover.

"I don't know," he replied, though the words tasted hollow. His eyes tracked the silent forms spreading through the plaza. He saw where Barry had been.

Erasing Barry wasn't a warning. It was proof—they were done waiting.

His hand clenched, nails biting into his palm.

He'd heard rumours for years, brushed them off as exaggeration. But now, watching their silent advance, he understood. They weren't attacking. They were executing a correction. That's how they saw it—erasing what didn't fit. Purging the Inducted, people like him, from the world.

These aren't people who believe in something. They treat belief like malware—and purge accordingly.

A heavy knot formed in his chest. He'd never fully accepted what he was—data, preserved thought, a consciousness mapped onto a substrate—but that was the truth. He was one of them now. A ghost in the wires. And OneKind had come to delete him. This felt different. Colder. Absolute. Not an argument, not a negotiation—an execution of protocol. But to remain here, fully present, facing down those who saw him as a system flaw? That was unfamiliar ground. The emotion hit all at once: anger, dread, and a grief too heavy for words.

He noticed the crowd pressed together, frantic, trapped by the perimeter. The soldiers aimed their weapons with tranquil menace, controlling every vantage. For one stretched instant, all motion ceased, as if sheer hope could summon a stay against what came next.

Barry moved—cutting through the unnatural stillness of the crowd. He raised his hands, trembling but trying for courage. "Wait," he called. "We're not a threat. Whatever you want, we don't need to be involved."

Alan's stomach twisted. He watched the soldier's muzzle twitch toward Barry—like a crosshair locking in.

"Barry, don't—" he pleaded, grabbing at Barry's sleeve and yanking him back. But a soldier raised an arm in warning, ordering them to "Stay Down."

Barry shook free. "Look," he said, glancing at Beatrice, who looked ready to break. "Most people here already died once today. Maybe we can let a few of them go to their realms. You don't need everyone to make your point."

He wanted to say something. Do something. Stop Barry from trying to parlay with OneKind. Instead, he stood there frozen.

The soldier tilted his head, as if weighing the request. But the moment passed, and the outcome was already decided. "You're right," the soldier said. "We don't need everyone."

He pulled the trigger. The shot landed hard. Barry staggered—his body breaking apart in a burst of static—he was gone.

The artificial announcement returned, "User deleted."

Beatrice let out a ragged sob. Barry had vanished—erased. A suffocating shock locked the plaza in place. The red perimeter held—no way out. The plaza was a cage now, and everyone knew it.

Alan felt Ruth's hand tremble on his arm, Jenna's slack expression in his periphery. Franklin's mouth had drawn into a grim line.

The lead soldier stepped toward Alan, rifle canted at a false angle of ease, the tension bleeding out at the seams. His helmet filtered the words into a dry, metallic burr. "Why're you scared?" he asked, casual as a knife twist. "You're already compost."

The word 'compost' hit hard and wouldn't leave his mind.

The OneKind goon angled his head. "Please give me a reason."

He didn't move. His mind caught up slower than the gun. Guilt arrived sideways—he'd never found the right way to meet Barry halfway. Gone before he even registered the sound.

Ruth, next to him, clung to the petition table, face chalk-white, eyes glued to the spot where Barry had stood seconds before.

Abruptly, one of the soldiers fired again. Alan closed his eyes as if closing them might keep him alive somehow. Time didn't pass—it suspended. He opened his eyes again.

A woman not five feet from him vanished, her outline stuttering before it dissolved.

"User deleted." The intonation confirmed.

A second shot followed; a man near the table buckled mid-sprint, confusion in his eyes as his body splintered into shards of static. A third shot found a random passerby mid-step, erasing him before his foot touched the ground.

More confirmations followed.

The air stank of panic, sour and mechanical. Anyone who ran would die. The screams came only after the third disappearance, rising in a collective wave of horror. The plaza wasn't frozen now. It was breaking open. People shouted names, flung themselves against the red barrier, grabbed anything for a shield—but there was no escape.

Instincts fired, but calculation rode alongside them. He yanked Ruth down hard, her knees cracking against stone. She shot a desperate look back at the table—as if outrage alone could overturn what had already begun. Jenna and Franklin were in cover.

Alan's mind continued to race. They were sealed inside the Gates, and every desperate thought clawed uselessly at the walls of his mind. Grief, fury, and helplessness flooded inside him.

He saw Ruth's hands tremble. He didn't have a strategy. He couldn't see or think of any way out. They were trapped.

CHAPTER NINETEEN
OVERCLOCKED

Remy ran—steady, focused, driven by the incursion to come. The space reconfigured with each step—walls realigning, halls bending, the system adjusting in sync with her motion.

The library waited ahead, centred by the golden tree—its brass leaves suspended in air. She slowed—barely. Enough to pass beneath the boughs.

The golden leaves shimmered, unmoving, their edges glowing with a warmth the code couldn't explain.

Her hand hovered near the surface, tracing the space she knew by feel. Hundreds of hours spent decoding beneath its branches, books stacked around her knees—always finding ways to stay longer than she should have. The tree didn't guide her. It witnessed her. And now, before the breach, she gave it a single, grounding beat—the kind that comes from recognition. The kind that says: I'm ready.

Books, tomes, scrolls, and special editions stacked in purposeful disorder surrounded it. She hadn't come to disappear. She was here to break through. At the back of the library, her safe waited—nested behind layers only she could unlock. It opened with a click, and Remy reached inside promptly, pulling what she needed: tools, not weapons. Each one chosen for function. Each one a step forward.

She took out the cloak—a sleek composite of tuned fibers and modular mesh. It wasn't designed to make her disappear, not exactly, but when aligned right it could scatter the field around her and let her slide past most sensors. Remy called it her cloak of cloaking, even engraving that into the metadata. She keyed the settings, primed it for movement and terrain, and watched the surface ripple once, then settle. It wasn't illusion or trick. It was built, refined, and trusted.

She pieced together the breach device from salvaged toy parts and code modules she'd been refining on her own time. It wasn't elegant, but it thrummed with potential—a force built to punch through a barrier when placed with care.

From the corner of the safe, she grabbed her wandboard—a handheld input wand, dense with mapped keys and pressure nodes—her fallback when the full rig was too slow. She was ready.

Her eyes narrowed—not in focus, but in entry—as if the world itself was a terminal waiting for her to log in. She extended her focus outward, visualizing not a portal or a standard spawn point, but the spot she'd locked in—exactly outside OneKind's red perimeter.

Coordinates solidified instantly in her mind, resolving intention into command. This wasn't teleportation. It was something subtler: the simulated fabric of space-time folding gently to bring two distant points seamlessly together. With a slight movement of her wrist, Remy released the signal. The response was immediate, seamless, silent. Reality realigned around her.

The jump landed true, but her balance wavered. She made a mental note to stick to portals from now on.

The Pearly Gates loomed ahead, their golden light pristine, yet distorted by a red glow at the border. What filled the air wasn't peace, but anticipation—the kind that gathers in the final second before impact.

She flexed her fingers and replaced her grip on the portal device, confirming its balance and placement. Her cloak sealed to her shape, anchoring at the joints as she moved.

She triggered the portal. A jolt of force hit the Pearly Gates, forcing them to absorb it mid-pulse. The whole frame shuddered.

The barrier wavered. Light skittered along its skin in broken patterns. This wasn't a simple breach.

The rupture widened, pulling at the simulated space like tension on a seam.

Three soldiers maintained formation, moving with practised unity. Behind them, system operators extended through the network—hackers and proxies running parallel processes, analyzing data far beyond human speed. Every movement followed protocol. Every command landed with intent. Remy saw the turn—their focus locked in, their priorities realigned.

A clipped phrase cut through comms. "That's no normal disruption."

Another followed—lower, tense. "Be ready."

The lead soldier advanced, head tilted, studying the rift. The gap wasn't breaking—it was spreading, slow and methodical. Uncontained. Unnatural. It expanded with tension winding through the rupture, straining at the limits of what the simulation grid could sustain.

"Hold your positions."

"Someone is here."

They tracked the perimeter's slow collapse, recalibrating the rules of the fight ahead.

Remy didn't wait for them to decide.

She moved through the gap before their minds recalibrated—shape slipping sideways in the haze, pace synced to their blind spot. The plan had worked. Their focus stayed on the damage. The guards held position, too slow to register what had already passed between them.

She struck without warning. A lunge compressed into a direct blow, her fist slamming into the first soldier's sternum. The armour's reinforced plating transferred most of the force, but not all. The kinetic dampeners slipped, and a fierce jolt rattled through his frame.

His stance fractured, leaving him open. She spun low, the cloak lagging behind her like an afterimage as she hooked her leg around the second soldier's knee. The joint gave under the force. A snapping crack.

His mass turned against him, pitching sideways. His rifle jerked up—too slow.

She knocked it free before he realized it was gone. By the time the first soldier regained his composure, she was already moving on him.

When she reappeared, she was behind him. He sensed the change, helmet jerking toward her, but his reaction lagged by half a second. Her strike landed true, driving into the gap below the ribline where the armour split.

He staggered forward, reaching for control that had already slipped away. They were fast. She was faster. The third soldier twisted, attempting to counter, but she was already inside his guard. A palm strike snapped his head sideways. A knee found his gut. A final twist of force sent him sprawling, his rifle slipping from his grasp before he could correct his footing.

OneKind's systems faltered. Targeting feeds jumped and stuttered, their predictive routines lagging behind what was actually happening. The coordination software—normally flawless—couldn't keep up. This wasn't what they'd trained for.

She wasn't matching their tactics. She was undoing them—pulling the fight apart before it could even begin. One strike at a time. One weapon at a time. Every step stayed ahead of their reach, every maneuver reinforcing the truth they realized too late. Except—it wasn't enough.

A soldier she had knocked flat jerked back to his feet, his weapon rematerializing in his hands as if summoned. Another, disarmed only seconds earlier, raised a fresh sidearm, perfectly placed as if plucked from thin air.

She moved faster, adapting, but every disarm, every blow, every hard-earned break she forced—vanished under a fresh layer of control she couldn't predict.

Their movements weren't human reflexes anymore. They corrected in time, as if unseen hands were patching reality on the fly.

That was when she understood. The soldiers weren't acting alone. They were proxies. The real fight was happening behind their visors—hackers, engineers, remote analysts stitching the battlefield back together faster than she could tear it apart. An invisible army, stitching the field back together in real time. She was fighting OneKind itself.

The soldiers only managed to keep up. Their enhancements gave them everything but an advantage. They moved with effort, but their support hive lifted them—corrected them—patched over every human error in real time.

Meanwhile, Remy was struggling to maintain her pace. The tree had taught her to slow time, but she was the one stretched thin. The fracturing red perimeter flared across the plaza, throwing shadows long and wild. The battle was never meant to be fair. It was meant to be inevitable. Doubt rose in Remy, but she crushed it. There was no space for second-guessing.

She launched into a flurry, moving through the chaos of data and combat. She was about to make her next move when her system stuttered—an unsettling delay. She tried to react, but her reflexes stalled, her body misfiring like a broken machine.

The nearest soldier turned. He saw the outline of a cloaking field and moved to take her out. He nearly caught her—but she slipped the blow, her pulse pounding in her ears.

She had seconds. She needed distance. But it was already too late. Her cloak glitched, leaving her exposed.

A cold shock ran through her. The delay had never been random. It was an attack. She twisted hard, scanning for an escape, but the soldiers were already on her.

Her limbs jerked once, seized—the signals jamming mid-path. She reached inward for speed, for strength, for any reservoir of force left in the rig, but it slipped from her like static through water. A soldier's grip locked at her back, the cold barrel wedged beneath her ribs.

"It's the Moreau girl," one of them confirmed.

She was trapped—conscious but unsynced, every command failing before it reached the surface.

"She shouldn't exist," another muttered, as if explaining an error they intended to erase.

Remy had spent eternity feeling like an exception, an error the framework had overlooked. But this was different. This wasn't philosophical. It was targeted—a correction already in progress. Her body refused to move, but her mind kept tearing through possibilities, grasping for any thread she could cling to. The disrupter stayed clenched in her hand—useless now. The cloak was blown. They hadn't neutralized her—they'd pulled her apart, line by line, like hostile coders stripping back her execution layer to raw syntax, exposing her at the lowest level, as if she'd been dropped into the In-Between itself. She clamped down on the rising panic, forcing her mind back into focus. If they wanted her gone, why hadn't they done it already?

Because she was more than a threat. She was useful—proof that even miracles could be broken and reclaimed. They weren't going to delete her immediately. But they were going to. The timing was the only question.

Her mind turned to Max—not in hope, but in reckoning. This was exactly what he feared she'd do, and she'd done it anyway. It would be easier, later, to say the system failed him. But she would know better.

CHAPTER TWENTY
REDLINE

Max stood alone in the sub-basement, staring at the bare spot where the Lazarus unit used to sit. Only the cradle remained—bolted down, hollowed out, every useful part stripped to the frame. A layer of dust traced its outline, like a chalk mark where his escape used to be.

He recoiled, throat tightening before logic conceded what he already knew. Harland did this—not only the workshop, but everything else. He'd come here to choose the moment—to enter Afterdeath by will, not desperation. But that choice—like so many lately—was already gone.

He forced himself upright, drawing on reserves he barely remembered.

The sprint that followed wasn't a sprint at all. It was a series of driven, uneven strides, a half-collapse in motion. The cancer was in his bones now. In his blood. Every step pulled life from him that he wouldn't get back in this realm. He pushed through the auxiliary corridor at a full sprint, his badge already in hand, his path set toward the executive elevator.

As he rounded the final corner, one of his own security team blocked his path. "Sir—wait. I've been instructed—" The taser was already half-raised.

Max didn't need words to understand. The man's posture was controlled, alert—already braced for a confrontation. His voice only confirmed what his posture had already warned.

He charged ahead—all force and desperation—and slammed his shoulder into the man's torso with the momentum of someone who'd already accepted the cost.

The taser hit him mid-roll—a white-hot jolt across his ribs that dropped fire into his lungs—but the impact carried him through. He hit the floor hard, the iron-heavy taste of blood behind his teeth.

The elevator doors parted. He dragged himself through on instinct and raw will.

A boot crashed into Max's solar plexus, flipping him onto his back. Pain shattered his focus, head smacking the floor, as the guard followed, already drawing a second weapon.

The elevator doors began sliding shut. His hand found the dropped taser. He didn't aim. He didn't think. He brought it upward in a wide, clumsy arc and slammed it into the man's pelvis. The charge fired, and the man fell beside Max.

It felt like minutes before Max could get to his feet, but he knew only seconds had passed. He reached for the panel behind him, fingers slipping as he searched for the close-door command. His other arm grabbed the railing, but his grip was weak, his energy draining with every passing second.

A fist landed. Another. Max twisted and drove them both into the far railing, using the last of his strength to shove off the wall.

The blow didn't drop him, but it staggered his balance—enough for Max to reach the panel. He hit the door control. The panel lit green. The elevator began to rise.

The guard lunged one last time—but the doors clipped him mid-step. The door barely slowed him before re-opening and attempting to close again. He twisted and drove his heel into the man's upper body, shoving him back into the hall before the doors sealed.

The doors sealed shut. Max sank against the railing, half-seated, half-folded, air scraping out in ragged gasps. A hot ache crawled across the intercostal muscles of his right flank, residual current sparking under the surface. One eye was swelling shut. The elevator groaned as it climbed—B2, B1, 1, 2—each stop gliding past with nothing more than a lurch and a scroll to mark its passing. He let himself believe—briefly—that he'd made it.

The cabin jerked to a sudden stop. The impact snapped through his spine and clacked his teeth together. The fluorescent lights wavered, before everything went black.

A chime followed. "All partners present in the building, please report to the Executive Boardroom for an emergency meeting."

Max slumped against the cold steel, heart pounding in uneven bursts. His fingers found the tremor at his throat, uncertain if it was fever, fear, or the aftermath. Harland had always played angles, but this was something colder—an endgame. And he'd seen it coming too late.

Every awkward beat, every sidelong glance—buried under the belief that he remained too vital to remove. That miscalculation had cost more than pride. Now it was collateral damage. He could taste not only blood, but failure.

He tried the panel. Nothing. A bead of sweat slipped down his temple, and he sank lower, chest tight with pained half-gasps. So this was it. Trapped between floors, pinned by Harland's cunning and his own arrogance, with everything he'd tried to protect hanging in the balance. No matter how he looked at it, each path led back to the point he failed to move.

Max closed his eyes, sweat gathering beneath his brow as the sting of ozone clung to each inhale. His side throbbed from the taser, nerves twitching beneath the skin, but it wasn't the pain that kept him frozen—it was the understanding.

Of course Harland was already up there. This wasn't a simple lockout. It was an installation. Not a malfunction, but choreography. Plan A had failed. Plan B had folded. He was inside a deeper trap now—a fallback layered beneath contingencies, the kind Harland would build for the kind of threat Max had become.

He braced himself against the wall and pulled out his tablet. The screen lagged for a moment before clearing. His hands were shaking, but he moved to answer swiftly as he could. The line opened without delay.

Paul picked up, face already half-lit by the amber light through his windows.

"Max? What's going on?"

"I can't move this elevator," Max said between coughs. "One of my own men tried to detain me. Harland's behind it." He tapped the frozen panel again, reflex more than hope. "Everything's locked down."

Paul's expression hardened. "What's he doing?"

Max glanced at the overhead bulb, its faint buzz drilling into the air between them. The elevator felt smaller by the second. "If I had to guess? The boardroom. Harland's calling a vote while I'm stuck down here."

The console flashed an error, then it went dark. When Max pressed his hand against it, there was no response. No pushback—only emptiness.

"Your health first," Paul said through the tablet. "Location?"

"Between fifty and fifty-one," Max muttered. "Breathing, somehow."

"Use the executive stairwell," he added quickly. "It runs parallel to the private elevator—no foot traffic, no cameras. Harland won't expect you through that side."

"Don't stop making noise. We're on the stairs."

Max shut his eyes against the tremor in his hands. The tablet dipped lower, and he let the gesture speak for itself.

Paul and Armand took the steps two at a time, heads down, drawing hard gulps in the close air. The only light was a patchy glow from above. After a few floors, Armand leaned against the wall at the landing.

"You okay?" Paul asked.

"Fine. Keep going," Armand said, barely slowing.

They pressed onward through the narrow stairwell, each step closer to the sound—and to Max.

Paul quickened his pace as the clanging grew louder with each landing—a blunt strike of fist against metal, more warning than signal.

He stepped into the hallway, footsteps echoing on the cold tile as he neared the elevator. Two men emerged, suits immaculate, stances practised, hands hovering at their belts as though waiting for a silent cue.

"Where do you think you're going?" one asked.

"My brother's in there," Paul said without slowing. "I'm getting him out."

"This floor's restricted," the taller one replied. "Mr. Reeves's orders." The name confirmed Paul's suspicions.

"I don't work for him. Move." They didn't. "My brother's dying in that elevator."

One guard swung first, a quick hook Paul deflected with a raised forearm. He countered, landed a jab to the jaw.

The second lunged, but Paul ducked low and drove him into the wall. Two elbows found their mark, and the guard dropped.

Paul straightened, heart pounding, knuckles throbbing. No time to linger.

He turned to the elevator, fingers scanning the seam. No panel. No manual override. From inside, another thud landed. Weaker this time. Fading.

He pressed his forehead to the door. "Hang on, Max."

Paul wedged his fingers into the seam and pulled, metal biting back with every inch. The groan that followed was deep and wrong, like something tearing that wasn't meant to open again. Armand joined him without a word. Together, they fought the doors open, arms straining, air rasping with effort.

A blast of trapped air spilled out—thick with heat and sweat. Max was inside, slumped against the wall, barely conscious.

"Max!" Paul shouted. A cough answered—faint, but real. Paul didn't wait. He wedged himself into the gap, reaching under his brother's arms. The balance was off.

Max didn't resist, didn't help.

"We've got you," Paul said, tightening his grip. Armand moved in from the other side, and they pulled

Max out of the elevator. Every inch was labour. His body didn't respond—slack, depleted. But his eyes stayed open, glassy, fixed.

The elevator doors closed with a mechanical thud. He dropped to his knees outside, lungs burning. His shirt clung to him, drenched.

"Thanks." His eyes flicked between them—drained, but aware. "Was starting to think you weren't coming."

Paul gave a dry chuckle. "We're Roys. We show up."

His demeanour was earnest, but it landed deeper than that. He saw someone ready to take his place, no conditions. That brought him back to a feeling he'd lost touch with.

Armand crouched, found his wrist, and finished pulling him up.

Max stood again, his brother doing most of the actual work.

"Can you walk?" asked Paul.

Max opened his mouth, then swayed. Paul grabbed his arm.

"That's a no," Paul half-joked.

They lifted him together. Max did what he could to help—while his body did its best to resist—but they got him upright. Paul on one side,

Armand on the other. He stood. Barely. But between them, he stood.

They were forced to stop briefly at a maintenance restroom. The door was scratched, the sign half-torn. Max felt the sting of shame, but didn't argue. He didn't have the strength to fake composure. Paul stood watch. Armand guided him inside. It wasn't delicate. Blood was wiped away. Sweat slipped down his face.

Max leaned into the sink, gathered himself, and let the water run. The overhead light buzzed—all clarity, no mercy. He met his reflection and winced.

Armand braced him, wiping the blood and grit. There was no blame in the gesture—only care. Max clenched his jaw, aware this was the closest thing to rest he'd get.

Back in the hallway, the pressure returned. The path ahead was long, and the situation worse than he'd thought. But he looked stable now—standing with help, relying on the two people who always showed up when it counted.

Armand repositioned his grip. "You're fading. Is this really worth burning yourself out for?"

The words rasped out of him: "People are dying. Harland's trying to bury it."

Paul didn't reply. His grip tightened, and his pace picked up.

They moved together without a word. Paul took on more of the effort. Armand did the same. Max didn't slip. He wasn't standing because he was strong. He was standing because he wouldn't stop. And they weren't helping him leave. They were helping him show up.

In a nearby boardroom, at the far end of the polished glass table, Reeves remained unaware that Max had escaped the elevator—or that he was already coming. His posture was exact: hands folded, back straight, every detail composed. Behind him, the mirrored wall returned his image: hands folded, back straight, every detail composed—the kind of order he never allowed to falter. The board was already seated. Unease pressed along the margins. Every member had seen the feeds. No one was here by accident.

Harland remained seated, spine straight.

"Thank you for assembling on such short notice." He watched their faces—waited for it. "You've all seen the breach. The hostage standoff at the Pearly Gates. This is the worst security failure Afterdeath has ever faced."

He glanced at the reports spread in front of him and looked up again. "Every second we hesitate, we lose control. Leadership must act."

A board member at the table tensed, about to speak—but Harland spoke first. "Maxime Roy is missing." He folded the report, then continued. "I've attempted contact," he said, folding his hands again. "No response. And in a crisis, the man at the helm does not vanish."

A low murmur rippled down the table. Harland allowed it. He didn't force agreement.

"We all respect what Max built," he said. His tone edged toward reluctant admiration. "But this company needs continuity. We need visibility. His absence exposes us at the worst possible time."

He waited, without playing to effect.

"For that reason, I believe it's time we discuss a leadership transition—for the sake of Afterdeath's stability, all of our executive power should be focused into one person. To keep us agile."

The mood didn't break—it bent, creeping in glances, in the reflexive straightening of backs and the tug of sleeves.

He made the pivot cleanly. "My role would be temporary. A stabilizing force during transition."

He met each pair of eyes in turn. "Afterdeath must project stability. To our investors. To the press. To the people inside. Right now, we can't afford to look fractured."

The partners around the table looked resigned. Marisol and a few others—those loyal to Max—traded glances, uncertain but watchful. Some gave the faintest signs of assent, more concession than conviction. The rest waited, postures rigid, as if any gesture might signal alignment before the outcome was certain.

The doors flew open, slammed back with a force that rattled the room. The impact echoed through the steel frame, drawing startled gasps from everyone seated at the table. Paul and Armand appeared on either side of Max, each with a firm grip on his arm.

The room went silent.

Max hung between them, drenched in sweat, but his spine was straight and his eyes were clear. He scanned the board without a word, eyes moving from one face to the next until they landed on Harland.

The energy in the room had collapsed. What had started to align, snapped back into place. Board members fidgeted in their seats, trading glances already rehearsing the fallout.

Harland spread his hands, patience carefully manufactured. "Max," he said smoothly, "We were about to vote on an emergency measure to grant all the boards power to me, during this time of—"

"Did you ask the panel to vote on attacking me and trapping me in an elevator, Harland?" He gave a short laugh, more reflex than release.

The boardroom of suits staggered at the words. The line between witness and participant had blurred. They were no longer watching from the sidelines. They were here to the jury.

The tension in Harland's voice cracked. "We face an existential threat. If we don't act now, the system will coll—"

"No. You engineered this breach. The hostages. The hackers. Every bit of blood is on your hands."

Panic briefly surfaced in a face accustomed to it, then vanished—replaced by a mask.

"That's a dangerous accusation," Harland said.

Some board members sat a little straighter, backs stiff with ambiguity—balancing between complicity and caution. Others turned to their screens—not to intervene, but to verify. Fingers scrolled, eyes darted, searching for language to match the moment. No one stood. But the ground beneath Harland's authority had started to slide.

Something clenched low in Max—deep, unignorable. It was the heaviness of all he'd hidden. Every decision, every failure, every fact he had hidden.

Paul moved. He reached into his jacket, pulled out a tablet, and placed it on the table.

"Maybe this will help." He nudged it toward Max.

Harland's hand twitched toward his own device—automatic, half-meant.

Paul had already clocked the move. "You won't be needing that."

Harland's hand stalled halfway to his pocket. That second was all Max needed.

He crouched low and collected the tablet without resistance.

Max had pulled the report earlier—trace code from a purged admin account, access privileges created and deleted within a ten-minute window. The ID trail pointed straight back to Harland. Worse, a separate log tied him to a closed-door meeting with OneKind exactly twelve hours before the breach. Two entries. Two facts. Not a full case—enough to strip the mask away. He sent it to the room.

The murmurs began again, but they weren't confused now—they were connecting. The glances that turned toward Harland weren't searching for leadership. They were searching for confirmation.

"You gave them your credentials," Max said, turning the display so the room could see it.

"You handed over Afterdeath's security architecture. You opened the door. You planned this breach."

A muscle at Harland's temple jumped, betraying the effort it took to keep his expression composed.

"Spare me the theatrics. You really thought I'd stand by while you wasted this company's potential?"

His thumb traced a small, restless circle against the table.

"You were so consumed with your legacy, Afterdeath didn't wait for you. I had to make all the hard decisions."

The murmurs thickened. Some withdrew back, others edged in, and a few finally looked at Harland like they were seeing the man beneath the polish—no longer mistaking him for the suit.

His expression didn't change—smug, absolute, immune to shame. "Before you start clinging to hope, listen closely. My safeguards go all the way down. Everything you've tried—wasted effort."

"Unless I personally shut them down," he added, eyes sweeping the room, "they'll wipe it all. Every sector. Every realm."

Max had braced for denial. Deflection. Maybe even a final appeal to optics. What he hadn't counted on was conviction. Harland wasn't dodging the accusation—he was trying to elevate it. To reframe sabotage as strategy. Treason as vision. The logic behind it wasn't slippery. It was sincere. And that—more than anything—was what broke the pattern.

He wasn't scrambling to protect himself. He was proud of what he'd done. As if razing both worlds was a necessary cruelty. As if history would sort out the rest. Genghis Khan in a business suit. A warlord of systems and scale. And maybe that was the worst part—not that Harland had lost touch with the time he lived in, but that Max had. Because in this room, the heat wasn't metaphor. It was momentum. And it was rising.

Harland went in for the kill. "And your little Lazarus side project?" he said, tilting his head. "Gone. Dismantled. Doesn't exist anymore." Harland studied him, hunting for fear, a crack, any proof he'd won.

"I know." Max said, gritting his teeth with all the force he wanted to strike Harland with.

"Your other side project. The Moreau girl, well you should know. I didn't plan for her to get involved."

Harland cleared his throat and straightened.

"But I'm damn sure glad she did. OneKind deserves a bonus don't you think."

With every word, Harland was inching out of the room, making his escape.

Armand didn't wait. He had spent the last few minutes melting into the background, moving into position. He closed the distance, seized Harland by the collar, and slammed him against the wall with a force forged from thousandfold days of labour. He wasn't letting go.

Harland barked a laugh—too loud, too thin. "You'll be dead before he is, old man. You know that, right?" The words came brittle, meant to wound—but fear cracked through anyway.

The first strike landed flat across Harland's face—no warning, no wind-up. Armand's open palm came backed by years of silence and one final verdict. The sound cracked through the boardroom like a misfired shot. Harland staggered, reeled—more insulted than injured.

The second blow came fast and close—knuckles tight, a compact right cross that snapped Harland's head sideways and sent him reeling.

He dropped to one knee, one hand catching the floor. Blood bloomed along his lip.

Harland clawed his way upright, expression warping. He lunged, low and reckless, fingers twisting into his jacket as he drove a knee toward Armand, trying to drop him by the hip.

Paul moved toward them.

Max tugged once at his sleeve. "Let him."

Armand grunted, off balance, but held. He turned with effort and drove his elbow into the joint of Harland's arm. He snarled and swung again, wild—a blind shot toward Armand's head.

Armand ducked under and closed the distance.

He moved like a man who'd worked fields and broken ribs—close quarters, no waste. One hand caught Harland by the collar. He yanked him close and drove a jab straight into his throat. No flourish. All muscle. The kind of strike that stopped things cold.

Harland dropped, jaw slack, limbs folding. Unconscious. Disarmed. The posture stripped away.

Armand stood over him, one hand braced on his thigh to stay upright. His breaths came ragged, but controlled. "Men like you never shut up."

A hush followed—shock, not silence.

Some stared at Harland's slumped body. Others stared at Armand. One or two had the presence of mind to check if Harland was alive. He was. Unfortunately.

Max closed the distance to stand at the head of the table. To be seen. He came to a full halt in Harland's collapsed eyeline. Conscious or not, the message would land.

"This board has seen the facts," Max said, his voice even but unmistakable. "You've seen the breach. The compromise. The cost."

He scanned the faces around the table. "I'm calling a vote."

He let the moment hold.

"All in favour of removing Harland Francis Reeves from his position—effective immediately?"

At "Francis," Marisol gave a short laugh she didn't mean to, and stifled it.

The vote began to form. Marisol's hand went up with the rest.

It wasn't all at once. Some slow. Some firm. But they rose.

"The ayes have it."

Max glanced down at the man who had tried to burn the future and call it vision.

"Harland Francis Reeves," he said, the weight of it deliberate, unflinching. "You're fired."

As if compelled by the charged atmosphere, the central screen activated. The Pearly Gates came into view—projected over the display: hostages huddled in fear, masked figures moving methodically. On the display, a gun pressed against Remy's head. The board stiffened as panic rippled through the room, surfacing in uneasy motion and darting glances.

Max kept his eyes on the footage.

"They're not asking for anything," he said. "This isn't about talking. It's about time. They're giving Harland a window. When they realize he's gone—"

"They'll unleash everything," Paul finished, stepping closer, the colour drained from his face.

Max bowed his head. When he lifted it, the answer was already there.

"We have to do what Harland feared most. I need to go in there, defend Afterdeath from the inside."

"But you heard him," said Paul. "Whatever method you had for visiting Afterdeath—Harland erased it. You think he was bluffing?"

"No. Well—yes, in part. But not about that."

"How—" Paul began.

Max interrupted, his voice calm but unshakable. "There's more than one way to access Afterdeath."

He could see it landing—slowly, but it was landing. "Everyone's gotta fall sometime. Figured I'd try for a controlled descent."

He let out a cough of a laugh—at the line, at himself. "One way or another, I was due."

Paul's grip on Max's arm tightened, his expression hardening. Armand, now composed, met his son's eyes with a look that carried more history than judgement. Neither asked for more—they understood what had been said.

Tension rooted him, body steeling for what was next.

"Alright," he said. "Let's go before I change my mind."

The showroom lights didn't so much as dim. Rows of Lazarus units stood like showroom coffins, lit for clients that would never come. Overhead, the branded loop kept running—Afterdeath™ – What Are You Doing After Death?—too late for irony.

Paul wedged the second cabinet into place, shoving until the metal groaned against the frame. Armand was already on the other side, bracing the opposite door with a bulk cart of boxed headsets and emergency medkits. It wouldn't keep the door closed forever.

Paul turned, the showroom's glare catching on the sweat at his brow. "What are you worried about coming through those doors—Harland's people?"

"I hadn't even thought of them to be honest with you." Max said as he continued to prepare. "I'm worried about the lawyers."

Paul blinked. "That's another joke, right?"

A single thud hit the reinforced door.

The corner of Paul's mouth twitched—either at the joke or the horror of it—but no sound followed.

Armand's eyes never left his son. "We've run out of time, haven't we?"

He met his father's eyes. "Yes. We have."

The second strike rattled the hinges. Max moved to the Lazarus unit.

He opened the side panel, entered the chamber, and began sealing the hatch by hand.

Paul hovered, unsure whether to intervene.

"You don't have to—"

"I do Paul," Max said. "We can't stall anymore. This is the only move I have left."

He pressed his palm flat against the inner surface of the tank door. A faint whine started in the base of the unit as the fluid began its rise, clear and cool, lapping at his feet like an incoming tide.

It came fast. In seconds, the liquid coiled around his calves, his thighs. As it climbed his torso, the nanites rushed in behind it—silent, ruthless. The first wave seized his spine. A bolt of heat roared through his torso, too fast to brace against.

His face twisted with the force as his muscles convulsed once. Again. His fists slammed once against the glass.

"I can't—" he tried, his voice pulled tight with strain. "Listen. I only have a few seconds."

"I should've been there," he said, eyes darting between them. "After Mom. I pulled away—and that wasn't fair. Not to either of you."

He spoke each word like it cost him—because it did. "You never owed me anything. But you showed up. Keep doing that—for each other."

Paul stood at the control panel, helpless, as the blue fluid blurred his brother's face behind the glass. Every part of him screamed to break protocol, to pull his brother out. But he knew he didn't know how to do that even if he wanted to.

Inside the tank, Max's expression tensed as a new wave hit. The nanites were past the surface now—crawling bone, rewriting marrow, unravelling muscle memory with microscopic violence. His neck jerked sideways before locking into place. A faint cry rose in his throat but died halfway out. His mouth opened, tried again. No sound. The fluid reached his neck.

He looked at them—Paul, Armand. There was fear in his eyes now, not of death, but of absence. Of not being there to help them through what came next. He tried to hold their gaze, but another ripple of pain tore through his spine and buckled him at the waist. His lips moved again, slower now. One phrase. Three words. Shaped, not said. I love you. It was all he had left.

The fluid touched his chin. His eyes fluttered. A tremor passed through his limbs, brief and total. The cables struck—temples, spine, palms. His body seized, mouth parting in one final exhale that never reached the surface. His skin had already begun to pale. He was suspended now—not in comfort, but in cessation.

Armand approached the tank. He placed one hand against the tank wall, fingers trembling where they met the glass. The blue light began to spread—a threaded signal tracing from panel to core, confirming what the room already knew.

Paul didn't move. His hands remained braced on the console, neck rigid, every muscle tensed against the flood inside him. The pounding on the barricade resumed, louder now, but further away somehow—irrelevant to the silence now binding the room.

Armand's mouth pressed shut for a long moment before he found the words. "Go finish this, son."

CHAPTER TWENTY ONE
KING'S GAMBIT

Max felt it before he saw it. His limbs moved freely, each joint smooth and responsive. He stood upright, regaining his balance mid-shift.

He'd woken in a meadow. Why was this familiar? He couldn't quite remember the details. The answer sat beyond total recall—like an iceberg, most of it was hidden from him. He'd never been here before—but he knew it all the same.

"Welcome, Maxime Roy. Please stand by—we are experiencing a momentary security breach." The mechanical voice felt familiar in a way he couldn't place. "I must ask you to remain here."

That's when it came back at once. Today. Yesterday. Tomorrow. Every reason that brought him here. The hostages. The breach. OneKind. Remy. Afterdeath. His death.

Focus struck like a switch thrown: not adrenaline, but alignment.

The meadow split ahead—clean. A line of light carved through the field, opening a corridor that hadn't been there before. Max moved at full stride. The corridor accepted him, light cresting his shoulders like a gate unlocking.

On the other side, the perimeter held firm, a red zone locked around the realm's core. There was no queue—only hostages and three armed users. People rarely volunteer for the frying pan.

The Pearly Gates marked the system's most fortified zone—its frame constructed by Harland Reeves himself, under the banner of intrusion prevention. But the deeper truth had become harder to ignore. This wasn't a security checkpoint. It was Harland's masterpiece. He'd built it to monitor passage, intercept patterns, weaponize entry itself. What he once called a firewall now looked like a funnel. And today proved it: Harland's long game wasn't made of vision—it was made of code. Endless, recursive, watching code.

Three black-clad OneKind soldiers held court.

The first—broad-shouldered, impatient, and by far the largest—adjusted his stance like someone waiting for permission to pull the trigger.

The second—a woman at the console—kept her hands mid-air, wrists locked. She wore her interface like armour, each scan a calculation, not a glance.

The third remained apart. No weapon raised. No signal offered. He tracked the hostages with the focus of someone counting fates, not bodies.

One by one, the proxies faced him. Their lenses came alive—each visor lighting in sequence as network protocol passed from one to the next. The name arrived like a verdict: MAXIME ROY.

Their comms caught a murmur—encrypted, clipped, not for his ears—but he heard the cadence of confirmation. A presence flagged. An identity resolved. Whoever had doubted was no longer in doubt.

By protocol, he should have been erased. No access. No authorization. No return path. And yet here he stood, accounted for.

The largest of the three—a brute with no sense for staging—lifted one hand, palm loose, gesture untrained. Either a question or a claim. "You're not supposed to be here."

Max kept his eyes on him. "Neither are you, if we're being honest."

A second voice came behind Max, circling him with a tricorder in her hands. "Scanning him."

Max registered the scan not as sound, but as a filament-thin charge threading through his marrow—clinical, inexorable, and utterly indifferent to his consent.

"You could at least buy a man dinner before peeling back his layers," Max said, deadpan.

It flowed through him—his heart, his lungs, even the fragmented, half-formed thoughts drifting on the periphery of consciousness—gathering data with deliberative, methodical precision. It wasn't attempting to understand him—only to confirm that every facet remained unaltered.

The result appeared above them—without preamble. DECEASED. Confirmation resolved before Max did. The air changed—tight, anticipatory. The hostages stiffened, their posture catching on something invisible.

The man they'd been built to destroy wasn't breathing anymore. Maybe they'd already figured out Harland wouldn't be joining them today. Max guessed their Plan A, B, and C—maybe everything through F—had gone out the window. Good. Because he didn't have a plan for what came next either. He had one last surprise. After that, he'd be a dead man.

They didn't lower their weapons. If anything, they held them tighter. The threat profile had recalibrated. Max was a ghost with a heartbeat. And ghosts weren't supposed to have access protocols.

He brushed at his lapel like it mattered. "I'm not what you're here for," he said. "You want money."

One scoffed.

"We have plenty," said the second.

The third didn't speak, but his head tilted as if listening for something deeper in the line.

Max stayed level. "No," he said. "You have whatever Harland told you you could have. I'm offering five hundred million."

A pause. The kind that lives in nerve and bandwidth.

"Lies," said one.

"Fabricated," the second added, flat.

The third cut in—"Verifying."

Max didn't stir. His hand flexed once—automatic, seeking something to hold. "Check the ledger," he said.

He didn't need the confirmation. One of them was already pulling the hash—standard protocol, probably her job. But the other two, both male, weren't verifying anything. They were watching him, trying to see the crack before it formed.

They weren't alone. These three were surface signals—fronts for something larger. Max could feel it now: a deeper quorum, layered behind them, dozens—maybe hundreds—tethered through burner relays, darknet threads, and buried chains. OneKind didn't show up solo. This wasn't performance. This was activation.

"You think we're that stupid?" the first one asked.

"I think you're smart enough to verify."

Another beat passed—the third OneKind goon looked up. "It's real."

"Half-chain. Verified signature. Origin node matches."

"You'll have it," Max said. "You do what I ask, and it's yours."

None of them moved. They stood in that half-second of disbelief that comes when the prize is too large, too easy, too perfectly placed.

"Fifty billion," the first echoed.

The second stared at him. "What's the real price?"

Max matched her stare. "That's the price."

They didn't lower their weapons. Their grips eased—barely. The kind of recalibration you make when the mission stops being about enforcement—and starts being about choice.

With a single tap, she initiated the transaction.

The moment the transaction cleared, it did more than move funds. It tripped a silent condition buried deep in the contract—a trigger Max had planted months ago. Not a kill switch. A signal. The ledger completed as expected, but underneath, something else activated—small, exact, and aimed outward.

A masked relay picked up the signal and passed it forward—first to a dead-drop server under Max's control, then out across encrypted lines. It reached inboxes and alert feeds from Cheltenham to Langley to Zurich. On paper, it read like a zero-day breach. In truth, it was bait—flagged, planted, and already being watched.

At the same time, the transaction carried something extra—disguised as a timestamp, harmless at first glance. But when the verifier's console processed it, the script embedded inside ran silently. One line was all it took. The query executed. Access followed.

It didn't need full access. It didn't need special permissions. All it took was for her console to open a single link—a planted request disguised as a refund. Hidden inside was a canary token, waiting to fire the moment it was touched. Her browser reached out, and in that instant, a small flaw let the signal slip through unmasked—like tossing a tracer into a tunnel and watching it bounce back. That was all it took. Her true address came through—location, OS, digital fingerprint.

Max exhaled through his nose, letting his shoulders fall a notch. One of the proxies—not the hacker, but the brute—twitched, head tilting like someone catching a glitch in his feed. The woman at the console froze mid-scan, eyes flicking to a secondary panel. A logout blip pulsed behind her—brief, unscheduled, unmistakable.

"That's one," Max said under his breath. No smile, but his mouth remembered the shape.

He lifted his gaze to the brute. "If you've got anyone left to warn, now would be the time."

No reply. No give in posture. But something behind their masks hesitated—tension not shown, but felt.

Beyond them, the breach kept crawling. The verifier's machine, now compromised, searched for shared relays, linked devices—anything still connected. Background tools. Team functions. Silent programmes meant to keep things running smoothly. It didn't act like ransomware—it didn't scream. It mapped. OneKind's internal web—spread across shadow networks and burner hardware—relied on shared systems. The virus knew exactly where to look.

Consoles blinked with strange behaviour. Logins broke. Commands failed mid-use. Old credentials reappeared in global records. Their cloak hadn't failed. It had been turned inside out.

At Fort Meade, the alert hit top priority. Max's beacon tripped a long-dormant fuse. Defences snapped awake. European scrubbing teams activated. Zurich's archive logs unlocked. They'd been waiting.

Interpol didn't send agents—they sent reflections. IPs unmasked. Transaction trails replayed in real time. Even the anonymity layers buckled. Every endpoint OneKind had touched lit up under machine scrutiny. Dead zones came alive.

And it all started with a hash. A simple string—no longer than a fingerprint—meant not to destroy OneKind, but to expose them. Max didn't need to win the war. He needed daylight.

Back inside the Pearly Gates, none of the proxies knew what they'd unleashed. But they felt it. Sync slipped. Weapons re-armed themselves without command. The hum of coordination—the invisible rhythm of a hive with purpose—shuddered and stalled. The swarm stood. But the unity was breaking down.

He watched as Alan and Remy moved toward the portal—a jagged opening where Remy's earlier code had forced the perimeter to break. One by one, the hostages stepped through, crossing into relative safety.

Remy halted, fists clenched, her arms locked like she might snap. Blame coursed through her—more than Harland, more than the OneKind stooges—she held herself responsible.

She tried to meet his eyes across the chaotic scene. Others passed her and crossed through the portal as she waited for the moment he saw her.

"Max—" His name, spoken low, more reflex than address—closer to clearing her throat than calling out. And yet, somehow, it reached him.

He shook his head before she could make another attempt. Pain coiled around his ribs, pressing behind his eyes. His mouth lifted—thin, reflexive, human. A shape meant for her, even if it didn't reach his eyes.

She needed to go.

"Kiddo," he shouted. "You did great."

Her defiance had nearly dismantled them. But she carried the blame like it belonged to her. He recognized that burden—he carried it too.

Remy couldn't answer. Her posture didn't change, but everything beneath it locked into place. It was the part of her that understood what it meant to leave without a word.

Alan reached for her arm. "Remy."

She let him hold on. Didn't move, either.

"Remy," Max said again, forcing his voice not to shake. "We need to hold their attention. That's the trade. Time for them—for you."

Her throat tightened. She couldn't look away.

Alan gave her arm the faintest tug. "We have to go now, Remy."

She turned toward the portal—not quickly, but with purpose. Her gaze met Max's one last time. Alan guided her through.

They were gone. That made the next part tolerable. He stood as the portal collapsed inward. They were safe—briefly. And for a single, hard-won second, he believed it.

Beyond the barrier, OneKind was already adapting. New portals emerged. New forms stepped through—more builds, heavier payloads. What had been a mere hive of minds was becoming a swarm of brutes—the kind that came when predators sensed blood and expected no challenge. He tracked the escalation, eyes narrowing with calculation. The others remained focused on their formation, blind to the change already underway.

He saw it first. The female proxy hacker stopped mid-step, as if something unseen had pulled her out of sync. The large one regripped their rifle instinctively. The unspoken leader didn't flinch. It wasn't caution. It was calculus—stillness held until consequence clarified. The kind of disruption that didn't come from noise, but from doubt.

The comms chimed in, confirming what he already sensed. "We've been pinged. All of us."

No one spoke. They didn't have to. It was already spreading through them. This wasn't panic yet, but the early signs of structural collapse.

He tracked the fracture as it spread. The brute pivoted, visor stuttering as the feed flooded with updates. The verifier glanced up from her console. The third stayed inert—calm past reason.

Max straightened his jacket—an automatic gesture, devoid of artifice—and rose. He had momentarily forgotten he wasn't weak anymore. He had cut cancer right out of the picture. That made the cost bearable. Now, with Remy gone, he was ready for whatever they had planned for him.

The second turned to him, visor unreadable. "What did you do?"

He didn't gloat, but he met her gaze.

The third spoke up, his tone tinted with resentment. "You rendered yourself useless."

Max fixed his attention beyond them. "That's the thing about people. We're all useless eventually. The trick is knowing when to go out swinging."

Through the closing breach, he saw the portal's flare—confirmation the last hostage had made it through. His mouth twitched toward relief—but it didn't quite make it.

"It's over. Do what you will, and then take your chances and run for it. You never know, they might not find you."

The third one laughed. The others followed. It took them a beat to decide how best to mock him. "You moved the clock up, Roy—but the event hasn't changed. Remy Moreau found us once. Now we return the favour. The signal loss you triggered cleared out dead weight. What remains is core. Focused. Unrestricted. We'll comb Afterdeath, top to stack—no safe realms, no exit loops. Everything burns until she breaks. Let them come. We've already uploaded our last words." The laugh came back—smooth, unbothered. In a heartbeat it fractured outward, multiplying into layered feedback—fractured, inhuman, self-assured.

Almost in unison, the words landed: "Now we hunt." A verdict, not a threat. And it told him everything. The deal had never been about Max. He was a placeholder, a stalling measure, a way to let the hostages walk away safely. Remy Moreau—that was the real hunt. The one they'd been waiting for.

And now, Max saw it too clearly. Maybe all he'd done was buy her time. Maybe that was all he'd ever sold—before, during, and even after death. Time. Leased, not owned. OneKind weren't dispersing. They were digging in. Preparing. His body protested as he forced himself upright—joints on fire, fingers twitching from strain—but the words came with difficulty. "No."

The third's visor turned toward him, its dark lens unreadable. Focused and locked—every line of code ready to strike.

Max met its stare. "That wasn't the deal."

There was no face to read, but their body didn't tense up, or show fear. It closed. It reached.

"We don't make deals with data packets."

The rifle struck hard—no warning. Pain split his skull—colour, sound, light scattering in its wake.

CHAPTER TWENTY TWO
STACK OVERFLOW

They stepped out of the portal and into fluorescent light and order. Everstacks opened before them—wide, spotless, indifferent. The glass doors parted without fanfare, accepting the survivors like any other foot traffic. Fluorescent light pooled beyond the store entrance and the air smelled faintly of lemon cleaner and fatigue.

Remy moved because there was nowhere else to go. Motion, not direction. But this place—this absurd shrine of aisles—sparked the first real plan.

Around them, the illusion of normalcy continued unbroken. Shoppers moved with the unspoken choreography of habit, sheltered from the world beyond the walls. Some moved in trance. Others fixated on trivial decisions—as if the right jar of coffee might keep the world from falling apart. A man lowered himself into a recliner while his daughter circled nearby.

Remy scanned the faces in front of her, reading the flicks of uncertainty they didn't speak aloud.

"I need your attention please. I know you're scared—I am too," Remy said. "If you stay here, near me, you're easy targets. You need to go back to your personal realms and hide. I can't promise safety for anyone who follows."

They didn't speak. Remy couldn't tell if they were weighing her words—or trying to imagine a version of this where she wasn't asking them to leave. Either way, not a soul moved.

"You didn't choose this war. But you can choose not to die, again, in it. Retreat—until the storm passes."

She didn't falter— she couldn't, even as fear kept pace behind her.

Beatrice stepped toward the group. "Barry meant a lot to me. I know not everyone saw him the same way, but I believe his life—and the lives of everyone who died here today—mattered."

She looked around. "We're standing here because of them. Because we won't let what happened to them happen to Max. Or anyone else."

The survivors absorbed it as they looked at each other.

Alan spoke up first, decisive. "Remy, you already put yourself on the line for us," he said, studying her face. "We can all see it—you're not done. But this isn't yours to carry alone. We fight with you. For Barry. For Max. For the others."

Remy squared her stance and looked ahead. "Okay. Okay. Here's the plan: we gather at the Pillow Aisle—defend it, survive together. That's how we save Max. And the system."

From the back, Franklin finally said what everyone had been thinking. "Pillows?"

Remy met it head-on. "Yeah. Pillows. Trust me—it's stranger than you'd expect, and we can make that work to our advantage."

That pulled a few eyebrows—but mostly, it got them listening. The confusion didn't vanish, but it cracked—urgency pulling them into motion.

Jenna took command.

"You heard her. That's the plan. Grab weapons along the way, supplies—whatever you've got. Let's move."

The survivors stirred—bags slung or dragged, hands snatching anything within reach. Near the entrance, a few lifted flashlights, collapsible crates, or pet supplies stacked by the checkout—plastic scoops, leash hooks, bins of hand warmers left partly ajar. Others pressed forward, tearing battery packs and folding canes off the impulse racks.

"I'll handle the King," Remy said as she pulled Jenna to the side. "But I need you to find someone named Jeff.

Probably near the bean bags—or wherever looks like a hideout made from store stock. If you find him, tell him—he's our only hope."

Jenna's brow lifted. "Jeff?"

Remy didn't slow. "I think he's a rebel, like the rest of us. OneKind's gotta be anathema to someone like that—has to be, right? All I know is, Bob and Jeff have been at war over something for ages. But if you tell him what's at stake, maybe he listens. If not—"

She opened a debug panel, keyed in a line of code, and materialized a PB Max bar into Jenna's hand. It flashed once in her palm before stabilizing.

"—give him this. I don't know why, but I think it matters."

Their eyes met for a heartbeat. Jenna turned to go, the doubt showing in how long she lingered. She didn't know if it would work—but she knew Remy needed her to try.

Alan, Ruth, Franklin, Beatrice, and the others scattered, grabbing whatever they could—tools, sticks, lawn darts—as Remy plunged ahead, drawing the others into Everstacks' labyrinth.

Shelves of forgotten inventory walled them in, the aisles winding in every direction. Footsteps pounded against tile. Clothing racks trembled in their wake. Others joined them—faces Remy had seen before, even if she didn't know their names. A woman in a weathered denim jacket yanked a telescoping curtain rod from a clearance bin, extending it with a snap before falling in beside Ruth. Further down, Franklin jerked his chin toward a man in a faded Blockbuster vest who hefted a cast-iron tortilla press like a war mallet. Beatrice moved with silent fluency, passing through like someone assembling a unit from memory—pointing one man to a fire poker display, handing a garden weeder to another. The group kept growing—by Home Organization, they were twice their number.

As Remy ran, she swiped at her console and opened Everstacks PA system. A chime rang overhead—the kind of sound usually reserved for daily deals and flash sales.

"Attention shoppers," Remy said, projecting her best middle school principal. "There's no flash sale. No manager's special. But there is a hostile force inbound—one that doesn't think we belong here." The overheads carried her words, and for a beat, nothing responded.

"OneKind is coming. If you're staying to fight, meet us beneath the banner of pillows—where the mattresses stack like battlements and duvet covers hang like flags. That's where we draw the line."

A few heads snapped up. Others froze in the aisles, fingers tightening around half-filled baskets and improvised weapons. The message had landed—not loud, but clear. It threaded through the overheads like a recall notice from a world that no longer applied. Some turned toward the sound. Some toward Remy. And some didn't move at all, but stood straighter, as if the words had found them where they already were.

Doubt thinned. Focus took hold. They weren't soldiers, and she wasn't a commander—but somehow, the floor beneath them stopped feeling like a store. It started feeling like the place where a line would be drawn. And Remy had drawn it.

"Keep moving!" she called. "Max doesn't have much time."

They swept deeper into Everstacks. It began as a blur. Shapes stacked in fuzzy columns, a palette of cotton and foam that didn't make sense until it did. Remy slowed without meaning to. It wasn't a store display. It wasn't even a refuge. It was a statement—deliberate, defensive, absurd, and proud. A castle built of sleep.

When they reached their destination, it was undeniable. Cushions rose in dense, layered walls—memory foam and down packed tight, arranged with intent. A barricade, not a display.

She spotted the changes immediately. Since her last visit, the defences had doubled: quilts hung from every corner, tied down as if to hold off a siege. Pallets, wrapped in blankets, formed a wide, arched entry. Decorative pillows had been strapped together into thick, reinforced slabs—less for comfort, more for protection. The whole structure had the latent force of something designed with care and built to last. It had outgrown being a mere hideout. It had become a fortress—Bob's last defence, built from thread count and sheer conviction, shaped over years until no part of it gave way.

Remy stopped short. Not because it was funny—it wasn't—but because it struck her. This was devotion in cloth form. A kingdom built from disregard, and yet it felt exactly as it should. Survivors pressed forward, urgency dissolving the last traces of doubt. Overhead, signs for Bedding, Home Essentials, and Clearance glowed with disconcerting normalcy, their bright letters standing in eerie opposition to the tension thickening the air.

Then she saw it—Bob's fortress, impossible and certain. Beyond a rough blockade, the stronghold spread across the aisle, its walls cleverly reconfigured into chokepoints, weighted blankets draped as makeshift ramparts, and an assortment of salvaged tools repurposed into a practical—if unorthodox—arsenal. It was no half-hearted structure.

Bob had shaped it with care and urgency, fashioning a defence that, despite its origins, offered the best chance for safety. Those who arrived next halted only briefly, letting the scene register: a refuge of blankets and barriers conceived from what the store had to offer. Some wore guarded acceptance on their faces, others a fierce resolve. It might have been strange to outsiders, but here, it was hope.

The "kingdom" held the centre of Home and Bedding, boxed in by Aisles 16 through 20. The chokepoint narrowed between mattress displays.

Near the entrance, Bob was already locked in a tense exchange with the latest arrivals, hands slicing the air for emphasis. His voice cut through the din. "That's far enough!" He spotted Remy approaching and scowled. "Dame Moreau, now's not a good time—"

Remy dropped into a sweeping, theatrical bow, one arm crossing her midsection with practised flair. "Oh, great and sovereign King Bob, keeper of the realm, defender of the plush and the weary, steward of these hallowed aisles." She rose to meet his eyes. "A dire threat approaches your borders. We come seeking safe passage within your walls."

Bob's scowl twitched, stuck between refusal and retreat.

Remy didn't give him the chance to decide.

"This isn't a scuffle, not a minor disturbance. What's coming will wipe it all—your fortress, your name, your claim to this place."

She straightened, her words plain. "We need your protection. And we're prepared to stand with you."

His scowl relented—barely. He squared his shoulders, setting them like a monarch shrugging into armour—more solemn than proud, steeling himself against the storm he'd never wished to face, yet refused to turn from—and dipped his chin in solemn assent.

"Then enter, Dame Moreau," he declared, sweeping a dramatic arm toward the pillow-gated entrance. "And may our enemies know discomfort."

Without a word, he motioned the survivors through the fortified gate—body pillows bound with duct tape, reinforced by conviction.

Inside, the room buzzed with urgency. People improvised with a kind of tactical grace, turning whatever they could find into something useful. One wrapped oven mitts around their forearms, bracing for impact. Another rolled a yoga mat into a tight cylinder and swung it experimentally, checking balance and reach. Blankets were draped like capes and pinned in place—more shield than comfort. A small group clustered around a homemade catapult at the rear—rigging the tension, fixing straps, bracing the frame.

Remy surveyed the chaos, her mind already spinning three moves ahead. Bob stepped closer. "Level with me—how bad are we talking?"

For an instant, Remy considered giving him the straight explanation: infiltration tactics, unyielding attackers, no margin for error. She answered plainly—then remembered who she was talking to—a man who saw the world in terms of plush forts and valiant cushion battles. Conventional logic might bounce right off him. Fine. She could speak his language.

"It's OneKind," she said bluntly. "Hackers who think none of us belong here—that we shouldn't exist at all. They were trouble before, but in this realm, they're worse. An army of grim reapers, ready to sweep this place bare."

Bob didn't move. He crossed his arms, expression flat. "Reminds me of when the Bean Baggers tried to siege the Leaning Tower of Sealy. Lost three pillows, two beanbags, and a sense of invincibility that day. After that, nobody underestimated a strong defence."

Remy swallowed a groan—of course he was in character. She inhaled and angled her tone to match his logic. "Bob," she said, trying to meet him halfway, "most of them don't even own chairs."

He visibly stalled, as though the phrase short-circuited his soul.

"Forget comfort," she continued. "No resting, no sitting. They're efficiency fanatics: standing desks everywhere, no pillows allowed."

She squared up beside him, speaking as though describing an ancient foe. "If they show up, they'll take your kingdom—and your right to sit whenever you want."

A beat passed, then Bob's whole demeanour locked into place. His expression hardened as he whirled around, barking fresh orders with redoubled urgency. "Reinforce those pillow walls! Triple layer—I want them thick enough to stop a freight train!"

A rustle of frantic motion rippled through the fortress as survivors leapt to obey. Bob stormed toward the barricades, gesturing wildly. "Find the heaviest blanket we have—if we fall, an enemy falls with us!"

Remy watched as the fortress sprang into motion around her, Bob rallying what he now saw as his troops with the grim determination of a man who had only now realized the true enemy. The entrance gate—a sliding barrier of duct-taped body pillows—was hastily reinforced, locking into place.

The defenders moved like they meant it—focused, fast, and without waste. Oven mitts were pulled tight over forearms, yoga mats slung across backs like jury-rigged padding. It wasn't elegant, but it was scrappy.

The first signs weren't loud—boots echoing on damp ground, dust unsettled in the air. It came, like the crack of a whip: a wave of black-clad soldiers, rushing toward them in flawless formation. They were like shadows made flesh—dark, uniform, relentless.

Franklin's voice cut through the roar, commanding. "Hold the line!" he barked, and the defenders snapped into position.

Beatrice, her eyes steely with purpose, reinforced the front with a hasty barricade of fire extinguishers and crates—anything they could get their hands on.

The defenders in the front took the brunt of the assault, their padded-together armour taking the first hits. The force of the first impact reverberated through the barricades, but Franklin stood firm, a rock in the surging tide.

The enemy pressed forward in unbroken ranks, testing the walls, but their advance buckled as the defenders, rallied as they were, didn't give an inch.

The first wave of OneKind proxy soldiers slammed into the front line, their momentum stopped dead. Bob's newfound force used this fault line to attack with everything they had.

In seconds, OneKind's vanguard was overwhelmed.

The troops guarding the chokepoint shoved back, boots scraping against the tile, while Beatrice bellowed orders, moving like a cyclone of urgency, directing fire and positioning with field-honed precision. It wasn't beautiful—it was raw, a brutal ballet of anticipation and speed.

Remy stood in the rear, watching the chaos unfold with tactical precision. The numbers scrolled by quickly, processing data, but all she saw were bodies. Hundreds of them, like a mass of shadows converging on a single point. The front line cracked under pressure, the defenders rallying each time the OneKind ranks pushed with renewed force. Each time they broke formation, the defenders gained ground, and Remy felt the strength of their unity reverberating through the code itself.

The chokepoint became a grinder—a meat grinder—and the defenders had the leverage. But Remy knew this wouldn't last. The second wave would come harder, faster. They had time—precious seconds. And that was all they needed.

Bob spotted a cluster of idle defenders. Instead of barking orders, he switched tactics—lobbing pillows like sacred weapons.

"They're not filled with fluff," he muttered. "Gravel, loose batteries, anything with heft."

The barrage transformed chaos into drive. Some rushed to reinforce the defensive barriers. Others sprinted for the chokepoint, swinging their improvised weapons with grim conviction. He kept slinging.

Remy tracked it all—her focus fractured; too many variables. She sat cross-legged, entirely intent on taking it all in through her senses, devices, and keyboard wizardry. The floor gave a small jolt. The air changed—slight, but unmistakable. Shadows crowded in from every entrance—black-clad figures moving in near-lockstep, barely short of seamless. The front line stopped in unison—movement honed to instinct, timing weaponized. More flooded in behind them, knocking over shelves and clearing paths as they advanced. This wasn't chaos—it was execution in motion.

Alan moved beside her, grip tightening on the fire extinguisher. "That's—a lot."

"We can do this. Stick together!" Franklin shouted.

Remy didn't answer. Her focus narrowed. Data streamed across her vision, unreadable to anyone else. The numbers doubled, then tripled—too many to track. OneKind hadn't sent operatives. They'd sent Jacobs. Hundreds of them.

The pillow braced solid in her arms. Decoder Girl locked into her decoder stance—feet planted, spine aligned, breath set like a cipher key. Built not to block, but to read. To register. To rewrite. She didn't brace for impact. She was the impact.

She closed her eyes. Fingers met the keyboard in practised sequence, each keystroke echoing hours spent beneath the golden tree. This was her rig—aligned to her reflexes, structured by her intent. The connection shuddered before stabilizing. The interface locked. The field tilted.

Her training unfolded in the In-Between Library, where time bent and silence offered answers to those who waited. She learned the rhythm of the codefield—its hesitations, its tendencies, its tells. She watched it fail and reform, fall apart and reassemble, until failure became predictable.

Now the code shifted with that same pattern: imperfect, uneven, but responsive. And listening.

They moved into place without speaking—bodies honed, nerves strung like tripwire. Knuckles whitened around crowbars and repurposed yoga mats, the ragged armour of oven mitts and pinned blankets pulling tight against bodies braced for impact. Bodies shifted into position, braced, eyes fixed on the aisle's mouth—where the first silhouettes would emerge. Tension pressed in from every side.

Franklin inched nearer to Beatrice, his jaw set like a locked dial, tension coiled like the moment before thunder. Ruth realigned her grasp on mop turned bo-staff, finding balance in its heft. Alan stood beside Remy, held in the way of someone who had decided to stay. They weren't trained soldiers. But the ground beneath them had been claimed. And they would not step back.

Black-clad figures spread in synchronized formation—helmets low, gear stripped of insignia. Some carried sleek rifles slung low on their armour; others gripped compact shields or lethal batons. They weren't uniform, but they moved like parts of the same machine.

Remy registered it instantly: this wasn't a contest—it was a reckoning. They'd brought knives to a gunfight, willpower to a machine war.

Bob's voice rang out, fierce and unshakable. "Make your stand! They can take the shelves, the walls—but not our restock!"

Remy anchored her stance, and the world aligned around it. Lines she'd followed without knowing clicked into formation. Every body, every weapon, every bead of sweat rendered. She saw the formation before it broke. Heavier weapons braced at the front, speed units peeling to the flanks, every movement drilled, executed without slack.

Simultaneously, the side gate buckled under pressure as more figures poured through, their gear flashing dully under the fluorescent lights.

Remy matched their advance head-on. Alan anticipated the path of the charge, extinguisher raised in both hands.

The lead attacker lunged, and Alan met him with a sharp swing that struck true. The body dissolved before it could fall. Alan exhaled once, reset his grip, readying for the next.

Ruth moved a heartbeat behind him, calm in motion. An enemy rushed low, blade gleaming, but she stepped into his path, hooked his ankle mid-lunge, and levelled him in one fluid motion.

Further down the line, Franklin kept close to Beatrice without crowding her, dropping an enemy with a calculated strike. Beatrice's weapon jammed mid-swing, she cast it aside, seized a metal hook from the wreckage, and continued, relentless.

Remy saw the break in formation before it hit. The improvised catapult slammed outward, hurling a dense pillow straight into the mass. The projectile hit hard, low and spinning, scattering the first Jacobs into bursts of light and static. For a second, the charge reeled—shaken, and from that break, the tide turned.

"Every shot counts," Bob said, repositioning a heavy pillow without turning from the fight.

She pressed deeper into the current, her awareness contracting to points of pressure and flow. Every step mattered. Every gap in the line burned straight through her vision.

The initial waves had been measured—now the flood came unchecked. OneKind bodies continued crowding, now pouring from side corridors, the mass of them spreading wider, until the defenders' positions strained against sheer math.

She marked it coldly—where Franklin anchored a slipping line, where Ruth absorbed a charge with brutal economy, where Bob's vanguard refused to give an inch. For every one they dropped, three more closed in.

The tremor hit with a clarity her body registered faster than thought. Weighted blankets and duct-taped barriers gave way with a groan, snapping loose like a muscle torn past recovery. The breach tore open fast. The handful of survivors nearby didn't stand a chance—shadows broke over them, swift and merciless, leaving bodies crumpled where the defences had once held. Remy marked the loss, recalibrating without time to grieve. The numbers mattered. The gaps mattered. Feeling the wrong thing now would get them all killed.

The defenders compressed instinctively, folding toward the stronger points of the barricade. Beatrice moved with raw force, every strike buying them seconds they couldn't spare. Alan dropped another operative with a hard arc of the extinguisher.

Remy registered everything—tracking vectors, anticipating failures, patching wounds in the defence as fast as her mind could process them. It was not elegant. It was survival straining against inevitability.

She dug in, but the code behind it frayed—patterns destabilizing, currents unravelling. She could feel the tension in her calves, in her spine.

Her digital view wasn't built to convey this much chaos at once.

Too many bodies, too many breaches, too much unsynced noise between her vision and the world. Small corrections slipped through her hands before she could finish them. One breach widened, another split off its axis.

She tried to send a command through the net—to pull the defenders tighter—but the signal buckled, bleeding static into her sight. Remy's grasp on the battlefield cracked.

Out of the storm, a figure snapped through the line. He moved faster than the current, faster than her tracking allowed—all intent, no warning. Remy barely registered him before impact. A short spear drove straight toward her ribs, cutting her straight out of focus. Pain lanced through her side. No time for thought, no code to call on. The world snapped tight and immediate—blood, bone, spit. She staggered back, half-blind, trying to brace for a second strike she couldn't yet see coming.

Remy pivoted instinctively, the pain in her shoulder white and tight. The hacker pressed in, relentless, switching angles faster than she could predict. His blade glanced off her forearm guard, carving a shallow line she barely registered. She gave ground in short, braced steps, refusing to break her concentration. When he lunged again, she trapped his wrist with both hands and twisted, using his own momentum to wrench him off balance—but he slipped free.

They circled, quick and brutal. Remy struck low, aiming for the knee, but he deflected with a pivot and answered with a rising elbow that clipped her temple.

Stars burst. She stumbled, slammed into a shelving unit, and forced herself upright before he could close the gap. Every inch felt carved from stone. Her muscles screamed.

She met him halfway, low and off-centre, and drove her knee into his groin with everything she had left. They crashed back toward the centre of the aisle, locked in a dead heat.

He recovered first, blade flashing up for the kill—but the strike never landed.

From the flank, a heavy bean bag—overstuffed with batteries and loose metal—smashed into him with a crack that folded his body mid-step. He dropped without ceremony, his form collapsing into static before it hit the ground. Remy turned, searching for the source.

They crested the fallen shelf in formation—seven shadows against the warm retail glow, their silhouettes sharpened by firelight and foam. The Bean Baggers. Not rumour. Not myth. Real. Ready.

Their leader, Jeff, moved like someone who'd never known comfort. His frame broad but tired, his stance carved from exhaustion and stubborn refusal. A long seam ran down the leg of his cargo pants, patched with duct tape and a stitched-in receipt. His jacket was military surplus—dyed sun-fade orange, layered with black marker glyphs and phrases that read like protest poetry. Stay seated. No kings. Rest is a right.

His boots didn't match. One was steel-toed. The other, strapped with floor mats. He wore a bandolier packed not with ammo, but energy drink canisters and spare batteries. A cracked visor hung around his neck, never worn. His face was weathered, eyes narrowed by years of fluorescent war.

At his flank, Jenna kept pace—her hair tied back with zip ties, face streaked with smudged eyeliner and effort. A duffel bag rode high on her back, its zipper half-split from weight alone. Her armour was whatever had held: a yoga mat pinned over one shoulder, elbow pads from a forgotten sports section, knee guards strapped on with bungee cords. She moved like someone who had learned to run while already bleeding.

Behind them, the rest of the Bean Baggers.

Bagger One wore a child's superhero cape, stained and re-stitched into a scarf. His weapon: a reinforced grabber tool, the industrial kind, its jaws scorched black from overuse.

Bagger Two had a rolling laundry basket welded to her back like a personal gear crate—bean bags poking out like munitions. Her gloves were oven mitts sewn over fingerless gloves. Her left ear was taped to her comms unit.

Bagger Three walked barefoot, toes taped individually. She carried a mop handle tipped with a steak knife. She said nothing.

Bagger Four wore no clear armour, only dozens of barcode tattoos. His vest stitched with one rule: NO RETURNS TODAY.

Bagger Five was oldest—bald, wrapped in a beach towel printed with a flamingo. His weapon was a croquet mallet wrapped in spiked zip ties, which he wielded with the grim serenity of a priest.

They didn't shout. They didn't pose. Their choices were already made.

They moved like insurgents of the absurd, forged in too many fights in a war no one else acknowledged—fighting not for ideology, but for the right to exist unmocked in a system that made a joke of them.

"What keeps us standing?" Jeff called.

"We take the hits," the group answered with conviction.

"And what comes next?"

"We come back harder." Jenna's voice came in a half-beat behind the Baggers' chorus.

Jeff and the Baggers closed in—pressing the line, firing from range, lifting the defenders at the gate.

Remy turned toward Bob. "They're respawning," she said. "Every time we knock them down, they learn faster." Bob's expression darkened, but he didn't argue.

Remy dropped herself back into code, centring herself in the storm. She pressed deeper—past pain, past noise—into the underlying currents of the fight. The tree's consciousness flared inside her, tuning the field into cleaner contrast. She could see more now—how the OneKind army moved, how each fracture widened, how the pattern of survival fractured and patched itself in seconds.

Near the gap, the Bean Baggers fought with ruthless aggression. Jeff moved like a man born to battle—angles efficient, strikes certain—his battered frame finding leverage where others saw chaos. A wild, stubborn fury shaping his every shove, every desperate reinforcement jammed into place.

Jenna danced through the gap he created, light on her feet despite the blood matting her sleeve, her staff cutting hard, relentless lines through the black-clad ranks. Bean bags, loaded with baggage, flew in brutal arcs—thudding into helmets, cracking ribs, carving space the enemy struggled to reclaim. There was a beat where the field bent around them—Remy amplifying every decision, slowing every critical strike to its purest frame.

But even at the height of clarity, she could not see it all. Beyond Jenna's edge, another wall caved, spilling debris and drawing defenders thin across too many fronts. A fresh column of shadow-dressed terrorists flooded the breach, faster than her pulse could track.

Remy compensated, but the tilt had already begun. For every enemy knocked down, another rose faster. She could feel the attrition taking root—a slow bleed they could not stop. And somewhere inside her overdrawn vision, the blind spot grew.

The strike came not from the front, but from the collapsed side—a flash of movement, blade-first, before warning could register. Jenna turned, staff mid-lift—but a beat too late. The blade severed her arm mid-turn—fast and final.

For a breathless second, everything stopped—Jenna's body realising what was gone. Her arm ended at the forearm, blood spraying from the torn edge into the white overhead.

She staggered back, choking on sound, knees giving as she grasped for what was already gone. Remy registered the loss, but not in time to prevent it. The sight scrambled her focus—lines dropped, nodes went dark. Her vision fractured into raw instinct, too slow to fix anything, too fast to fully feel it.

Bob caught Jenna before she hit the floor, the impact jolting through him. Jeff was already there, taking the other side, his face set grim and pale. Between them, they hauled her away from the crush of bodies—back toward the centre, where Remy stood ready, hands clenched in urgency. Bob braced himself against the wall, blood smearing his sleeve, every muscle drawn tight.

"Thank you for coming, Brother," he said, voice rough but proud. "After this, we parley—as kings should."

Jeff gave a firm tilt of his head. "We should have done so long ago."

They clasped forearms—tight, unflinching—the ancient grip of brother-warriors who had fought through a thousand imagined fields and one real one. For once, it wasn't theatre. It was truth.

Remy took it in from the wreckage—what was left of the pillow fortress now scattered and torn. The defenders were worn down to their last reserves. The opposition pressed in—rebuilt bodies launching without pause, undeterred by damage or delay. Nothing had changed. The fight kept looping, brutal and exact.

Remy dropped deeper into the current, plunging past anything the underlay had been built to contain. The world around her slowed—halting, fragmented, but usable. She could see the slight coiling before bodies moved, the fine fractures in resolve before attacks formed. She matched the tempo of the battle, locking tighter with every second she stole. Her mind balanced at the edge of something massive, and for now, did not tip.

Bob and Jeff moved as one. Jeff hurled another dense bean bag overhead; Bob snatched it mid-arc without looking and hurled it like a cannon shot, breaking two OneKind heavies out of formation.

Franklin charged in low, wielding a broken shelf bracket like a hammer, clearing a path through the onslaught.

Alan closed ranks around Ruth, moving faster than sight could follow—dropping one hacker, then another, precision without waste.

Remy widened her perception further, stretching each second into what felt like entire minutes. Around her, the defenders fought not with control, but with the kind of raw refusal that could break better armies.

A Bean Bagger near the outer wall was cut down—blade buried deep in his gut and twisted once. He crumpled instantly, gone before help could reach him.

The gap he left yawned wider, and Ruth, trying to close it, took a blow to the side that dropped her to one knee. The blow that came next went right through her.

Ruth paused, her body slid, and she fell out of sight.

Alan turned immediately. He was moving before his eyes could take it all in—crossing the distance like a tether had snapped taut.

Beatrice saw it too. Her jaw clenched, and for a split second, her next strike landed too hard—more rage than follow-through. She pivoted to cover Ruth's flank, her expression flat with focused fury.

But it was Bob's face that changed most. He saw Ruth from across the battered aisle, arm raised for the next throw—and broke stride. Transfixed on the sight of Alan tending to Ruth, and others rallying to their side. The chaos narrowed around that gap, and the absurd kingdom he'd built felt less like a joke and more like a debt.

Remy registered the fall, the fallout, while trying to glimpse what came next. It wasn't fatal. Not yet. But the pattern around Ruth was destabilizing in a way Remy had never seen before. She flagged it, trusted Alan and returned her mind to the battlefield.

Ruth tried to rise, teeth clenched, bracing against the shelf for balance. Her body failed her, but her grip didn't—one hand clutched the broom, the other found Alan's arm as he helped her beyond the front line.

Alan reached her first, pulled her in, and didn't let go. Beatrice moved beside them, guarding with a raw, defiant intent. Bob didn't break rank—but his next throw hit harder. Sharper. Like he'd reclaimed why he built it in the first place.

He flanked wide, dropping three attackers in swift succession with bean bags packed heavy enough to crack bone.

Franklin rallied Beatrice and the others into a tighter knot, forcing the OneKind hackers to spend precious momentum on every inch. The losses hurt, but the line didn't break.

One attacker slipped through—angled fast toward Franklin's exposed side, blade raised.

Remy registered another change—minute, yet exact. The enemy's code swam against the current, breaking formation, recalibrating mid-strike. She had a second, maybe less. Beatrice was nearby—pure force in motion. Remy created a pocket of time and placed it in the path.

Beatrice felt the opening before she understood it—a thread pulled tight inside the chaos. Her hand closed around the shelf bracket mid-fall. The swing came fast, brutal. The metal struck the attacker's temple with a crisp crack, snapped his neck on contact, and dropped the body flat.

Time resumed. Beatrice turned, bracket raised, already tracking the next threat. Franklin hadn't flinched—but his glance met hers. Brief, exact. From then on, they moved as one.

Remy traced the arcs of motion across the battlefield—where the pressure mounted, where the cracks would split if she faltered. Her focus carried Ruth clear of the worst of it. Beatrice kept moving, driving enemies back with a relentless series of strikes that grew harsher as the seconds stacked. But Remy could sense it now—the slow, mounting price of what she was forcing. Time was no longer slowing for her alone.

Somewhere deep in the code, Remy saw the golden roots recoil—not break, but retreat, pulling inward like nerves recoiling from strain. Something within her snapped taut, and a cold numbness lanced down her spine.

She reached again—presence thinning, too far to follow. The conduit hadn't vanished, but it had gone inert. Numb to her. She could reach no deeper without risking fracture—of the interface or her own mind. The last thread slipped from her grasp. She was on her own.

The breach yawned wider where the northern wall of Bob's kingdom had given way. OneKind footsoldiers pressed forward in ceaseless ranks—pouring through the gap, clambering over broken shelving and fallen bodies as if pulled by some remorseless will. Their features vanished behind darkened visors, but purpose radiated from every stride. More arrived by the moment, streaming in from the sides, turning confusion into siege. For every defender who drove them back, two more crowded in, boots hammering the tiles, shields striking against the scattered defences. The air thickened with static and heat, a single overwhelming current that reduced everything to survival. Remy saw the line fray and understood too late—the pressure wouldn't ebb. It mounted with every passing second, a force that refused to break.

No matter how fiercely they fought, the onslaught showed no sign of faltering. The gap remained open, spitting more enemies into the field, feeding the churn at the chokepoint until every defence strained toward collapse, caught between fatigue and force.

The fight had become hopeless, but someone forgot to tell Franklin and Beatrice.

Franklin crashed through the breach like a living battering ram, shattering the press of bodies and cleaving the enemy line wide open. Beatrice was right on his heels, striking with a speed that left only impact behind. She moved with the raw force of a faultline finding its moment—direct, brutal, exact. Where grace might have faltered, conviction burned through; each blow a refusal to vanish, every step a living answer to erasure. Together they forced the wave back, a two-person wedge driven deep into the surge. They stood against numbers, fatigue, the logic of defeat—and refused to fall. For a moment, the unstoppable force met something that refused to move.

And around them, defenders realized again: it was possible, after all, to break the cycle.

Jeff and Bob drove forward as one body, a cyclone of thrown bean bags and strikes that folded enemies where they stood.

Remy dropped her eyes to the aisle map. OneKind's respawn markers glowed hot—too hot—crowding the backend loop behind the front lines. She didn't hesitate. Her fingers danced across the console, bypassing protections, forcing admin clearance through sheer refusal. The grid stuttered, then reformed.

She overrode the delay.

Return-to-Shelf Protocol: ENGAGED.

The floor shook. From beneath the vinyl tile, shelving units erupted like sprung traps—metal arms unspooling, sides folding out in precise, mechanical motion. The protocol didn't see enemies. It saw misfiled product. Misplaced stock. Items out of category.

The shelves didn't wait for them to move. They erupted upward and outward, boxing in squads mid-form, compressing others into the frames like they were soft goods caught between price points.

Dozens of Jacobs vanished in flashes—boxed, crushed, sorted for deletion. Remy tracked the surge point—drove the sequence there. Stack by stack, the machines obeyed. Not to kill. To reshelve.

Behind the lines, OneKind froze.

Some turned to run and were overtaken by the shelves as they closed. Others stood too long and were swallowed in silence. A few simply logged out where they stood, gone in a flick of static and shame.

It wasn't the blow that hurt them—it was what followed. Watching others break and realising they would too. One by one, the formation fractured. Discipline cracked into doubt. And the ones yet standing? They looked back, watched the field eating itself, and knew: they'd lost the battle.

Bob saw it. He straightened, planting one foot atop a broken pallet like a war general surveying the field, and shouted, "They're retreating!" with everything he had left.

Around them, OneKind began to pull away from the remnants of their fortress—some moving cautiously toward cover, others stumbling, plainly exhausted or injured. Several simply vanished—logging out in bursts of uneven static. It was clear the fight had drained both sides, physically and emotionally.

Bob's fortress had caved—its comforting walls reduced to torn layers of blanket and foam. The trebuchet lay buried in the wreckage, its usefulness spent, already gathering dust.

Jenna lay in a recovery position, her severed arm lost somewhere beneath the wreckage. Her good hand remained clenched around the base of her staff, as if part of her hadn't noticed the fight had ended.

Alan struggled to keep Ruth upright, exhaustion visible in the trembling of his grip.

Franklin stood nearby, vigilant but uneasy, scanning the scene for threats.

Remy watched as Bob bent down without a word, retrieved a fallen pillow from the rubble, carefully dusted it off, and placed it gently atop what remained of the barricade. It was a small, reflexive gesture, an unconscious refusal to abandon what they'd fought to create.

She navigated the battlefield with care, her body burdened by fatigue. By a shattered checkout counter, she halted—her focus fixed on a pair of sneakers, upright and neatly tied, as though their owner had vanished mid-step. Remy opened her mouth to speak, but no sound came. Her eyes lingered on the others. Their faces showed only weariness and uncertainty. She exhaled slowly, steadied herself, and reached again for her keyboard.

Her thoughts had already moved on. They had endured—for now. Max was out there, and the fight wasn't done.

CHAPTER TWENTY THREE
BLACKOUT

Mathieu Moreau crossed into the waiting room—deep inside Afterdeath HQ's fallback command node, now running on reserve power. The walls were bare, lit only by the hum of backup systems threading the air.

He had followed the corridor without asking questions. The guards didn't stop him. Either someone had cleared him, or no one had the energy left to argue.

On the far side of the room, Marisol paced, eyes darting between screens and her tablet. His mom had once called her "the one person who is human over there." Today, her tension said it all.

The room was filled with different kinds of silence, and each one asked to be heard.

His parents stood at the far side, hands linked more from habit than comfort, their posture drawn tight with attention. They didn't turn. Their eyes stayed fixed on the monitors, faces lit by the cold, ghosted light.

Mathieu didn't speak. He studied them—their motionless forms, the way the screens pressed light into their backs.

His mother's face looked bleached in the glow. He could feel the way she used to squeeze his shoulder during bad news—a signal that she hadn't let go. Now, she was fixed in place, unreachable.

His father's face had that same tension he wore before every piece of bad news—bracing without words, as though sheer will could stop the whole frame from buckling.

They hadn't noticed him. That was okay. Some distances weren't ready to close. He looked at them, then let his eyes move to the rest of the room.

Armand Roy sat near the centre, upright despite the cane resting lightly against his knee. His expression was carved from something weathered—an old man's restraint worn down into bone. Paul Roy sat opposite him, rotating a whiskey glass absently between his fingers, the ice already water.

Red and blue light flashed faintly through the windows, emergency vehicles painting streaks along a skyline that had lost power. Outside, the city kept moving—slower now, unsure. Inside, monitors cycled on and off and vents pushed air that smelled like dust and ozone—functional, but far from alive.

He saw Remy. She was on-screen, composed and unshaken, her familiar chestnut tumbling into her eyes as she worked methodically. Her voice wasn't audible, but he could nearly hear it. The way her eyes moved, assured, gave him something solid to stand on.

She wasn't here—but somehow, she was holding the room together.

It wasn't that he thought she couldn't die—again. He couldn't picture it—not the girl he knew, someone who already knew the ending and refused to stop. She looked like the version of herself from every story he ever made her the hero of—except this time, no one was pretending. This time, the monsters were real.

Of course it would be Remy. Unravelling what everyone else thought unbreakable. She didn't treat boundaries as fixed—especially not the ones adults swore were real.

Armand turned, catching Mathieu's eye.

The moment jolted him—quick, instinctive—but something in Armand's posture eased. Recognition passed between them, unspoken but clear.

Armand looked back to the screen, voice low. "Your sister—she believes in the kind of impossible Max used to chase."

He stayed with it, eyes fixed. "Some people would've given up by now. She hasn't."

The words hung in the air, without pressure. Mathieu said nothing. He didn't need to answer. He'd watched Remy outpace every limit they set—never asking permission.

He stayed beside him, not to comfort, but because it was the only answer he had right now. His eyes drifted to his parents. His mother's hands were clenched, knuckles white against her coat. His father's eyes stayed locked on something he couldn't hold. Mathieu recognized the effort—grief packed tight inside a body trying not to fold.

A burst of voices from the screens broke Mathieu's concentration, news anchors struggling to make sense of the unfolding chaos.

A fragile stillness rippled through the room as the footage cut abruptly—to Maxime Roy, trapped in something Mathieu knew instinctively was wrong, unfair.

Armand's hand pressed down against his cane, knuckles white, gaze fixed, his expression steady—effort keeping everything in place. He had seen this coming, that much was clear; the space for this moment had been made in him long before it arrived.

"That's my son," he said, barely more than a whisper.

On the feed, Max broke into a run—free of his restraints at last. He didn't break stride. He ran straight for the glowing portal Remy had opened and dove through, arms tucked, a clean leap into what they all assumed was safety.

But the next frame hit like a blow. He didn't land. He fell—emerging high above the earth, suspended in open sky. His body turned once, loose and unresisting, as if he trusted the fall.

A loud gasp rippled through the room. Armand whispered, "Oh my—" but didn't finish it.

Meanwhile, on the screen, Max kept falling. His crisis one of many, the monitors cycled through names and rolling footage, each critical update dissolved before it could land.

Mathieu barely registered the headlines as they scrolled by—one reporting continued breaches throughout Afterdeath, another noting that a key suspect had left the scene before authorities arrived. The phrases blurred into static, but the implication sat uneasily in the background: someone important had slipped away.

Mathieu moved. Not because he was ready—but because staying felt wrong. His legs felt shaky. But he kept going—past the monitors, past the shadows of people bracing for a version of the day that no longer existed. He stepped between his parents and closed the distance—shoulder to shoulder. Not to be protected. To show them: I'm here too.

Outside, the city kept failing. Blackouts rippled through the skyline like dominoes falling sideways. A plane skimmed too low before vanishing behind a tower—no crash, no signal, gone. Sirens lit up corners of the dark streets like warning strobes. One feed caught a fire punching through a parking garage roof, the camera whipping sideways before cutting out.

The streets below were chaos—automated vehicles locked in motion, hazard lights blinking like warning beacons with no meaning. A few human drivers tried to weave through, dodging wreckage, stranded cars, and each other. Looters moved through darkened shops brazenly.

Through the thick glass, all of it was silent. The motion was real, but the muted nature of his view made it worse—like watching the world end from underwater. He saw looters bolt from broken windows, glass catching light as it scattered across the pavement—and none of it reached him.

Was it the blackout? Was it terrorism? Or had this always been waiting—people on edge, held together by power grids and morning routines, now boiling over?

Mathieu didn't know. But he knew this much: someday, he wanted to be out there—calming, protecting, helping to rebuild. Not yet. Not today. His instincts, his training, his preparation—or lack of it—wouldn't make him useful. They'd only get in the way.

He stayed right there—between them. Watching. Staying with it. Not pretending it was over. Not looking for answers. The world was changing shape in front of them, and he wasn't ready. He was here.

He didn't know what came next. But he knew this much: he wanted to stand where she would've stood—if she could.

CHAPTER TWENTY FOUR
DEADFALL

Maxime Roy dropped through open air—fast, untethered, but not helpless. His body angled instinctively, minute corrections of arms and legs carving his fall, holding his line true against the slipstream.

It had been years since he jumped under his own power—years since those reckless twenties when he learned to pack his own chute, to trust the mechanics—and his own judgement—over gravity's indifference. But muscle memory stayed stitched into the bones. You didn't forget how to fall. Not when it mattered.

Max summoned the parachute pack early, materializing it from his clearance privileges before the auto-trigger could even warn him. The rig snapped into place with a mechanical slap. Every decision that led him here hit him in a blur, a jagged chain of cause and consequence, accelerating faster with each second. He had no illusions about where this ended. But until it ended, he was in the fight.

Remy's voice came through the comm. "Well," she said—not quite laughing—"that's one way to make an exit."

He corrected his rotation, easing into a controlled descent.

"Thanks for the assist back there."

Remy's tone darkened. "Heads up. The three stooges are back."

He didn't need visuals to confirm it. Three figures broke through the ruins in tight formation—armoured cores, trailing heat signatures, zeroing in with purpose. Remy marked them with names anyway. "Larry, Moe, and Curly. You're welcome."

"You're serious," he said, almost laughing.

"Dead serious. They're stooges," she quipped. "Low ping, trained to kill, wrapped in a manifesto they didn't write. OneKind doesn't send soldiers—they send conviction. That's why they can't adapt. They follow the plan. You see through it. That's what makes you dangerous."

He'd been called a genius, a moron, a saint and a devil, but no one ever bothered to call him dangerous. Until now.

Tucking his arms tighter, he angled into a shallow track. The retreat bled off into controlled drift as he repositioned himself, slicing through the air to fall in line with the operatives above him. "Understood," he said as he dropped.

The cold, digitized air tore past him as his trajectory carved through the simulation's layers. Every second narrowed his focus. He wasn't playing defence anymore. He was shaping the end.

Curly descended with cold efficiency—every input razor-tuned, every line tight, like someone executing a rehearsed drill. Moe hovered—scanning the airspace with practised intent, as if working through a puzzle already half-solved. But Larry—Larry strained. He lagged, overcompensated, always trailing, always grasping. Like a competitor chasing a scoreboard no one else was watching.

He spotted the imbalance at once. Larry wasn't undisciplined—he was eager to make a name for himself. That made him predictable. Leaning into a wide bank, he cut across their altitude. The air tore past his helmet in shearing bursts, but he threaded the curve like a needle. Below, Larry reacted. His ascent tilted a few degrees—barely, but it put him in reach.

Remy's voice clicked in. "If you're trying to bait him, it's working."

A flicker of satisfaction curved his mouth.

Larry narrowed his descent path, drawing in fast. As he crossed the point of no return, Max launched a heat-ghost—crude, but it fooled any lock-on or aim-assist.

Larry's visor and gun snagged on it. His aim skipped on the fragmenting signal. In chasing the ghost, he had coasted wide—and into Curly's field.

A half-second later, a bullet meant for Max passed straight through the faint trace of heat and grazed Curly in the leg.

"What the hell was that?"

"Sorry," said the terrorist labeled Larry.

Their formation staggered. Moe tilted instantly, realigning without thought. But Larry—he was choking on his big stage moment.

Max tucked tight and aimed himself like a spear in the wind. He launched himself downward in a tight corkscrew—arms locked, frame compact—a compression dive built for speed and minimal drag, nearly impossible to track once fully committed. The angle cut air resistance to the bone and built pressure fast.

Larry tried to reorient, but he was playing catch-up. Unknowingly, falling into a trap.

Max broke through the gap and hit hard. He summoned a dagger, clutched it in both hands, and struck true, angling through the line where Larry's profile was mapped. He ended it.

Larry had believed too deeply in his own momentum.

The killframe buckled. His form spasmed in a quick burst then folded in on itself. Game Over, Remy thought. Signal dropped. Level cleared. Two left.

The muzzle flash flared—he twisted before the round passed his ribs, peeling air from his side like a knife dragged through fabric. It didn't hit—but it didn't miss by much either. The sound followed half a beat later: a blunt force that rattled his chest and left his nerves buzzing.

His blade spun from his grip—lost to the fall before he could track where it landed.

He twisted through the drop, reorienting mid-descent. The next shot came closer.

Remy whistled, low and impressed. "Moe's putting in the work."

Max exhaled through gritted teeth. "And I'm not?"

Another shot flared—Moe had already committed to her line. She was tracking ahead of him now, leading by instinct and training.

Max didn't dodge this time. Because he knew this wasn't winnable at range. Not like this. He'd never been much for guns. Not on the ground, not at a range, not shooting cans off fence posts. Timing always came more naturally than aim. So the idea of firing a weapon while plummeting at terminal velocity, wind screaming, no stable platform in sight—it felt less like strategy and more like gambling with math he didn't trust. But if they were trying to line up the perfect shot—maybe he could line something up too.

He rolled once through the drop, not to evade but to fine-tune his line. Pulled slightly to the left, gave Moe the line she wanted. He tracked Curly's vector—predictable, mirroring Moe's lead. Max waited. One second.

He tucked, rolled, and twisted, pulling himself clear. For the two tracking him, it was a blur of motion. The shot meant for him tore through the air—and into Moe's side.

The impact folded her midsection. Her body didn't spasm or cry out. It—paused. Suspended. The comms went silent. Her figure locked in place for an instant, like the render thread lagged—caught between input and response. Her tether severed.

As the simulation confirmed the kill, her form began to splinter, breaking apart like glass under pressure. She didn't look at Max. She looked to Curly—a final vector tilt, carrying more meaning than motion. She was gone. Deleted.

He righted his descent. The sky around him churned in layers: scorched clouds, trailing debris, broken geometry collapsing in freefall. He scanned left, below. Nothing but the roar of altitude burning off his suit.

The fight had honed to a one-on-one. But the one was nowhere to be seen. That was, at least until it was too late.

The final strike didn't come from far. It hit like a current—silent, close. Curly crashed into him, rifle gone, replaced by speed and force. The hit drove straight across Max's back, wrenching the air from his lungs and throwing them into a spiraling plunge. Limbs collided. Orientation vanished.

Max absorbed a second blow to the chin, pain cracking through his teeth.

He struck back on reflex—elbow, forearm, anything to force their tangled bodies apart in the rush of freefall.

Curly stayed on him, tireless, relentless.

Remy's voice cut through the channel, trying to lighten what she couldn't reach. "Want me to hum the Jaws theme for motivation?"

Max barely pulled in a breath. "Don't think he needs the encouragement."

The joke had been for Max to be Jaws—but the way he heard it told her everything. He didn't need humour. He needed her to show up.

From her position—too far to intervene—Remy tried something she'd once overreached and broken: slowing time itself. That time, she'd pressed too far—the thread gave, leaving only silence where power had been.

Now, she eased in. Not with force, but attention. Whether she succeeded or he adapted didn't matter. Speed thinned around him. Patterns emerged. Motion simplified into lines and angles.

He veered left, bleeding speed to throw Curly wide. The man followed instantly.

A punch slammed into Max's ribs.

He countered with a twist, dragging his knee upward into Curly's centreline—felt the force rebound through his own frame. They spun again. No ground to catch them. Only air, inertia, and whatever each of them had left.

The exchange grew tighter, more brutal. A fist deflected. An elbow clipped his neck. Another blow landed near the temple, jarring but incomplete.

He didn't reach for a weapon. He reached for that unspoken connection every skydiver learns to feel—the subtle tension in the air between two falling bodies, more real than anything else at terminal speed. He leaned into it, letting the distance draw him in, every movement calibrated to trust the physics more than the panic.

The moment their vectors aligned, he turned, seized Curly's arm, and spun him through the air. He pivoted—one clean kick off the man's chest, not to escape, but to turn velocity into force, motion into impact, and the fight into something he could finally control. Curly reached for what wasn't there anymore.

Max fired once, with exacting force. The round tore through the centre of his frame. The simulation confirmed. Light overtook him, and he was gone.

He exhaled as the momentum resolved—strain, speed, decisions made at the limits of reflex. His body remained coiled, muscles braced long after the danger had passed. Internal diagnostics lit up around him: minor tissue tears, superficial bruising, elevated neural stress. All within acceptable limits. Stabilization was already underway.

Remy's voice returned, lighter but clear. "Damn. I was actually worried for a second."

"Yeah. Me too." His limbs ached, fatigue mapped across every joint, but diagnostics held green. Systems recalibrated. Recovery was underway.

"That everyone?" he asked, not expecting reassurance.

Remy reviewed the data. "Lazarus signatures are gone," she said. "You locked them out for good."

OneKind was gone. Their anchors severed. Their grip failed as access protocols shut down.

The battle had ended.

Max refocused, and this time his vision steadied without resistance. The land below came into focus, familiar lines emerging—the worn arc of a dirt path, the tilt of the barn roof, the battered fencing, worn in all the right places, looking more natural than it had any right to.

His reconstructed family farm rose into view—not imagined, not the original, but more and more real every update.

He pulled the chute. The harness cinched against his torso and legs, the canopy blossomed with a crisp mechanical snap. His velocity slackened—air pushing back against him with measured resistance. His limbs retained their strength. His lungs expanded without friction. The ache that had followed him for years was gone. For the first time in memory, his body moved in full accord with the world around it—and for once, everything held true.

The wind flattened against him, losing its texture, its grip. Colour drained from the sky without dimming its brightness, as if contrast itself had been stripped away. His instincts flared, old systems trying to read a world already breaking. His display shuddered, telemetry slipping out of sync, onboard corrections hunting wildly for a ground that no longer answered back.

The parachute vanished. Weight hit, slipping away before he could react. It wasn't torn—it was erased. The sky offered nothing. No grip. No delay. Gravity clutched him raw and unfiltered, and he dropped. His body responded faster than thought: arms pulled tight, legs speared downward, spine locked into delta form to fight spin. His eyes raked the empty ground for any slope, ridge, or contour—anything that might slow the fall—but there was nothing.

He twisted his shoulders, fighting the pull, but the sky refused him. Terminal force seized him. Time drew in—tight, final. Harland's voice cut through the buckling airframe.

"You thought you'd get to choose the ending. You won't even see it."

He barely had time to process it. The ground surged upward, swallowing distance in a rush too fast for counting. Wind tore the strength from his limbs. He angled his body sideways, an instinctive attempt to slip the worst of the impact, but it made no difference.

The collision came fast and final. First came heat—blinding—followed by the severing—a depth without light, without pain, without anything he could grasp.

CHAPTER TWENTY FIVE
ASH AND HUSK

Franklin arrived at the field's boundary, the dry husks crunching underfoot as he surveyed the wreckage. Remy skidded to a stop beside him, breath catching in her throat. Together they spotted Max, crimson code pooling into the torn soil where he'd fallen.

"Max."

She dropped to her knees beside him.

"Hey, you miserable wretch," Remy said, voice cracking with something like warmth. She steadied her trembling hands. "Wake up!"

Code shimmered beneath the surface of his skin—fractured threads, damage points glowing red. She could try to repair it, but some breaks ran too deep. Quick fixes risked making things worse—an arm rewritten on unstable logic might move, but not when it mattered. Max's injuries went further. Vital systems, buried deep—organs, structural bones—had taken the worst of it. She couldn't swap those without risking catastrophic failure. Arms were doable. This wasn't.

Max coughed and tried to push himself upright, pain warping his face. His eyes, unfocused at first, found her.

"You're—getting overtime," he rasped, a crooked line of something like a smirk pulling at his cracked lips.

"Overtime, a raise, and a bonus." She shot back, doing her best to hold back tears that were equal parts anxiety, relief, and madness.

"Knew you were—only in this for the money."

"Says the only billionaire in the realm."

Remy activated her portable console. "Next time, don't make us dig you out of a damn cornfield," she chided.

Max managed a rough, bitter chuckle, pain etching fine lines into his forehead. "Let's pretend there won't be a next time," he said.

Franklin approached, his voice low but steady. "Remy, we should get him inside."

They each took Max under an arm—barely stabilized—and headed for the farmhouse. Each step drove home the truth: bones, muscles, pain. There was no shortcut through reality.

The farmhouse loomed—new but made to look old—its faux-worn boards and freshly painted windows standing strong. Inside, order offered little comfort. Cushions and scattered medkits lay hastily arranged. Beatrice worked with clinical precision, checking injuries with swift, practised hands. Bob scanned the room for structural weaknesses, while Jeff's remaining crew leaned into each other for balance more than support. Alan, Ruth, Jenna, and the worst of the injured hadn't reached this fallback point.

They weren't sure what to expect. OneKind had lost the battle. Everyone was wondering if they were truly locked out now. The crisis was global—power grids down everywhere. No one inside the simulation knew what horrors were unfolding beyond Afterdeath; imagination supplied all the fear they needed.

Remy and Franklin lowered Max onto the couch, cushions yielding under his weight. Sweat pooled at his hairline, eyes clouded with fatigue that cut deeper than pain. His jaw clenched, the shallow rise of his chest all that revealed how much he'd held together to make it this far.

Remy set her kit down, hands shaking as she worked—threading sensors, scanning with practised speed, no longer narrating every variable aloud. She pressed fingers to his wrist, checked the rise and fall of breath, trusted the small tells that spoke louder than diagnostics. She patched what she could, improvising. Colour-coded strings meant nothing if the body wouldn't hold.

Franklin watched the door, boots planted. Jeff stacked medkits, silence stretching between each clatter. Beatrice moved from patient to patient, wrapping gauze and tightening splints with a steadiness that was more reassurance than medicine. Bob muttered about a cracked rafter, voice barely above a whisper. In a corner, someone set out mugs of water, steam rising from a single chipped kettle. They moved the way people do when there's work left and no one names what comes after.

Max gritted his teeth, forced himself upright without help this time, and flexed his fingers—watching them move, as if surprised they even obeyed. He found Remy's gaze and let the smallest smile break the tension. "Enough. I don't need to feel any better than functional."

Remy pressed the last patch into place, then wiped her eyes on her sleeve. "That's the first time I've heard anyone complain about me fixing them up."

Max gave a low grunt. "Well, let's call it even. I think I've had my fill of repairs for this century." He looked at her again, his tone level. "Are you okay?"

Her answer failed in her throat. She shook her head, unable to speak.

Max opened his arms. "Come here."

She buried her face against him, and he didn't move. For the first time in too long, she wasn't left alone in the aftermath.

A faint ripple passed through the glass on the table. Neither noticed.

After a moment, he tried for humour. "If you're hiring, I'd like to audition for estranged uncle. Maybe extra grandpa, if there's an opening."

Remy laughed into his shirt. "You're hired. Pay's terrible, though."

He squeezed her once before letting go. "Yeah, but the benefits aren't bad."

A picture frame on the shelf gave the slightest of tremors.

Remy drew back, drying her eyes. "Thanks, Max."

Franklin crept to the window, peering between the weathered slats of the farmhouse's outer wall. Light slipped through in angled shafts, slicing dust in the air. Over his shoulder, Remy finally saw the thing that had shattered the horizon.

Her breath caught—not only from the scale, but from what it confirmed. Harland hadn't changed. He'd been revealed. The simulation wasn't inflating him. It had stopped masking him. It was Harland

Reeves—grown to impossible scale, cast in shadow and authority, risen from the fields like the simulation itself had forged him. He was dressed in the same black suit he'd worn into every boardroom, but now it ran the length of a mid-rise. The fabric refused to wrinkle, the lapels held perfect geometry despite the wind. A blood-dark tie, knotted at sternum height, cut a clean line down the front of his torso. He was immaculate, but at a scale the world had never seen.

His left boot, polished leather as black as engine oil, pressed into the soil so deep it had flattened part of the cornfield into a shallow crater. Dust spiraled up in waves around it. The barn, not fifty feet to the right, looked like a diorama prop.

The torso was a wall, sleek and unbent. His posture hadn't changed since the last time he stood at the head of a table. Shoulders back, arms relaxed but never slack. One hand hung at his side like a programmed metronome. The other was raised—wrist flexed, palm half-closed, not in greeting, but in selection. His index finger curled slightly. A gesture meant to imply power without needing to perform it.

Above it all, the face.

His jawline was square, expression cold. His thin lips stretched into a grin devoid of joy—a simple declaration of inevitability.

Behind him, clouds thickened, bunching in rows as if gravity deferred to his position. The sun should have cast his shadow across the entire property, but the light bent wrong. As if it feared showing the full shape of him.

Through heat-sensing vision, Harland scanned the inside of the farmhouse. The survivors retreated farther inside, scrambling for cover. Bob and Jeff King—brothers, irrelevant—flanked Beatrice and Franklin, who shielded the last of the so-called beanbaggers. The movement was panicked, but he picked out the ones who mattered—Max and Remy, the reason he was here. Their defiance was obvious. He raised a hand, ready to finish it.

When he finally spoke, the sound did not pass through the walls so much as arrive inside them—like an announcement piped directly into the architecture of the world.

"Max Roy," he said, voice tectonic. "Now. Or this unravels fast."

Harland kept watch. "I can see many of you are inside. I'm willing to leave with only Max. That's the offer."

No exclamation. No heat. This was how gods wrote ultimatums.

In the house he built, Max didn't have to look up to know all eyes were on him—every pair drawn toward the centre of the room where he sat, breath catching, body rebuilt but far from whole. There was no sound in the room except for the small, involuntary things: a scrape of heel against floorboard, a wrist flexing against a wrap. But beneath it all, expectation coiled.

He looked toward the door.

Every thread of him had been trained to recognize the moment when one life had to be exchanged to secure the rest. He'd watched that equation play out more times than he'd admit. This time, he was the variable.

He hesitated only long enough to feel the weight of their gazes. Then he rose, slow but certain.

"I'll go," he said, voice stripped of theatre. "You know he won't stop unless I do."

Beatrice placed herself in front of him before he rounded the corner. Her frame didn't block much, but her voice did.

"Don't fool yourself."

Remy planted one hand on the back of a chair, the other already halfway to her wandboard. "Sit down, Max," she said, not angry—certain.

Franklin didn't look up from the window, but his voice landed with finality. "He has no intention of stopping."

Max angled his head toward the field. "Have you seen him?"

"I have," Remy said. "And if that coward wants a body count, he can work for it."

There was heat in the words—not bravado, not defiance for its own sake—but something close to love, expressed through refusal.

He started to reply. To argue. To insist that this was the cleanest route, the least disastrous. But every rationale crumbled under how much they believed in him. No one here was ready to surrender him. No one here was willing to stand down.

That realization didn't relieve him. It humbled him. These were not the same people who followed orders. They were no longer his employees, or even his allies. They were survivors—and survival had bred something stronger than hierarchy: commitment.

He closed his mouth and nodded once.

Around him, chairs dragged closer to the table. Scraps of plans surfaced. No one raised their voice. The energy wasn't calm—it was bracing. Like swimmers tightening their strokes before the undertow hit.

Max eased into the nearest chair, fingers tapping along the edge of the table. "Alright," he said. "No one walks out alone."

They began. A map unfolded. The fight wasn't over.

Compliance wasn't expected; Roy and Moreau had surrounded themselves with precisely that brand of foolhardy defiance.

Harland lifted one massive foot and crushed a rusted truck beneath it, debris scattering like startled insects.

"Ready or not," he taunted.

The farmhouse groaned as Harland advanced, each monstrous tread rocking the foundation. Windows popped from their frames, glass splintering, floorboards buckling under pressure that defied every rule of structure and stress.

Someone shouted, "Out! Move!" Panic turned to survival. Chairs toppled, boots thundered against boards. Franklin threw open the nearest door, waving people through, voice raw with urgency.

Beatrice hurried the weakest toward the back exit, herding them with one arm while firing a desperate volley from her beanbag rifle—more warning than deterrent.

Jeff vaulted the counter, rifled through the cabinet, and liberated a smoke canister. He cracked it open as Harland's shadow spilled across the porch, then sent it skittering toward the threshold.

The device activated mid-roll, pumping erratic pulses of light and signal-dirt meant to jam visual filters. It didn't stop Harland—but for a second, he slowed as his filter suite parsed the interference, then nullified it.

Bob seized the moment. "Out the side door!" he shouted, body-checking the old oak pantry flat to reveal the narrow crawlspace between walls. He grabbed a lanky kid—barely a teenager—and shoved him through first. Three more followed, crawling toward the east wall and the open shed beyond.

A massive hand cracked through the front wall. Dust exploded inward as a section of ceiling came down in waves, beams splintering down in a thunderclap of plaster and shards.

Jeff grabbed Beatrice by the collar, yanking her back as a support column splintered beside her. "You got two clips left?" he barked.

"One and a half," she answered, tossing him her backup. He caught it with one hand, jammed it into the beanbag rifle he'd snagged off the floor, and kicked open the cellar door. "Beanbaggers! Down and out!"

Three more survivors barreled down the stairs. The cellar had a broken wall—half collapsed during the last simulation quake. It opened into a root cellar, then out through the under-foundation vent into the west pasture. Jeff motioned the others through, then looked up. The rafters groaned. Harland braced himself again.

Above them, the roof peeled open like tin under a storm surge. Harland crouched, barely needing to bend as he forced his way inside. The ceiling gave way in slabs, not slats. His head and shoulders punched through like a wrecking ball given form.

Beatrice aimed high and fired into his face—not hoping to harm, but to distract. "Come on, you corporate golem," she hissed. "Look at me."

He did.

The beam of light from his eyes was silent but total. The table between them ignited and shattered. Beatrice rolled sideways, shoulder slamming into the wall, and vanished through a side hatch one of the others had cut with a code torch minutes earlier. A beanbagger behind her laid down suppressing fire.

Out back, Bob dove behind a rusted cultivator left near the edge of the rear field. Its massive wheel well provided three seconds of cover. He unwrapped a slingshot with microcode-pellets packed into glass. With no time to test aim, he fired at Harland's neck—the only exposed seam visible above the second-floor wreckage.

The pellet struck, disintegrated, and failed to do more than draw a flicker of notice.

Behind him, two survivors made it to the barn. One took cover behind the corn harvester; the other scrambled into the seed shed and barricaded the door with feed bags. A third ran low along the row of rolled hay bales, dragging a scorched toolkit behind her. Her rifle bounced against her spine as she raced between the bales.

Harland stepped through the shattered kitchen wall, crushing the table flat beneath his heel. The ceiling collapsed onto his back, debris raining down as the staircase splintered under his weight. Jeff and a beanbagger fired from the porch; their shots dissolved harmlessly on impact.

He didn't even turn his head.

Remy slipped into the trees, chest heaving. Harland's shadow swallowed the broken farmhouse behind her. Beatrice pressed flat against the rain barrel, rifle ready. At the edge of the clearing, Jeff and Bob edged toward the silo's mouth, spacing themselves so they wouldn't share Harland's next impact.

Remy keyed the wandboard, working by instinct. The scan ran, reaching for heat, movement, code signatures—anything. But nothing came back. Not silence. Not resistance. The signal didn't stop—it bent, veering around Harland like the space itself had been warped to keep him hidden. This wasn't jamming. It was a hard-coded reroute. A design choice to make him impossible to track.

Harland stood where the front of the house had been—immense, unmoved, a fixed shape in the ruin. His gaze combed the clearing with surgical focus, hunting the one anomaly he couldn't see.

Right behind him, the last remaining farmhouse door blew open as Max broke into a sprint, headed straight at Harland's left leg, shoulders hunched, as if he was about to body check a redwood tree. Reckless. Desperate.

Harland hesitated, thrown by the move, then fired. A focused eye blast cut through the air, hitting Max dead centre.

Max vanished in a burst of data fragments.

For a moment, Harland felt the win.

Then more figures appeared across the field—clones of Max, darting and weaving, each one harder to pin down. Their paths crisscrossed like a scrambled simulation, confusing even the field's physics engine. Harland pivoted, frustrated, locking onto the nearest doppelgänger and blasting it into vapor. Another raced for the barn; he swung low, cleaving its path with a horizontal beam.

A crack of fire came from the silo. Jeff's head popped over the rim, launching two beanbags in quick succession. One pinged off Harland's temple. The other bounced off his collar. Harland didn't flinch. He didn't even blink. He raised one arm and loosed a wave of searing heat in their direction—not enough to level the structure, but enough to send Jeff diving backward with a grunt.

From the far side, Bob took his shot—firing from the back of an overturned tractor, rifle braced on the axle. He landed a hit against Harland's cheek. Harland wheeled toward the tractor and raised his hand. A miniature construct flared in his palm—half-formed fireball, then fully armed. He hurled it at a cluster of Max decoys near the haystack, vaporizing them and igniting the stack in a flash of code-flame. Bob rolled off the tractor an instant before it was shredded.

Beatrice fired again from the rain barrel, this time aiming for the eye. Her beanbag missed, but the follow-up shot landed in Harland's shoulder seam. No damage. But she saw his head rotate—calculated, unfazed. He extended one foot and drove it down, aiming for her—earth quaking, barrel upended. Beatrice scrambled out, rolling into the furrows behind a rusted combine. Harland's next stomp drove a shockwave through the field, throwing clumps of soil in every direction.

A Max-clone leapt from behind a chicken coop and slapped Harland's shin. Another ran between his legs and tried to climb. Harland growled and swatted downward with both hands, swiping two of them into static.

Then he looked down. His internal overlay displayed health at 94%. He chuckled—low, cold, resonating through the air.

"Feeble," he muttered, amused more than angry. "Ants with firecrackers."

Another Max darted past, drawing fire away from Remy. Harland tracked it, and fired again.

As the last decoy dissolved, Harland's eyes swept the farmhouse ruins. Scanning the ruins, Harland spotted Remy hunched over her console, hands moving fast.

Her distractions were clever, but he saw one simple fix now. The field fell silent as he advanced, the simulation compressed around him—every thread of code dragged inward, bending to his signature, every path narrowing toward her.

Remy didn't run. She couldn't. Her body wouldn't move, caught between memory and the moment. Harland's shadow fell across her, but it was his eyes that broke her—cold, blank, impossible to mistake. She had seen that look before, once, and never forgotten it.

A shape moved beside her—a brush of motion, almost missed in the chaos. At first, she thought it was debris or another decoy. But then she heard the strained breath of someone hiding close.

It was Max, the real one. He crouched behind a fallen log, out of Harland's line of sight, clutching his side. Blood—too red for this world—leaked between his fingers, but his eyes found Remy's, and for a split second she saw clarity. Not a ghost, not a glitch, not a copy. Him.

Harland was closing in, his attention fixed on Remy. She typed with one hand, heart pounding. The tension stretched thin, every muscle locked as if one twitch would reveal everything. She couldn't run away in time, she couldn't summon anything to stand in his way.

The ground shook. At first Harland thought it was his own weight, but the tremor grew, off-pattern, wild. The battlefield seemed in shock, as Harland stopped to try to track what was coming.

At the top of the hill, a herd of impossible beasts thundered down—thick fur, single horns catching the light. Elasmotherium. Even Harland's code flagged them as extinct. Three riders: a figure in old robes, one in a lab coat, and, at the centre, Alan Prescott.

Alan raised a battered brass horn and sounded it. The call split the air. Leo and Reed flanked him, knuckles white on their mounts.

Leo grinned wild. "Next time, we pick something with seats!" he yelled over the din.

Reed said nothing—eyes fixed forward, jaw clenched.

Alan steadied himself. "Too late now!"

The charge hit Harland like a wave. Alan drove his unicorn forward, the horn catching Harland at the knee—joints buckling, code flaring. Harland staggered, snarling, and swung his arm wide. The beasts scattered, regrouped, circled for another pass.

Alan barked, "Again!"

Leo darted to the right, Reed swerved left, each drawing Harland's focus. The giant stomped, sending up a plume of shredded data. Leo's mount dodged, barely clearing the blow.

Alan wheeled around and plunged in from the side, driving the unicorn's horn into Harland's shin. The code cracked. Harland recoiled, grabbing at his wounded leg.

Reed finally shouted, "Focus fire—don't let up!"

They circled, pressing the attack. Hooves hammered the earth, horns driving again and again at the giant's weak spots.

Harland lashed out, his heel catching Leo's mount—code exploded, Leo tumbling free.

"Keep moving!" Alan shouted. They drove in again, horn meeting code, but Harland swept them back effortlessly.

Harland's palm ignited, releasing a fireball that scorched the unicorn line into ashes. Alan seized the opening and struck Harland's ankle. Code shattered, but Alan's beast collapsed beneath him, throwing him to the dirt, vision spinning.

When he hit dirt, Alan tucked himself under the form of a downed unicorn, hoping he could repair himself without being spotted.

Around him, fragments of elasmotherium code flickered and dissolved—pixelated horn tips, broken brass fittings, saddles with no riders. Dust hung in the air like suspended ash. Glowing remnants drifted downward, catching light but casting none. The ground was scored with deep ruts from hooves and impact craters where fire had struck.

Harland stood at the centre of it, immense and unhurried, steam rising from his frame where code burned off. Circuits rerouted. Armour realigned. His overlay read: 81% integrity. He absorbed the damage as if it registered beneath his threshold for concern.

Her next move was pure gamble—untested, unstable, patched together in the dark. She ran a buried script she'd found weeks ago in a half-broken corner of the net. Nobody ever got it working. It became her obsession: a puzzle with no answer, a broken blueprint for a machine no one could finish. Until now.

Parts flew into place around Max—wheels locking, wings folding, ballast systems anchoring him down. The frame convulsed as three designs—land, air, and sea—competed to shape one body. Nothing matched. Tracks from an old scout rig fought with glider struts. Deep-sea code sank the centre of gravity like it wanted him underwater. It shouldn't have stood up.

But Max did.

He found balance in the chaos, barely. Remy caught a flicker of the old myth this thing was based on—a robot made from pieces that didn't belong together. Dairugger XV, the build that never worked. Until now.

The body moved awkwardly—like a mech learning to walk mid-battle. It wasn't elegant, but it was alive. Max flexed his hands. One gauntlet dragged, the other pulsed with unstable light. His chestplate throbbed with heat. The whole thing looked ready to fall apart.

But it didn't.

Fifteen modules, scavenged from fifteen forgotten projects—each built for a different war, never meant to share code. Somehow, they were speaking now. Somehow, they stood.

Max grinned behind the visor.

"Fifteen parts, no plan, and a prayer. That's more than I need."

He charged—a monument to unfinished work, unfinished logic, unfinished hope—assembled not for victory, but for the sheer, reckless refusal to collapse.

Harland loomed, titanic, code billowing from his form. The field behind him was a wasteland of ruined unicorns and splintered avatars. He closed on Max with machine-like precision, power distilled into certainty.

"You think this pile will stop me?" Harland's voice crackled, seismic.

Max rebalanced his stance—one leg tuned for speed, the other for brute weight. "You never respect the builds nobody else can finish." His own voice was split between three competing audio streams, but his intent was fixed. He advanced in time with the discordant cadence.

He went first. Every module converged as one—shoulder dropping, arm swinging with rough intent. The hit landed hard, ground buckling, Harland rocked back on one knee, corn and debris spraying skyward. Max's armour groaned; alarms flashed, a sensor mast sheared off and hit the dirt.

Harland rose, seamless and unbroken, eyes cold. He struck first—his counterpunch hammered Max dead centre, hurling the suit backward. The impact gouged trenches in the dirt. Max's chestplate shrieked with stress.

He absorbed the hit and twisted hard, answering with a backfist—wide, clumsy, but forceful.

The blow staggered Harland—only a step, but it opened the lane. But the rig's joints were fighting each other. Coordination lagged behind intent. Max pushed through.

Then came the flare.

Harland lifted one hand, fingers spread. Code coiled around his palm, spinning fast into an orb of blistering heat. Fireball, yes—but worse. The space around it shimmered, wrong. Corn blackened before the heat even arrived.

Max dove, shoulder-first, soil spraying as the blast shredded the air overhead, vaporizing the field behind him. He staggered upright, fighting the mismatched modules, before Harland's kick sent him spinning, overlay blinking out to darkness.

A back up light triggered. Static, then Remy's voice, pinging in his feed. "You've got maybe two seconds. Reboot. I'll hold the block."

Harland's fists crashed down—each hit bled through as an alert—his feed lighting red, the ground-and-pound relentless. Armour dented, module connections threatened to break. Through it all, Max could barely feel his limbs. The mechanical body was slow, stuck in a partial shutdown. Harland knelt over him, his full weight driving every punch. The sound in Max's ears wavered between code and violence.

Harland's voice cut through the haze. "Did you think this scrap could hold me?"

"I'm really not trying to make you angrier. But my power was out. I didn't hear any of that." He forced the suit to roll, enough to break the cycle. "Say it again if it matters."

Harland hesitated, more insulted than surprised. Another blow rained down, glancing off a gauntlet. Remy's signal sharpened—her voice now stretched and strange, echoing through the feed. Time itself slowed. The rhythm of the fight changed. Harland's fists descended slower, every punch tracing an arc that could be seen, mapped, and dodged. Remy bent the tree—straining her own code, pulling time thin. She could feel the stress in her own mind. Reality split—colours bleeding at the edges, like the code strained to hold shape. But for Max, every second doubled, then doubled again.

He moved. With time to see each attack, Max locked both arms, blocking a punch, then another. He heaved sideways, knocking Harland off balance.

The rig rolled—every module groaning like it had a different opinion—but he found his feet. Harland pressed in, trying to pin him, but Max caught the next arm, twisted, and fired the flight module's thruster. Max's rugger-tied torso lurched upright, sending Harland stumbling backward.

A cluster of warning lights bled across his command view, but Max was already in motion. He pivoted, spun, and drove a full-body elbow into Harland's side—one module after another, improvising on the fly. The arms, so mismatched before, now worked in sync under Remy's manipulated clock.

Harland swept for Max's legs, forcing an awkward hop. Max absorbed a wild punch, then countered—modules firing in chaotic sync, staggering Harland.

Max took space, breathing heavy. Heat surged through the frame, but the rig held—scattered machines finally pretending to be one. He hammered a punch into Harland's midsection, the impact knocking his admin shell into the dirt.

For a beat, both giants held—Harland, now frustrated, saw his chance for total victory slipping. He cast a glance at Remy, calculation breaking through his composure. He understood. If Max kept standing, if Remy kept bending time, he could not win.

He unleashed another fireball—raw, apocalyptic, the air screaming with pressure. But now, with seconds stretched by Remy's intervention, Max saw it coming. He sidestepped, the blast missing by inches, scorching the world behind him to cinders.

Harland reset, his anger distilled now into cold calculation. He drew back, summoning one last fire construct—terminal heat, the kind that erased everything in its path. But this time, his attention snapped to Remy. The construct's arc angled for Remy. She saw the intention a split second before Max did.

Max caught it—a blink in his targeting view, the angle of Harland's lean. He overrode every fail-safe Remy had installed, dumping every ounce of power left into forward motion. Stabilizers screamed; modules risked catastrophic failure. He didn't slow. He dove between Remy and the attack, driving the rig's battered frame to intercept the blast.

The fireball hit him point-blank. Searing. The force tore through the suit, peeling armour, erasing code, every layer burning away before the world even caught up. The last alerts fired off in unison—then darkness, pure and absolute.

Max's body hit the ground on one knee, every last circuit spent, but Remy was untouched. He'd taken the full force. Harland's aim never found her.

Max Roy, the man who conquered death, died a second time. And this time, the old-fashioned way.

Remy's scream tore from somewhere deeper than memory—something older than the body, older than the code. It didn't summon him back. It was the first thing her body allowed—some instinctual scream that broke through even the code.

She stumbled, wandboard lit in her hands, code ready. As if any of it mattered now. The space where he'd stood burned in her vision. Her knees hit the ground hard. She didn't feel it. Couldn't even look at the spot—not while it burned.

She drew in a breath that scraped on the way down. Grief didn't stop. It settled in, rewriting her at the roots. She ran through every scenario she could think of—how to save him, recover remnants of his code, anything. Max was gone. She couldn't bring him back. But that didn't mean she couldn't do something about it.

Across the shattered fields, Harland stood tall, his form smouldering with deadly potential, yet carrying a hint of something perverse: satisfaction.

Remy closed her eyes. In the dark behind them, she saw Max again—standing in a workshop, tripping over words as he tried to explain why he'd saved her, why he'd broken every rule to do it. She saw his mask slip, the pain in his expression no longer guilt, but fear—fear of losing her again. She remembered walking into fire because no one else would. Jess, Darby—all of them inside her now, part of what came next.

When she opened her eyes, her grief had sharpened into a blade.

Remy moved with intent, one hand gripping her newly decoded weapon, the other wrapped around the wandboard—her tether to the code itself, honed through relative weeks of practice, calibrated to respond at the speed of thought. She didn't speak an incantation. She typed, swift and silent. The realm broke open, not with thunder but with a line scored through its surface.

A clean-cut seam split through Max's personal realm, carving open a rift that glowed at its edges, revealing a plane beneath the surface: the In-Between.

The structure beneath all realms—a slate-coloured platform suspended in nothing, flat as logic and stripped of ornament.

She crossed the rift in realm-time, leaving ash and husks behind. The space welcomed her back: removing from her the very few layers that had not been built here.

The ground ahead stretched, colourless, fractal, exact. The air absorbed her exhales, dissipating the data until none remained. Her shadow slipped away, as if the space acknowledged mass but not ego.

This was not a battlefield. It was a final destination: the layer of raw code reserved for those who had root access to fear.

"Harland," her voice came flat, emptied out.

"You killed Max. You crossed your line. Why stop now? Come on. Wipe me out. Burn the trace. Or run—run forever from something you can't overwrite. I'll be here. I'll be the error you can't bury. And I'll wait. Right here. Until you're tired of pretending you're not afraid."

Harland didn't move at first. His posture remained statuesque, but his eyes tracked fast—scanning the breach, parsing telemetry, issuing silent commands. Nothing returned. No signature. No terrain. No protocol attached. It didn't look like a trap, he couldn't see anything except Remy's shape.

"Where the hell are you," he muttered, half to himself. Everything he reached for—landmarks, signals, even memory—came back null. The more he reached, the more absence stared back.

Remy said nothing. She watched it unfold—the first misalignment in his posture, the set of his jaw hardening, the thin sliver of doubt that widened.

Harland moved forward and cut through the seam—a forced entry. The moment his foot crossed the boundary, his codebase convulsed like a body rejecting invasive code. His frame stuttered. Protocols unraveled in sequence. His admin shell caved inward, collapsing layer by layer until only the raw human baseform remained. One moment he was massive, bloating out the void, the next, Harland Francis Reeves.

The suit dissolved into low-resolution scraps before reforming into something that could only suggest seriousness. His hands opened, expecting a response. No scripts triggered. No input returned. His shell broke. His control unraveled. In this layer, he was neither designer nor dominator. He was exposed.

Harland didn't panic or charge ahead. He circled—slow, rehearsed, buying time. One hand drifted low, fingers curling toward a ghost-interface only he could see. He was building something, line by line, the way old gods might have tried to remember prayer. The script sparked to life. A fire construct: summon, shape, deploy.

Remy recognized the flourish for what it was. With her longsword in one hand, the wandboard in the other, she began counter-coding in parallel—silent, recursive blocks designed to intercept and nullify.

Harland, attempting to stay a fraction ahead, hurled another kind of barrage at her.

"You lost them both, didn't you," Harland said. "Darby quick. Jess slower. Messier."

Remy didn't answer. Her body betrayed the hit.

"She looked surprised," he added. "Like she thought someone might come."

Remy's anger fused into focus as she gripped both blade and board. She knew what he was doing. Yet knowledge didn't dull the pain. Memory was wired with nerves—and he knew how to find them.

Harland's construct finished compiling. A searing pulse of heat formed in his palm, unstable, hissing like pressurized steam. He lifted it with effort and hurled it towards Remy. The white-hot fireball ripped across the gap.

The first trigger tripped, and time compressed around the fireball. Remy's eyes fixated on the oncoming flare. It burned white, fast, and absolute.

Three feet from her—too late to brace, too soon to miss—it fractured. Broke apart midair, evaporating like a shooting star snuffed in the atmosphere. To Harland it was impossible. To everyone else, it was magic. To Remy, it was the opening she was waiting for.

"You lost the moment you followed me in here." Her voice filled the void.

Without fanfare, she exploded into form—longsword angled low, wandboard drawn close. Every part of her was aligned—body, thought, and will.

She crossed the last of the dying heat she had summoned moments before. Time flexed—sound thinning. She closed her eyes and phased into code mid-stride. Her fingers swept the wandboard, stretching the localized temporal throttle—shaving fractions from reality, slowing everything but her own thread. The underlayer of the In-Between expanded in response. Remy's mind reached deeper, past framework, past interface, into the undercurrent connecting her to the golden tree that loomed unseen. The roots answered—slowly, with effort.

She was in full sprint now—she opened her eyes in the final strides. Remy drove the blade through him, a full-bodied, diagonal cut—from left hip to opposite shoulder—surgical, final. The sword didn't drag. It didn't need to. Her strike carried no waste, no hesitation—only form, speed, and an edge written to cut what couldn't be reasoned with. It entered. It crossed. It ended.

Harland didn't fall right away. His admin shell failed first—pixelating into strips, his commands broke off mid-transmission. One hand tried to reload a vanished script. His mouth twitched, mid-sentence, with nothing left to say. The body split along the cut. Limbs folded wrong. The pieces dropped.

The impact forced her off-balance. She skidded across the monochrome surface of the In-Between, slowing near its far edge, blade down, lungs burning. Behind her, Harland staggered once. He didn't scream. He seized. His body tried to obey old commands, but nothing answered. The wound was grotesque—warping past realism, opening him like torn geometry, bloodless and red all at once. His limbs spasmed in incorrect directions. For half a second, he remained upright—like he might stabilize. His frame buckled inward, light consuming form, until all that remained was particulate scatter.

Harland Reeves was dead.

Remy stepped back into the fields of Max's farm and closed the tear. She lifted her head and let in the sky—knowing Max would've said something absurd, nearly funny, to cut the tension. "He died doing what he loved—controlling absolutely everything."

Around her, the survivors began to regroup. Jenna leaned into Franklin; Ruth found Beatrice's side without a word. Bob and Jeff met at the field's boundary—whatever passed between them didn't need saying. Alan caught Leo and Reed on respawn and walked toward them. The field filled slowly with motion—hands clasping forearms, shoulders pressed together, short embraces that lasted longer than their touch.

No grand declarations were made. But in every glance and gesture, a silent understanding passed between them: they had come through. Not unscathed—but together.

Peace wasn't something handed down by victors, or secured by the closing of wounds. It was a standoff with memory, a refusal to carry the weight of what she'd lost. But now, standing among the others, she felt the design of the world realign: the field stilled, the sky unburdened, the code no longer straining to predict her next move, and neither would she.

Franklin and Jenna reached her first, dust streaking their clothes. He stayed close without speaking. Jenna touched Remy's shoulder, then let go—like releasing a thread she'd held since the fall.

Beatrice arrived next with a nod—something between respect and relief.

Bob raised a hand in lazy salute, less flair than usual.

"You honoured yourself, Remy Moreau," he said. Jeff stood beside him and didn't argue.

Across the field, Leo and Reed lifted their hands—wave, salute, something in between. Ruth stood between them, smirking the way only someone alive could.

Alan came last. He stopped in front of her.

"Didn't know the guy well," he said, glancing past her. "But I get why he broke the rules."

"Yeah," Remy said. "He made sure I'd live long enough to hate him for it."

There she was again—joking at a time like this. But it wasn't humour. It was heat and grief, sharing the same breath.

There'd be time for the rest later. For now, this was all she had. And she let it burn.

The crisis that would forever be known as Zero Day had ended inside Afterdeath. In the days that followed, global power grids were restored, reinforced—declared unhackable. At least in the media.

People would write books about how this moment changed the world—white papers, biographies, histories sold to school boards. But those stories never reached this far. They always ended with Harland: the monster, the collapse, the patch notes.

What followed was quieter, harder to narrate. Not triumph. Not healing. Continuance.

She stood where he fell, the air still faintly scorched. It felt wrong that everything around her seemed almost normal now, as if the ground itself could shrug off what had happened. As if Max's sacrifice was a temporary scar already fading into memory.

"I didn't say thank you," she said softly.

No audience. No echo. Only words.

"You taught me how to hold things together when I was falling apart. You never tried to fix me—you just let me build something better. I don't think you knew how much I needed that."

She pressed her palm to the heat-warped ground, tracing the edge of the burn as if it could speak for him.

"I hope you saw it. I got him good. For you."

She paused, waiting for something—some trace, some whisper. Nothing came.

Remy straightened, guilt heavy in her chest like a stone. She closed her eyes one final time, memorizing the shape of his absence. But guilt wouldn't bring him back, and she wouldn't waste his final lesson. You carry the weight. You keep going.

She took one final look, breath catching.

"I'm sorry, Max," she whispered. "I'll do better."

And walked away.

ACT FOUR

CHAPTER TWENTY SIX
SNOW GLOBE

Toronto, Forest Lawn Cemetery, Christmas morning. Remy Moreau—present only by the grace of borrowed circuitry—knelt in the snow at her best friend's grave. The marker sat beneath a leaf-bare cedar, a dusting of frost turning JESSICA MARIE TURNER • BELOVED DAUGHTER silver in the weak December light.

Remy brushed the name clear with gloved fingers and set a small, capsule-sealed letter beside the flowers Jess's mother must have left at dawn. "I missed the part where we grew up," she said. "Figured you might want the highlights." She exhaled into the cold. "I'm doing the frightening thing—trying to make a life after death."

The words hung softly, fogging in the cold, before drifting away. Her gloved hands rested in the snow, the capsule held between them, the cold pressing against her palms with no effect.

The irony wasn't lost on her. Here, in the waking world, she was a visitor now. Somehow, in this body, nothing about the world felt real—despite embodying the proof that it was.

She felt the tears come—unmistakable, even if they never formed. The ache welled from a depth she couldn't mask, grief moving first. She didn't cry for Jess alone, or even for Darby, or Haskins. It was for the grief stacked beneath Zero Day, for every name she didn't have the voice to say out loud—for Max, because he was next, and she already knew.

She accepted it. Let it pass through her without restraint or apology. It was easier, here, in a body that didn't flush or tremble the same way. Easier to hide the traces once it was done. But in the moment itself, she let it be human.

A black sedan waited at the cemetery gate, engine idling, windows already defogged. The driver—a broad-shouldered man in a dark coat—stood holding the rear door. "Ms. Moreau," he said with practised deference, like she signed his cheques. "Where to?"

Remy stopped, cold. "Home."

The door closed behind her, the car pulled away, and the cemetery receded into snowfall.

As they travelled toward her family home, she fought the old habit—the need to work, to fix, to retreat into function. She didn't win the fight.

For less than a second, she halted her android body's movement. In that brief pause, she was back in the koi-pond office she rarely used but never abandoned. Six monitors hovered before her, casting reflections across the water. One displayed orbital telemetry, tracking the quantum relay satellite—her final Afterdeath upgrade, now nearly in position. Another mapped Wall Street volatility in real time, a jagged graph tracking the market's convulsions in the wake of OneKind's collapse. Two more displayed patch queues, traffic rerouting, and reruns of policy debates.

But her vision snagged on the last feed: a model of the Welcoming Committee, finally implemented. No Alma. Fully decommissioned—at least officially. Except for the hundreds who had refused replacements.

Some had grown dependent. One had even married their Alma. Others clung tighter now that it was forbidden, hoping scarcity might someday restore value. Remy didn't blame them.

A checkpoint chime sounded. She slipped back into the android body seamlessly.

The sedan nosed onto Bogert Avenue, headlights slicing through snow that lay thick and muffled like felt. From the back seat, Remy traced each landmark with a caution close to reverence. Halfway down stood the brick house whose number she'd once inked on her preschool arm so the world could return her if she wandered. That small memory hit harder than expected—proof of how long it had been, even if the calendar said otherwise.

The front maple—felled this past summer—had left a pale disc in the lawn like a missing tooth. She hadn't known its genus, never needed to, but it had framed her whole childhood. Now it was gone. And it wasn't the only thing.

Next door, the Kovács porch light burned steady. That couple—immigrants in their fifties when they arrived—had folded her family into theirs like it was instinct. Best neighbours she'd ever known. Her friends used to ask if the families were actually related. It had taken a few confused conversations to realize that wasn't normal.

Across the street loomed the tall wooden fence of the neighbour who'd once sued over a replacement panel that dared to look better than the original. She'd called the cops over baseballs, towels on the fence, and once, a badly hung snowflake banner. Every neighbourhood had a villain, but Remy's had filed paperwork.

Memory stacked itself on every eave and walkway, weight pressing against the titanium ribs beneath her coat. She lifted a hand to the curved monitor that served as her face, readying the expression her parents would try to recognize when the car rolled to a stop at the curb.

Each porch step groaned under her boots, wood cold enough to bite. She knocked—harder than she intended—and waited as snow drifted past the door. Footsteps approached. The door opened.

For a long moment, Élise didn't speak. Her eyes widened, then focused—recognition that had waited too long to be surprised.

"Remy." The name landed tentatively, as if her mouth remembered it before her mind arrived.

"Hi, Mom."

They had spoken before, but never face to face. Before Remy could react, Élise pulled her in. The hug landed harder than intended—tight, sudden—but she didn't let go. Her hand brushed the smooth ridge of synthetic fabric along Remy's back, colder than it should have been. Elise held her there, not letting go.

Remy's arms responded a beat late, then closed around her mother. The warmth didn't belong to her new body, but she stayed in it anyway.

Denis stood in the hallway, posture composed, eyes rimmed with a grief older than sleep. He said the only words that felt solid: "Welcome home. Come in."

Inside, the house smelled of cinnamon and pine. The gilded tree tilted a few degrees off centre, as if no one dared to fix it. The fire cracked in the hearth. Everything appeared unchanged, but Remy registered each detail differently—familiar, but warped with distance. The living room wasn't frozen in time. It had endured time.

From the back hall, Mathieu emerged. He looked taller—older in a way that wasn't only height. "You really went all in on the holiday spirit."

"Felt like I had to," she said. "Hallmark only goes so far."

His arms closed around her with a care he hadn't shown before, and through the chill of synthetic fibers, she felt it. They hadn't hugged like this before. And neither of them needed to say why.

He had never asked for explanations. He simply stayed. She had learned to trust that. Now, she was returning the favour.

They gathered in the living room, the mugs radiating heat between their hands. They left space between them, and no one moved to close it.

Remy studied it, the lean of the tree, the low crack of the fire that had always sounded the same.

She set the gift bag on the coffee table and looked at the faces watching her. "I brought some gifts," she said. "Don't worry, it's not an Afterdeath t-shirt. It's a tool."

Élise cradled her mug more tightly than she realized, the heat pressing into her palms. "A tool for what?"

"For keeping in touch," Remy replied. "Only—differently."

She set four sleek, light-reactive capsules on the coffee table in a tidy row—pieces she could no longer carry herself.

Mathieu's eyes narrowed as he inspected the nearest one. The tech looked untouchable, streamlined, precious, probably expensive.

"So like one-way voicemails?" he asked.

"Kind of," Remy said. "No delivery receipts. They exist on their own terms—floating."

Denis picked one up and studied it, thumb brushing the groove at its centre. It felt balanced. Thoughtful. Over-engineered in exactly the way that suited his daughter.

"This is what you've been building," he said, not quite asking.

Remy dipped her head. "One of the things."

They all looked at her, waiting. She didn't fumble for words. She'd rehearsed this, edited it down to what would hurt least. "Legacy Link was helpful. These calls, this visit—it matters. But trying to keep showing up like this—it isn't landing the way any of us hoped."

Élise's frown came gently—a look that belonged to the kind of love that knew when not to interrupt. She wanted to ask what Remy meant, but part of her already knew. "Why?"

"Because time moves differently in there," Remy said. "For you, I've been gone a few months. For me—it's been longer. Some days feel like years. And you're living every day here. Grieving in real time. And I'm elsewhere."

She drew a breath before looking at them—her mother clutching her coffee, her father turning the capsule.

"Trying to live in both places—it's pulling me apart. Maybe you feel it too," Remy said, not to convince them—to finally give it voice. No one rushed to disagree.

"I'm not saying goodbye," Remy said. "I'm asking for solace—a space where grief can happen on its own terms, in whatever shape that takes—for all of us."

Mathieu, who had kept to himself until then, kept his thumb tracing the seam like it might click open or light up if he got it right. "Does that mean no visits anymore?"

"For now, yes." The words landed without edge—steady, composed.

"This body goes into storage after today. I don't want to show up at your door out of habit. And I don't want you waking each morning unsure whether I'll be standing there."

Élise winced at the word "storage," barely hiding the way it landed. Her fingers tightened around her mug, its heat fading too fast. She kept listening. That was the deal—hold it together so Remy didn't have to.

"They're a bridge," Remy said. "One-way, by design. You place a memory if you choose to. Or not. It belongs to you."

Denis gave a short nod, firm enough to land. His eyes stayed elsewhere at first. What passed between them wasn't space; it was the unspoken acknowledgment that Remy no longer needed guidance.

"You've thought this through," he said, tone even.

"Yeah," she said. "I had the time."

Mathieu finally looked up, brows pulled in. "What if we miss you?" He tried to ask it flat, but the words betrayed him.

"You will," Remy said. "I will too."

He looked back down at the capsule. Turned it once more. "And if we change our minds?"

"We change the rules," she said. "But for now, let's keep it easy."

Élise reached for one of the devices and rolled it slowly between her grip. It felt smooth. Like it had been engineered to remove all friction—except the kind she yet carried. "What do we say?"

Remy met her mother's eyes without flinching. "Anything you want. Whatever feels honest. Or ridiculous. Or yours."

The room went silent. Denis exhaled, slow and deep. Mathieu sank into the cushions and pulled his knees up, barely curled, but smaller than before.

"I don't like it," Mathieu said. "But I get it."

"That's been my motto for years," Remy said.

"I'll probably send you nonsense."

"Good," she said. "I could always use more nonsense."

Remy folded her hands and held the room in view. "Let's take today. The fire, the cookies, the tree. Christmas. We don't need to solve everything."

Élise reached across and found her daughter's hand. The contact was cautious at first. "We never did."

Remy squeezed back. "Exactly. Let's keep the streak alive."

She took in the room—the stockings hung crooked, the cushions slumped, the tree's glow spilled softly onto the floor, its imperfect shape echoing the warmth and untidiness of the season.

"And today?" said Élise.

Remy didn't answer right away. She looked around the room, then leaned back into the couch.

"Today is ours. A Christmas like we used to have. Let's take our time and enjoy it. Though, to be clear: I have to get this body home before midnight."

"Let's make it count," Mathieu said. Not as a statement—more like an anchor. Something he could offer that wasn't wrapped in fear.

Remy offered her hands without words. Their fingers found hers, not all at once, but gradually—hands meeting at angles, thumbs brushing unfamiliar seams. The prosthetic joints adjusted instinctively, but she still had to focus, guiding pressure, softening grip. The touch didn't feel like skin, not exactly—but it held. They stayed connected, uncertain in shape but sure in purpose.

Grief remained, but it had stepped aside. What remained was tempered. Sturdier. Love, maybe—but not the fragile kind. The kind built over time.

The day unfolded on its own terms. The cinnamon rolls burned on the bottom—Mathieu's fault, though Remy took the blame with a shrug. They played cards without keeping score. The snap of shuffled decks mixed with Nat King Cole drifting from an old speaker in the corner, cinnamon hanging in the air. Go Fish turned into war, turned into whatever came next. No rules. Only presence.

Remy observed more than she participated—but for today, being there was the point. Her body didn't tire. It tracked motion, found its footing, responded as designed. She saw her mother dry her hands on a towel she didn't need, then rest one palm flat on the counter and stay like that, steadying herself. She noticed Denis leaning in during the lulls in conversation, his laugh coming easier than it used to. She saw Mathieu glance at each of them in turn, as if confirming who remained.

By dusk, the sky had gone pale behind the windows. Remy stood beside the tree, one hand resting near the trunk, the other tucked loosely into the sleeve of her synthetic coat. She stayed at ease, the peace around her feeling earned. Words weren't necessary. Everything that mattered was already here.

Mathieu spoke first, arms folded the way he always did when trying to work something out.

"We'll be okay, Remy."

"I know," she said convincingly.

He didn't look away. He watched her longer than she expected, studying her with the kind of care she used to take for granted.

"Will you?" he asked.

The question lingered, drawing them closer together even as neither spoke.

"Eventually," she said as she reached for his hand and gripped it.

"Promise me one thing," asked Mathieu.

"Anything."

"Don't lie to yourself about how you're doing. Don't pretend it's fine when it isn't. Even up there."

"That's a dangerous level of insight," she said, not bothering to hide the affection. "You got smarter while I was gone."

"Don't get carried away," he said. "Hey, I haven't read that last chapter of the book you were reading me. I've been waiting for you."

She gave a low chuckle. "Maybe I'll record it for my first story in a bottle."

"I'd like that." He hesitated.

"But on that note," she teased, reaching for the bag she'd set behind the couch earlier—unlabelled, soft-wrapped, clearly placed with intent. She handed it to him without ceremony.

"Though, if you ask me, final chapters are overrated," she said, now waiting for him to unwrap it.

Mathieu peeled back the paper slowly. Inside was a slim, dark-spined book with no familiar branding. The cover was matte black with a title pressed in faint, metallic type. It was something new—he had never heard or seen it before. It immediately felt exciting.

"The beginning's the only part you read without anyone telling you how it ends," Remy said. "And after that, it's yours to understand at your own pace, in your own way."

Mathieu ran a thumb along the book's spine, stepped to the hearth, and set it upright on the mantel—spine out, title squared to the room.

CHAPTER TWENTY SEVEN
LUNCH AND LEGACY

Alan Prescott—former field archaeologist, reluctant revolutionary, newly minted greeter of the dead—stood in Afterdeath's hand-built break room, wrestling with a collar that refused to look casual or sincere. The mirror above the cracked sink threw his uncertainty right back at him: how does a man who once dug up lost civilizations learn to relax inside a digital one?

Behind him the vending unit gave a spiteful whir, the coffee station sputtered, and somewhere a fluorescent tube buzzed like an insect that wouldn't quit. None of it cared that Alan was trying to look like he belonged here. The noise was honest, at least; honesty he could live with.

He and Remy hadn't set out to build a break room—it had started as a place to catch their breath. A mismatched couch, a detuned radio, a salvaged brewer that ran hot and smelled faintly of electrical burn—little acts of refusal that shaped a space into something lived-in. Over time, it became theirs—scuffed, cluttered, and unmistakably theirs.

The vending shelves buzzed gently, lined with the usual suspects: limp sandwiches, tired donuts, and, now and then, a slice of pie that no one ever stocked. The coffee burbled again, releasing the scent of overcooked grounds—awful, yes, but oddly grounding.

Against the far wall, a small analog clock ticked—a tether to real time, not Afterdeath's internal cycles. In the corner, a whiteboard was crowded with half-finished to-do lists, doodles, and inside jokes, faintly traced with the scent of dry-erase ink. The clutter was curated. Thoughtful. Stupid. Human.

Ruth stood beside him, easing into place. She ran a hand through her silver hair—less for vanity than for ritual. A small act of gathering before movement. They always arrived early. Time for a questionable coffee.

She nudged him. "You haven't let that unicorn go, have you?"

Alan turned from the mirror, a grin tugging half-hearted at one corner. "Siberian unicorn. Technically. I offloaded it to an old rival—let him chase that forever. Don't get me wrong, I kept enough of them Barnacles—I had Reed plot out some grazing lands for—"

"You mean unicorns, right?"

"Right—What did I say?"

Ruth reached across the counter and tapped the cufflink once. "You're fine," she said. The hand stayed a second longer than it needed to.

Alan glanced at the Polaroid again. "Turns out there are more important 'species' to look after these days."

The door banged once and the late-shift crew spilled in together—Jenna's theatrical stretch, Franklin already hunting sugar, Beatrice quiet but watchful. Their chatter tumbled over itself: donuts vs. sandwiches, recon jokes nobody entirely got, a brief silence that settled when Barry's name surfaced and fell away. Bob King followed, eyes sweeping the room in a quick perimeter check that doubled as hello.

"Night watch," he pronounced, clapping Alan on the shoulder. "Retirement suits you, Prescott."

Laughter rinsed the lingering ache, the machines kept their low growl, and the break room filled with ordinary comfort—a cluttered sort of togetherness that made the day easier to carry.

The equipment around them gave off a tick and churn, more background than presence. Yesterday's notes clung to the whiteboards—smudged and half-set. The couch in the corner sagged like an old dog—familiar, defeated, but present all the same.

Between the beat-up thermoses and the bitter bite of overbrewed coffee, they'd managed to build something that stuck. For Alan, that was enough.

He squirmed in his seat and rubbed the back of his neck. "You honestly think this qualifies as retirement?"

Bob shrugged. "Call it whatever you want. You belong."

He paused at the door and added over his shoulder, "And remember—on time is late."

Jenna side-eyed the hallway and offered, "We're gonna need a manual for the new Bob."

A few of them laughed, the kind that sticks around for a second longer than it should.

Somehow, they'd all ended up here: Alan himself, Ruth, Jenna Powell, the comic-book visionary, Franklin the relentless pragmatist, and Beatrice, always unobtrusively steering things along. Even Jeff had worked here for a while—until he created a new daytime routine, wanting to keep the peace with his brother.

Now, standing among those only trying to find their way, he wasn't bringing back the past—he was standing with the living. A simple peace washed over him, not an ending, but a recognition of where he was needed.

Bob checked the wall clock, rolled his shoulders. "Night crew—hold the fort."

A loose chorus answered him at once. Jenna muttered about being talked to like a kid; Beatrice shot back that it counted as praise; Franklin snagged a donut and mentioned Armand Roy's crossing as casually as weather. Their voices overlapped on the way out—boots scuffing tile, laughter bouncing down the corridor—until the break room settled into its steady hum of vending motors and fluorescent buzz.

Alan's gaze lifted to the sign above the door: WELCOME COMMITTEE. The words felt deliberate.

He and Ruth stayed behind—two veterans of late shifts, long since fluent in each other's small rebellions.

He reached for the door, but Ruth caught his wrist and, with zero ceremony, dipped him into a kiss that stole half his balance. His eyes went wide. Then he laughed—louder than he meant to, the sound catching in his chest on the way out.

"So we're doing the full dip now?" he asked, breathless and smiling.

"Daily drill," she confirmed for him.

She'd kissed him like it wasn't a question. And he was trying to believe it wasn't.

He hadn't pictured an afterlife built on coffee rituals, inside jokes, and shifts wrestling stubborn furniture. He'd spent years chasing lost things—always moving, always searching. But here, surrounded by these people, the need to chase had finally eased.

Retirement. Afterdeath. Alan had never quite understood the words—had spent years circling them like an orbiting satellite, never landing. But this? This wasn't an epilogue. It was the next chapter.

CHAPTER TWENTY EIGHT
THE ARCHITECT'S GHOST

Armand surfaced slowly, first aware of a gentle lightness—the lifting of mass rather than the absence of it. It was not erasure, but a careful uncoupling. He had anticipated the transition, the unwinding, ever since Remy Moreau had explained what to expect. A better place, she'd said. Not perfect. But kinder.

Apparently, her transfer had been anything but smooth. In the years since, changes had improved the experience. She suggested there might yet be some fog as he awoke, but when he saw her next, he knew he would tell her it felt even clearer than before the transfer.

His last memory had been Paul's firm hand holding onto his, a solid anchor until the very end. Now that comforting pressure was replaced by the textured surroundings.

The meadow of awakening.

He pressed a hand to his upper torso, expecting the old pain—the tightness, the lung strain that had followed him for years. But the air moved freely now, rich with fresh grass, sun on soil, and wood retaining the day's heat.

He waited, bracing for the pressure that used to live there. It didn't come. Only lightness. The kind Remy had promised.

Carefully, he sat up, flexing his fingers experimentally. They no longer trembled; his hands were firm, strong, his own again. He wore clothes he recognized—faded grey shirt, worn corduroys, familiar boots—but they felt fresh, free from hospital scents or memories of illness.

Standing came easily, naturally. Armand rose to his feet, balanced and effortless, a sensation he hadn't known in years. The sky stretched open above him, clear and vast; afternoon sunlight rested on the fields around him.

He drew a slow, steady breath, feeling the weight and possibility of every step—earth packed beneath his boots, sun warming the back of his neck. Each sensation arrived unfiltered, impossibly vivid. Far ahead, a familiar shape drew his focus—a gentle roofline at the horizon, framed by distant trees.

The constriction across Armand's upper back released, and his heartbeat found its pace.

He began to walk, drawn toward a small rise ahead. Trees lined the crest, their shadows long. Despite the small incline, it was the easiest walk he'd taken in years. He reached the top of the rise, the path opening to a wide clearing where the farmhouse shone in the afternoon sun.

A man stepped out from the trees. Armand stopped dead in his tracks. He didn't need to squint or move closer. He saw something he recognized in the man's walk, his frame, the set of his head.

"Max," he said. He recoiled at the name, like saying it aloud might cause him to vanish.

They stared at each other. It didn't feel like shock. It didn't even feel new. It felt like a truth that had waited until now.

Armand had imagined this moment more times than he dared to count. On the porch in the hours before dawn, in the tractor cab while fields drifted under a sleeping sky, in the long years after the funeral when memory rose without warning.

He'd pictured Max arriving with a shout, or in tears, or folded by grief. He had rehearsed what he might say, how he might fail to say it. But none of that belonged here. Across the clearing, there he stood, as he lifted his hand slightly, as if he wasn't sure whether to wave or reach out.

His voice reached him—familiar and unforced. "Hi, Dad." Armand stayed where he was, reading every line of him—the broader frame, the same tilt to his stance, the old flannel softened at the collar. The years between them no longer stood in the way.

Armand crossed the distance and gathered Max close, his grip firm, complete. One hand landed between his son's shoulders, where instinct met memory and held its ground. The imagined versions fell away. This was the one that endured—the one he hadn't dared to prepare for, but recognized all the same.

He found his hands shaking—this time, not from weakness, but from a disbelief so sharp it almost hurt. For a long moment, neither spoke. The world seemed to hang in the space between breaths.

Max stepped back, his face thoughtful. "Remember Grandpa's knife—the one he made from that old broken shovel?"

Armand nodded. He could see it clear as day: his father in the garage, sweat on his brow, filing the blade until the steel caught the light.

"He always said he never wasted good steel," Max continued. "Melt it down, reshape it."

"You're saying you're the knife."

Max nodded.

For a moment, neither spoke. Armand simply looked at him, his face unmoving as his thoughts sifted through the words. Armand laughed—a sound that cut the silence, like the breaking of ice.

Max hadn't expected laughter. It knocked him off balance. "What?"

Armand shook his head, eyes bright. "No, son. He never melted the shovel."

Max tilted his head, confused.

"He cut it," Armand corrected. "Used a hacksaw. Made two, maybe three knives. Said melting it down was wasteful—more trouble than it was worth. Kept the grain of the steel intact. Gave each blade its own character."

Max furrowed his brow, starting to speak—but stopped himself. "I could've sworn he forged it."

Armand reached out, laying a hand on his shoulder. "Doesn't matter. You got the truth of it. Same steel, new shape."

Max exhaled and lowered his eyes. "Huh." He wondered, briefly, how many other important memories he might have filed wrong.

Armand watched the break take place—small, uncertain, but real. That trace of doubt in his son's eyes didn't unsettle him. His restraint gave way. He reached for Max and pulled him into another firm embrace.

Max closed the space between them.

Armand kept him close, eyes shut against the pull of it. Fresh hay. Autumn wind. And Max—solid and unmistakably here.

Maybe this was his son, whole and returned. Or maybe it was recall, code—some careful reconstruction. Armand couldn't say. But after that small flaw, that imperfect recollection, he believed it was Max. That, on its own, brought Armand more peace than he expected.

He released a low, tentative laugh, gauging the sound as he flexed his fingers. They moved easily. No pain.

"I feel good. Better than I have in years." He looked down at his hands, and back at Max. "They really pulled it off."

Max met his eye. "Exactly how Remy said it would go."

Remy Moreau. She had come to see him when the doctors couldn't promise anything. She'd told him he wouldn't wake up alone, and here he was. He didn't know the details yet. But he knew she meant it. And she'd been right.

Together they walked the path that led them home. At the verge of the meadow stood a gate, its frame worn smooth by time and touch. Armand ran his hand along the grain, feeling grooves carved by years he recalled but couldn't fully identify.

Armand placed his palm against the gate. "This is home."

He eased it open. The hinges creaked—with the drag of faux-worn metal finding motion again. Beyond the fence, the land opened wide. The barn was where it had always been. Somehow, that felt truer than it should have—more convincing than any simulation had a right to be.

Golden grass swayed in the breeze, and the trees along the fence line stood unmoved, placid in the afternoon light. Armand stepped through first. The place didn't feel frozen in time. It simply waited—and now, they had returned.

He let the view wash over him. This place hadn't been rebuilt from code alone—it had been shaped with care. With love. He drew in the air, not out of necessity, but because it felt good. "So this is it," he murmured. "Afterdeath."

"One version, anyway," Max said after a pause. "I started building it a while back. Remy helped finish it," he added, quieter now. "There were pieces I couldn't find on my own."

Armand studied his son, noting the unassuming mannerisms, the subtle honesty behind his words. The details felt comforting, carefully shaped by hands he trusted deeply. "You didn't simply fill gaps," Armand said gently. "You built something real."

They continued onward until a hand-painted sign emerged at the cornfield's perimeter: Roy Grove Farm—Est. 1954. Armand reached out slowly, tracing the letters, fingertips brushing over carved initials worn smooth by time and touch. The scent of fresh earth and sun lingered lightly in the air. Recognition landed—unmistakable and full.

Moving along the dirt path, Armand's fingertips brushed against the tall stalks of corn, their leaves parting under his touch. The field opened ahead. Armand could hear the laughter rising, could almost see Max disappearing into that same summer haze. Armand glanced aside and found Max already watching him—present, knowing—sharing the moment without needing words.

"You sure you're okay with all this—being here?" Max asked.

Armand stared out toward the fields, bathed in late-afternoon sun, the farmhouse ahead welcoming, the windmill silhouetted gently against clear sky.

"Yes," he replied simply. "We're both here, and nothing hurts. What more do I need?"

Some old fear seemed to fall off Max, and he met Armand's gaze fully.

"They told me you'd come soon," he said, voice tightening as he took his time with the words. "But I was scared you wouldn't."

He looked away for a second. Looked back, eyes shining now, one tear slipping free before he could stop it. "Not after everything with Mom."

"Well, I'm here now. And I'm not going anywhere." He tapped Max lightly on the cheek, a familiar gesture of affection. "You're stuck with me, kid."

Max laughed, the tension easing from his shoulders.

They walked the rest of the way in a worn-in silence. As they neared the farmhouse, Armand stopped, resting his palm on the wooden gate. The grain was aged, marked, confirming that it had been closed before. He felt presence—not absence—etched into every mark the years had left behind.

The wooden steps creaked beneath Armand's boots, setting him up for a chuckle. "Those steps always gave me away. Every time I snuck out, your mother heard." He grinned faintly, amused. "Guess you two reconstructed more than I realized."

He studied his son's form, registering the small differences—the way his shoulders held less tension, the unshaken clarity in his eyes. But it was Max, unmistakably so. Whatever code had amounted to this, it hadn't replaced anything critical. They'd done a damn good job.

They pushed through the screen door and walked in. Lamplight filled the farmhouse interior, casting familiarity on the space—the kitchen table worn smooth by years of shared meals, the rocking chair angled near the window, a well-loved quilt folded with care across the back of the sofa.

He took in each detail. It wasn't nostalgia—it was recognition. Max touched his elbow—lightly, firmly—letting the moment sink between them. The ache of loss hadn't vanished entirely, but had reshaped itself—smaller now, easier to carry.

Max spoke. "Welcome home, Dad."

Armand tasted the word slowly, savouring its simplicity. "Home."

He didn't know if this place counted as home—code or memory or something in between—but the feeling it gave him was real. It lived in the weight of Max's shoulder under his arm. Maybe home had never been a place. Maybe it was this—a sense of being known, and not being alone. Whatever it was, he didn't feel the absence of it anymore.

From the kitchen, a voice rose up.

"You two have impeccable timing," Remy said. At the stove, she turned toward them mid-stir, casual, steady. "Supper's almost ready."

Armand made a beeline for the kitchen table, the chair greeting him with a comforting creak as he dropped into it.

"Smells incredible," he said, already feeling the hunger that had nothing to do with food.

She worked with the fluency of someone who'd done this before, timing each dish, drink, and quip with the finesse of a maître d' who didn't need to announce herself.

"Figured you might appreciate something you actually recognize. You recall all those conversations about favourites?"

"You slipped them in so smoothly, I didn't even catch it. That's real spy work." Armand laughed—low and sudden, like he'd expected pain but found breath instead.

Remy set the plates down with a little flourish that wasn't showy so much as fond. "Learned from the best," she said.

Armand dug in, lifting a forkful of golden-topped Pâté Chinois and inhaling like a man who hadn't eaten in a decade. The first bite hit hard—savoury beef, bright corn, creamy mashed potatoes crisped to the cusp of perfect. It wasn't only good. It was damn good. He looked up, the fork pausing midair.

"Remy," he said, his voice hitching, "this is—better than you led me to believe."

Remy shrugged, a flush rising to her cheeks.

"We've had plenty of practice," she said, shooting a mock-glare at Max. "He endured the early disasters."

Max propped himself against the counter, grinning in the easy way of someone who'd fought long and hard for a place at the table.

"You don't know the half of it. Whole kitchen looked like a bomb went off some nights."

Armand laughed—a full laugh this time, deeper. His gaze roamed around the room again—the cluttered counter, the slouched dish stack, the scent of warm herbs thickening the air. Remy dropped into a chair beside them, brushing a lock of hair back from her face without thinking.

Max pulled another chair close with a scrape of wood. Armand sat back slowly, plate half-forgotten, and took them both in—this unlikely family, this second chance, stitched together not by design, but by stubborn, beating will.

When he spoke, his voice was coarse but unyielding, shaped by everything it had taken to get here. "You know," Armand said, smiling faintly, "I could get used to this."

The room answered with its own coded language—lamplight glinting, forks clinking softly, chairs drawn closer, a thousand small declarations that none of this would ever be taken for granted again.

ABOUT THE AUTHOR

R. P. Gage is a Canadian author whose fiction defies categorization, weaving together elements of speculative fiction, mystery, science fiction, and fantasy. His stories are built on character—grounded in grief, memory, and the unfinished work of living. Noetic Gravity is part of a larger project exploring what lies beyond traditional genre boundaries, where narratives don't simply entertain but disrupt, question, and linger long after the last page.

If this book stayed with you, the best way to support it is to leave a review—whether online, in a bookstore, or wherever readers still gather. Honest reviews help stories travel further, reaching new readers and communities. For independent authors, there is no greater reward than knowing a story has made it into your hands and your memory. Thank you—for this step, the next, and the ones still to come.

If you'd like to reach out directly, we welcome your thoughts at GageForcePublishing@gmail.com.